The Improper Governess

The Improper Governess

Carola Dunn

G. K. Hall & Co. • Chivers Press
Thorndike, Maine USA   Bath, England

This Large Print edition is published by G.K. Hall & Co., USA and by Chivers Press, England.

Published in 2000 in the U.S. by arrangement with Zebra Books, an imprint of Kensington Publishing Corporation.

Published in 2000 in the U.K. by arrangement with Kensington Publishing Corporation.

U.S. Hardcover 0-7838-8974-7 (Romance Series Edition)
U.K. Hardcover 0-7540-4133-6 (Chivers Large Print)

The text of this Large Print edition is unabridged.
Other aspects of the book may vary from the original edition.

Set in 16 pt. Plantin by Elena Picard.

Printed in the United States on permanent paper.

British Library Cataloguing-in-Publication Data available

Library of Congress Cataloging-in-Publication Data

Dunn, Carola.
    The improper governess / Carola Dunn.
        p. cm.
    ISBN 0-7838-8974-7 (lg. print : hc : alk. paper)
    1. Governesses — England — Fiction. 2. Actresses — England —
Fiction. 3. Large type books. I. Title.
PR6054.U537 I4 2000
    823´.914—dc21
                                                          00-021605

The Improper Governess

One

The tall, dark gentleman was watching her again. Despite the glare of the gaslights on the stage, Lissa was quite certain his gaze was fixed on her from the shadowy depths of his box. Among the dozen skimpily clad odalisques holding uncomfortable poses about the Turkish Sultan on his bejewelled couch, she alone was the object of his attention.

A tremor shook her, a thrill of mingled alarm and excitement. New as she was to the profession, Lissa had already learned that when a gentleman regarded an actress in that particular fashion, he had only one thing on his mind.

The sole question now was whether to reject outright his forthcoming offer of "protection," or to risk an attempt to carry out her plan.

"Stir your stumps," Minette hissed in her ear. "It's your turn."

Belatedly Lissa realized that the music had changed. As Nicole, her sensual solo dance finished, rejoined the harem, the orchestra struck up the introduction to Lissa's song. Her steps a compromise between a hasty trot and the much rehearsed languorous glide, she moved to the front of the stage, her long brown hair, worn loose, floating behind her.

It took all her self-control not to peep up at the gilt, crimson-velvet draped box whence, she knew, the dark gentleman was staring. Suddenly her gauzy draperies seemed all too scanty, as if the thigh-length chemise worn beneath to satisfy the Censor had vanished. Willing herself not to blush, she launched into the mournful ballad about how she had been torn from her home by pirates and sold into slavery in Constantinople. Set to a tune adapted from Mozart's *Abduction from the Seraglio*, the song brought the usual storm of applause.

Next came the dance of the concubines, greeted by more hearty applause along with the whistles of the vulgar in the galleries and cheers from the dashing blades in the pit. The *Grand Asiatic Ballet* was proving a popular piece for the opening of the new Royal Coburg Theatre.

A troop of Janissaries marched onstage and the slave girls fled, with coquettish backward glances.

Safely hidden in the gloom of the wings, the odalisques slumped onto benches to rest their aching limbs. Nicole and Minette joined Lissa.

"Lord Ashe's got his glims on you all right, Lissa," whispered Nicole, a voluptuous brunette, "and it ain't your voice he's after, neither, you lucky hen."

"Lord Ashe?"

"The dark swell in the third box on the left, second tier. Di'n't you notice him ogling you?"

"She noticed awright," said Minette with a hushed giggle. "Nearly missed her turn, she was so busy making sheep's eyes back at him."

Lissa forbore to correct this misconception. "I didn't know his name," she explained.

"He's a baron, he is," Minette told her. "Plump in the pockets, too — not one of them lords as lives on the banks of the River Tick — and generous with it. They say he gave the Skylark a river of emeralds the other day when he cast her off."

"The Skylark? Miss Carew of the Royal Opera House?"

"That's her, duck, the high-flyingest bird of paradise on the town. She's been Lord Ashe's light-o'-love these six months or more but he's tired of her at last, just like the rest. He's in the market for a new *chère amie,* and it looks like you're the one to land in clover."

"Lucky hen," said Nicole again, with envy.

Lissa could not tell them she had no intention of becoming Lord Ashe's mistress. If she asked their advice about her plan, as she longed to, they would think her positively crackbrained for spurning a young, handsome, wealthy nobleman. Still less was it possible to explain that she had not yet sunk so low as to exchange her virtue for gold and jewels. They would be insulted. Neither Nicole nor Minette made any secret of their lovers. It was expected in the world of the theatre. How else was a poor girl to survive?

"I cannot understand why Lord Ashe should be interested in me," Lissa said honestly, recollecting her visit to Covent Garden during a rehearsal, in the course of her search for employment. "I have seen Miss Carew. She is a true beauty, with a superb voice."

"Your voice'd be as good if it was prop'ly trained," Minette assured her, "and you've got a genteel way about you. They say he goes for that."

"Your looks'd be none so bad neither," added Nicole, "if you wasn't so skinny. 'Spect his lordship's planning on feeding you up."

Lissa's empty stomach chose that moment to growl loudly. All three girls burst out laughing.

"Hush, ladies!" the stage manager hissed at them, though there was little fear of the audience hearing them over the martial music accompanying the Janissaries' dance.

A clash of cymbals brought the slave girls to their feet, ready for their next entrance. Lissa vowed to herself not to cast so much as a glance towards Lord Ashe's box. Sheep's eyes, indeed! He must not be able to claim justifiably that she had encouraged him.

He had survived his third viewing of the tedious *New Melodramatic Spectacle* and the *Grand Asiatic Ballet*. At last the *Splendid Harlequinade* called *Midnight Revelry* drew towards its close. As Janissaries, now transformed into particolored Harlequins, chased squealing odalisque-

Columbines from the stage, Robert Ashe's gaze followed the little singer.

He shook his head in puzzlement. What was it about her that attracted him? As different as a female well could be from the gorgeous, flamboyant Skylark, she was scarcely even pretty except for those wide grey eyes in her thin face. To one who considered himself a connoisseur of music as well as of feminine pulchritude, her voice was mediocre — strong, sweet and true but unpolished.

Yet something there enchanted him, the graceful turn of a wrist, a glimpse of a slender ankle, a certain air of fragile, virginal innocence.

Though she was new to the London stage, years of experience in the provinces must have honed the art that looked so artless. Her apparent youth had to be the result of the clever application of cosmetics. She intrigued him.

He wanted her.

Well, he'd try her out tonight, and if she pleased him it would be time enough to consider a long-term arrangement.

He reached for his hat and gloves, blessing the impulse which had brought him back alone to the Coburg Theatre tonight. No need to make excuses to guests for deserting them the instant the performance ended. No need, in fact, to keep his seat until the end. The final scene between the chief Harlequin and Columbine and the jealous Pantaloon was almost over. He'd slip out during the Grand Finale and be waiting in the

11

Green Room when the girls emerged from the dressing rooms.

Ashe found himself neither the first nor the last gentleman with the same notion. Half a dozen others preceded him, from a pair of sprigs scarce out of short coats, blushingly agog at their own daring, to an elderly lecher more in need of a nurse than a lightskirt.

A fair, foppish gentleman a few years older than Ashe sauntered up to him as he entered the room.

"*On dit* that you have given the Skylark her *congé*, Ashe," he said in a languid drawl, staring disapprovingly through his quizzing glass at the two abashed youths.

"Even the best grow tiresome in time."

"True, alas." He lowered the glass, restoring his eyes to their normal size above the round, rather full cheeks which dominated his under-slung chin. "Might have a try there. There's nothing in this crop to match her."

"The Skylark's not your usual style, is she? I thought you preferred less ripe charmers." Ashe had always regarded with distaste Lord Quentin Teague's pursuit of young, unsophisticated damsels, though he had no evidence the man was actually a corrupter of innocents. Now that he found himself drawn to the little singer, he had lost his grounds for disapproval.

Of course, her unworldly air was a mask, he told himself. No doubt it enabled her to exact a higher price from her lovers than her meagre

12

figure otherwise allowed.

"I fear you are too late for *la belle* Carew, anyway, Teague," he continued. "She has already accepted *carte blanche* from Bosworth."

"Ah well," sighed Lord Quentin philosophically. "Daresay it's all for the best. She's an expensive bit of muslin and my pockets ain't quite as deep as yours."

"Not to mention that my sister would be bound to hear of your taking up with so prominent a Paphian," Ashe noted, his tone dry.

"My eternal devotion to Lady Orton has nothing to do with such affairs, my dear fellow. Besides, she won't have me."

"Daphne has the deepest doubts about your suitability as a step-papa for Colin."

"Justifiably, *mon vieux*, justifiably," Lord Quentin admitted with the greatest good humour. "Were we wed, I'd pack the squalling brat straight off to school. Ah, Waddingham," he addressed one of a group of gentlemen just entering the Green Room, "I've a bone to pick with you."

He drifted away. Ashe was accosted by another of the group. By the time they finished discussing the merits and demerits of a horse he was considering purchasing, the room was crowded.

A sudden lull in the buzz of conversation announced the arrival of the performers. A bell-like laugh rang out, and the babble resumed as admirers and well-wishers gathered about the principal actors and actresses. Excusing himself, Ashe made his way through the mob. Over their heads, he saw the girls of the chorus coming through the door from backstage, a fluttering, twittering flock of bright-hued ladybirds.

Amongst them, he sought in vain for his songstress.

Then he spotted her. He might not have recognized her had she not raised her bowed head, revealing those luminous grey eyes beneath the brim of the dowdy black bonnet hiding her beautiful hair. In contrast to her colourful companions, she was dressed in an ill-fitting, Quakerish grey gown, long-sleeved and high to the neck, and she carried a dark brown cloak over her arm.

Ashe grinned. She was carrying the pose of innocence almost too far. Few gentlemen in search of a bit of fun would pay her the least heed — which was all to the good, since it meant he'd have few or no rivals for her favors.

Except Teague. Damn the fellow, he was heading straight for her, a determined look in his protuberant blue eyes. The hint of competition whetting his blood, Ashe hastened his pace, but he was farther off by several feet and several obstructive couples intent on their own affairs.

"Sorry," he muttered, brushing past a dancer whose plump bosom quivered in an apparent attempt to leap from her brief cherry-striped bodice.

Teague stopped, his arm caught by an acquaintance. Ashe forged on.

"No show tomorrow, Lissa," cried the wearer of the cherry-striped bodice from behind him. "Make the most of it."

The girl — Lissa — half raised her hand in acknowledgement, blushing. Close to, she appeared not a day older than she had on the stage. The top of her head scarce reaching his chin, she gazed up at Ashe with combined defiance and appeal.

He frowned. "You're very young."

Lissa drew herself up proudly. "I am nineteen, sir."

"Well out of leading-strings," he agreed with a smile. "Will you give me the pleasure of taking supper with me, Miss . . . Lissa?"

"F-Findlay, my lord. Melissa Findlay. I . . ."

As she hesitated, Lord Quentin joined them.

"Stolen a march on me, eh, Ashe?" he said, trying without success to hide his annoyance. "Not *your* usual style. You'll not keep his interest long, my dear. Do better with me."

She recoiled a trifle, almost imperceptibly, but her voice was composed. "I thank you, sir, but Lord Ashe was beforehand with his kind invitation."

Shrugging, Teague reached into his breast-pocket for his card-case. "As you will," he said indifferently, handing her a card. "When he tires of you, you may contact me here. It's just possible I may still be interested." He turned away.

Ashe took her cloak and draped it about her shoulders, which drooped a little beneath the

15

weight of the thick, heavy duffel. If she satisfied him, if they reached a satisfactory arrangement, he would clothe her in velvet and cashmere against the chill of the spring nights, he thought.

Tentatively she laid a hand light as a butterfly on his proffered arm. He noted with complacency that she had let Teague's card drop to the floor.

To Lissa's dismayed eyes, the cushioned couch against the far wall dominated the candlelit private parlor of the Piazza Coffee House, Covent Garden. As big as a bed, it loomed threateningly beyond the table in the center of the room.

She had assumed a change of scenery before the third act of this farce. No matter, she assured herself stoutly. The play was to be booed and hissed from the stage before it reached its dénouement.

Nonetheless, she could not quite suppress a tremor of anxiety. What if the principal actor refused to retire into the wings, turning her planned comedy into a tragical drama? Though Lord Ashe had thus far treated her with courteous consideration, she could not but be aware of a forceful masculinity held in check.

The heat of his gaze contradicted the mildness of his tone as he handed his hat and gloves to the obsequious waiter and said, "Allow me to relieve you of your cloak and bonnet, Miss Findlay."

Paradoxically, the fire in his hungry brown

eyes made Lissa shiver — and not entirely from alarm.

Divested of her outer clothing, she somehow felt as exposed in her modest kerseymere gown as she had in the diaphanous stage draperies. She crossed to the fireplace and held out her hands to the flames.

"It is chilly for May," Lord Ashe remarked. He turned to the waiter. "Turtle soup to start with, and asparagus, and then the finest delicacies from tonight's bill of fare. Miss Findlay, do you care for creams and jellies?"

Creams and jellies! After a moment of yearning, Lissa said firmly, "I prefer pastries, sir."

"Pastries it is, and whatever hothouse fruit you have." He ordered wines with exotic names, which Lissa promised herself not to so much as taste, then he added, "Bring everything at once, if you please. We shall serve ourselves."

The waiter cast a curious glance at Lissa as she uttered an involuntary, inarticulate protest. She had counted on frequent interruptions from servants.

Lord Ashe nodded dismissal at the waiter and came to join her by the fire, smiling.

"Did you wish to be waited on hand and foot?" he asked in a caressing voice. "Never fear, I shall be your *cavaliere servente*." In answer to her look of enquiry, he explained, "Your willing slave, a slave of love."

If only he meant love, not mere passion! Lissa

was swept with a wave of longing to be truly loved by this man, or at least to be able to trust him, to let his broad shoulders share the weight of her self-imposed burdens. Impossible dream.

"I am perfectly able to help myself, my lord," she said primly.

He laughed, but turned the subject as a pair of waiters came in to set the table with a snowy white cloth, gleaming silver and sparkling crystal.

"Is the Royal Coburg a satisfactory employer, Miss Findlay?"

"I was fortunate indeed to find a new theatre about to open its doors when I came to London. It is very difficult to get a place in the established companies."

"You are a newcomer to the metropolis? I guessed it."

Afraid he was going to ask whence she came, Lissa frantically racked her brains for a polite but uninformative answer. To her relief, he merely asked whether she had yet viewed many of the sights of the city.

He seemed rather startled to learn she had seen nothing but St. Paul's Cathedral and West-minster Abbey. She nearly explained that, after visits to the great churches upon her arrival, all her time and energy had been spent on the search for work. How close to despair she had often come! How close to despair she was now, for even if tonight's scheme succeeded, the suc-cess would be no more than a temporary remedy.

She nearly explained, but she could not bear that Lord Ashe should suppose her to be making a deliberate play for sympathy. So she smiled, with an effort, and said she had heard there was to be a balloon ascension from Hyde Park tomorrow which she hoped to attend.

"I trust the weather will cooperate," his lordship observed. "In my experience, these events are postponed as often as not. Ah, here is our supper. Will you be seated, ma'am?"

He held her chair for her, facing the fire not the couch to her relief — relief spoiled when she realized his place was laid adjacent to her rather than opposite. She tucked her feet back under her chair for fear of colliding with his ankles.

However, the savory odor rising dizzyingly from the tureen before her drove all fears of the baron's expectations from her mind.

Whether to eat her fill was the only remaining doubt. She glanced calculatingly from the dishes crowding the tabletop to the figure of her host. Broad shoulders and powerful chest tapered to slim waist and flanks: Lord Ashe did not look as though he was given to overindulgence in food. There would be plenty left whatever inroads she made, and she would regret not having taken full advantage of the bountiful supply should he fail to fall in with her plans.

Turtle soup; asparagus to dip in melted butter; turbot in lobster sauce; cutlets of spring lamb with minted new peas and new potatoes; a fricassee of chicken and mushrooms; stuffed fillet of veal in a pastry case — Lissa sampled everything. She had never eaten such well-seasoned, deliciously sauced, beautifully garnished dishes before.

Lord Ashe watched with an air of amused tolerance. Recalling Minette's jest about his wishing to feed her up, Lissa almost giggled aloud. He himself ate little, though emptying his glass with some regularity. Lissa took a sip or two of wine after a rather salty mouthful. She did not care for the taste, so was not tempted to drink more, despite his lordship's occasional gentle urging.

He was a charming host. Besides keeping her plate filled, as promised, he made her laugh with a droll review of the Coburg Theatre's melodrama, ballet, and harlequinade, always exempting her own performance from his wit.

He went on to tell fascinating stories of the London theatre world, of Sheridan and Byron, of Kemble, Siddons, and Kean, and the great soprano Catalani.

"You ought to take singing lessons," he said, "if you wish to advance in your profession. I daresay I could arrange for one of the best teachers to accept you as a pupil. Ah, you have reached the sweets stage, I see. Try one of these *petit puits d'amour.*" He reached for a plate of jam tarts, the crimped puff paste circles glazed to a golden shine around the jewel-bright centers.

Lissa took one. *"Petit puits . . . ?"* she asked, nibbling.

"You don't speak French? No, of course you don't." Lord Ashe looked a trifle disconcerted.

On the point of informing him that, though ignorant of French, she read Greek, Lissa held her tongue. It was bound to lead to unwanted curiosity, and he already sensed something smoky about her antecedents, or he would not have unconsciously expected her to know French.

Before she could think of some way to distract him from the subject, Lord Ashe pushed back his chair and took her hand in his. At the touch of his lean, warm fingers, a shock ran up her arm. She froze.

She had almost forgotten his purpose in treating her to supper.

"*Puits d'amour,* 'little wells of love.'" His burning gaze moved from her eyes to linger on her lips, then down to her bosom. "I am eager to discover what you have hidden behind that Puritan costume, my Lissa. If you have eaten your fill, it is past time to plumb the Well of Love."

Two

Lissa dropped the remains of her tart. "W-what do you mean?" she faltered through suddenly dry lips.

Lord Ashe raised dark, sardonic eyebrows, tightening his clasp as she attempted to pull her hand free. "Exactly what I said, my dove. I spoke English, not French, did I not? I wish to try whether we shall suit before I offer you my protection. I have already dismissed your predecessor. It is a common enough situation."

"For you, perhaps!" Indignation warred with embarrassment. "Just because I am an actress, it does not mean I am a l-lightskirt."

"No? Why the devil do you imagine I invited you this evening? Don't plead ignorance, pray!" he added dryly.

Abashed, Lissa stared at the crumbs on her plate. "I confess, I did not suppose you wished to congratulate me on my performance."

"So why did you accept?"

"I was hungry," she muttered, her face aflame. Then her spirit revived as she reminded herself how much practice she had had at standing up to browbeating. She raised her chin and squared her shoulders. "And I hoped to be able to take some scraps home for the children."

"Children!" Lord Ashe pounced on the word, his grip now painful. "I knew you could be neither so young as you look nor so innocent as you claim."

Biting her lip, Lissa managed not to wince. Show fear and they had you where they wanted you.

"I told you I am nineteen," she said quietly. "The children are my brothers."

At last he let go her hand. "Brothers?" His penetrating stare held her gaze for an endless moment. She was glad she was telling the truth.

He reached for his glass, drank, then lounged back in his chair. "You are supporting your brothers?" he asked, his tone conversational now.

"I do my best." Against her will, her lips trembled. She felt for her handkerchief and twisted it nervously between her fingers to stop her hands shaking.

"A poor best, I take it," he said gently, "if you are reduced to deceit to feed them. Well, I'll not make matters worse. Come, put on your bonnet whilst I ring to arrange for our leavings to be packed up."

Her heart too full for words, her eyes misty, Lissa could only look her gratitude. She hastened to obey, glad to hide her face within the depths of the drab bonnet.

The waiter received with astonished resentment Lord Ashe's order to bestow the broken meats in a basket to be removed from the premises. The sullen glance he cast at Lissa, who was no doubt robbing him of his perquisites, quickly changed to a pitying sneer. Obviously his lordship, disillusioned by the dowd's lack of hidden assets, was casting her off kindly.

The real wonder, Lissa thought wistfully, was that a gentleman of Lord Ashe's manifest superiority had for a brief while desired so plain and dowdy a female. Now the false glamour of her stage appearance had worn off, he must be glad of an excuse to retreat.

Though not accustomed to catering for outside parties, the Piazza found crocks and cans enough to accommodate every morsel. Lord Ashe brushed aside apologetic explanations of the necessity of charging for the loan of the containers. A potboy lugged the heavy basket out to the lamplit street where his lordship's hastily summoned town carriage awaited.

Lissa's plan had worked. She had eaten well and had enough left to feed the boys for two or three days. So she could only attribute her low spirits to the prospect of the long trudge home carrying the spoils.

Curtsying, she breathed a heartfelt "Thank you, my lord," and reached for the basket.

He forestalled her, slipping a coin to the lad, who dashed back to his work. Hefting the basket, Lord Ashe enquired, "Where do you live, Miss Findlay?"

"On the other side of the river, sir, in Lambeth,

near the Coburg Theatre."

"Back to Lambeth, Burr," he called to his coachman.

"There is no need to take me so far out of your way, sir." Lissa was not at all sure she wanted him to know her precise direction. Worse, what might he not attempt in the privacy of his coach, with none but a loyal servant to hear her cries? "I can very well walk."

"*So far out of my way* is far enough to walk, burdened," he said mockingly, as if he guessed her thoughts, "and the streets around Covent Garden are far from safe for a lone female at this hour of the night. By the new bridge, Lambeth is no great distance to drive. Besides, I am curious to meet your brothers. Come." He held out his hand.

Short of engaging in an undignified and undoubtedly unsuccessful struggle for the basket, Lissa had no choice but to abandon it or obey. He handed her into the carriage. Following, he set the basket beside her and sat down opposite, thus relieving her immediate apprehensions.

She was very tired. As the horses trotted along the Strand, she drifted into a half-doze, from which Lord Ashe roused her only when, at the far end of Waterloo Bridge, the coachman needed further directions.

Much of Lambeth was still laid out to market gardens, but the streets of mean tenements were gradually encroaching. Here streetlamps were few and far between. For a few minutes Lissa was

25

too busy directing the driver to worry about what to do when they arrived at her lodgings. Then the carriage pulled up before the dark doorway and it was too late to prepare a speech.

"You do not really want to come in?" she pleaded, trying to make out Lord Ashe's expression by the light of the carriage lamps as she stepped down.

"I do," he said firmly. "Wait here, Burr."

She unlocked the door and led the way up the dilapidated stairs. The lingering smell of boiled cabbage seemed worse than usual tonight, perhaps because she had for once eaten her fill. On the first landing she picked up the tallow candle left burning for her by a kindly landlady, adding its fumes to the fetid atmosphere. Lissa knew there were worse odors she might yet have to endure if she had to remove to cheaper rooms to save a few pennies on the weekly rent.

Behind her, Lord Ashe made a choking noise, hastily smothered. His firm tread followed her up the second pair of stairs, up and up, till they reached the door to the garret under the roof.

The door creaked open. By the light of her candle, Lissa saw Peter in his nightshirt slumped at the battered deal table, his fair head pillowed on his arms, fast asleep.

Swiftly she turned, finger to her lips — too late.

"You live here?" said Lord Ashe, his voice harsh.

She nodded. "You *would* come," she whispered.

"Lissa?" Peter mumbled drowsily. "It was getting dreadfully late. I was worried. I couldn't sleep."

"I'm sorry I'm so late."

He sat up, blinking at her. "Here, we saved you a bit of currant bun. Michael found a penny in the street and bought a bun, though I *told* him bread is better value. There's not much left, I'm afraid. He was dreadfully hungry so I let him . . ." Catching sight of the figure in the shadows behind Lissa, he stopped and stared, then jumped to his feet. "Who's that?"

"Lord Ashe. He . . . he brought me home from the theatre." She prayed the boy would not guess her escort's original intentions. At eleven, Peter was as fiercely protective of her as of his younger brother, and a few weeks in London had taught him far too much about the ways of the world.

She cast a rapid glance around the narrow, chilly attic room. It was as tidy as it could be with her pallet bed in one corner and their few books neatly piled in another, as clean as borrowed broom and scrubbing brush could make it. Moving aside, she let Lord Ashe step in.

"Good evening, my lord," Peter said, executing his best bow.

A faint smile lightened his lordship's grim expression. "Good evening, Master Findlay," he responded.

Peter started, glanced at Lissa, and said quickly, "Thank you for bringing my sister home, sir."

"Lissa?" Rubbing his eyes, nightcap awry

and dark hair tousled, Michael stumbled through from the inner room, little more than a closet, where the boys slept. "Did Peter give you your bun? It's just a little bit. I had more'n my fair share," he confessed guiltily, " 'cause I got so hungry I had a pain in my pudding-house."

"You had *what?*" Lissa enquired, laughing.

"A tummy-ache."

"Oh dear! Well, make your bow to Lord Ashe and then you shall have a treat. I have brought home a midnight supper for the two of you."

She took off her bonnet and cloak and hung them on nails behind the door as Lord Ashe set the basket on the table and the boys delved into it, exclaiming, "Now don't eat too much," she warned, "or you will get another tummy-ache and there will be none left for tomorrow. And eat first the things in sauces that will not be so nice when they grow quite cold. Lord Ashe, may I show you out? I am sure you are anxious to leave, and I must bolt the front door."

He made an odd grimace. "I daresay I had best not keep my cattle standing," he admitted. "Good night to you, gentlemen."

"Good night, sir," said Peter. Michael, his mouth stuffed with a *puits d'amour,* waved cheerfully.

Lissa lit a stub of candle for them and took the other with her to light the way down the stairs. Lord Ashe trod unspeaking behind her, whether out of consideration for slumbering lodgers or because he had nothing to say. At the bottom, she stood the candle on the stained table in the front passage and turned to thank him.

"My lord, you have been more than kind . . ."

Stepping forward, he took her in his arms. His lips sought hers. Taken by surprise, she did not think to turn her head until his mouth crushed her own — and then it was too late. Her bones and her will turned to jelly, melting in the fire that swept through her veins. The hardness of his body pressed against her set every nerve atingle.

Abruptly he released her and moved back, regarding her with a strange look. Gasping, she slapped his face.

He raised his hand to his cheek, startled. Then he laughed softly. "Very good, Lissa," he congratulated her in a low voice, "but that will not deter a determined seducer. Indeed, there are those whom it would excite."

Breathless with indignation, and perhaps some less comprehensible feeling she did not care to dwell on, Lissa snapped, "I care not, my lord, so it deters you."

"Then you waste your effort," he said with heightened color. "I kissed you merely to demonstrate your danger. Promise me you will not accept any further invitations, nor allow anyone to know where you live."

"I thank you for the lesson, sir," she said doubtfully. Her shoulders slumped as she turned away to open the door. "Yet maybe I but struggle against the inevitable. I must feed the children."

"Can you find no respectable occupation?"

"Seamstresses and milliners earn even less than actresses, and who would hire a governess or companion without references and with two dependents?"

"I had not considered." He paused. "You are right. But be careful, I beg of you, Miss Findlay, and should you change your mind, pray consider my offer open."

He laid a visiting card upon the table, bowed without looking at her, and left.

Lissa slowly closed, locked, and bolted the door. She picked up his card and scanned it unseeingly through a haze of inexplicable tears.

Later, when the boys were asleep, she hid it away under the loose floorboard with her mama's pearl necklace. She took out the necklace and contemplated the sheen as she turned it in the dim, flickering light of the dying candle. It was her last resort. Only in desperation would she attempt to sell it, for so fine a string of perfectly matched pearls was bound to lead to suspicion of theft, to probing questions.

And questions could only lead to discovery and disaster.

In the middle of the delicate business of knotting his cravat, Ashe paused, his eyebrows raised at the sight of a lady's handkerchief lying neatly folded on his dressing table. "Where did this come from, Mills?"

"I found it in the pocket of your evening coat, my lord," his valet informed him stolidly, "the one you wore last night. It being all crumpled up, I had it washed and ironed. I hope I did right, my lord."

"Yes, of course."

Ashe picked up the small cambric square, edged with inexpertly tatted lace. Lissa Findlay's; now he recalled retrieving it from the floor as they left the private parlor. It was monogrammed in white on white, he saw, also by inexpert fingers. *FM?* No, *MF* — she had said her christian name was Melissa. She had stitched the wrong letter first.

Low wages were not the only reason she had not sought work as a seamstress, he thought with a smile.

He ought to return it. In her poverty, even so insignificant a scrap of material represented an asset, to be sold for a penny, perhaps, to buy a currant bun for her brothers.

But instead he found himself opening the small center drawer of his dressing table. Into it he dropped the handkerchief, amongst his keepsakes: a bundle of letters; ribbons; a glove; a withered rosebud and one of pink crepe; three locks of hair, each wrapped in tissue paper; a silk stocking; and half a dozen other handkerchiefs, embroidered, trimmed with genuine Valenciennes lace, still faintly redolent of sensuous perfumes.

The drawer shut with a click. Ashe frowned at his reflection in the looking glass.

"Damnation, I've ruined this neckcloth."

31

Wresting the offending length of starched white muslin from his throat, he reached for the fresh cravat the patient Mills had waiting for him.

Having achieved a neat Osbaldeston knot, Ashe allowed Mills to assist him into a close-fitting morning coat of blue Bath superfine. His dark hair brushed into the fashionable Wind-swept style, he descended the stairs to the break-fast room.

And all the time, that handkerchief nagged at the back of his mind.

It was absurd, he told himself, to feel the damn thing did not belong with the mementoes of his amorous conquests. To be sure, it represented a defeat, but after all it was only a bit of cloth, inca-pable of sensing the affront of its present com-pany. Why the devil did he keep all those odds and ends anyway? He'd tell Mills to dispose of them.

"Good morning, my lord," his stout butler greeted him in the vestibule.

"Morning, Halsey. Another fine day, do you think, or are we to expect rain?"

"Fine but chilly again, I believe, my lord. Your lordship will find Lord Quentin in the breakfast room."

"Teague? What the deuce . . . ?"

"I understand his lordship has an appoint-ment to drive out with Lady Orton, my lord."

"At this hour? He's mistaken the time, depend upon it. My sister won't show her face for hours." Striding into the breakfast parlor, a

32

small, sunny room at the front of the house, Ashe repeated his query to the blond head half hidden by the *Morning Post*. "At this hour, Teague?"

"What?" The paper dropped, revealing shirt points of extraordinary height, an intricate neckcloth, a green coat with padded shoulders and wasp-waist, and a sunshine yellow waistcoat. "Oh, beg your pardon for intruding so early, Ashe. Lady Orton desires my advice on a gown she wishes to wear to the Jerseys' ball tonight. I'm to accompany her to the modiste as soon as she comes down."

"Rather you than me. I hope she won't keep you waiting too long. She breakfasts in bed. Have you broken your fast?"

"Yes, yes, thank you, before I came out. Your butler provided coffee. Pray go ahead and don't mind me."

Annoyed by the unwanted company at his breakfast table, Ashe filled a plate at the sideboard. At least Teague had the grace to bury himself in the *Post* again rather than demand conversation or watch his reluctant host eat. Taking his seat, Ashe opened the *Times*.

For a few minutes he ate and read without interruption. Then Teague again lowered the *Post*, folded it, and set it aside.

"Must congratulate you on your conquest," he said, suavely but with a hint of disgruntlement. "Your personal charms certainly carried the day — or the night, I should say. The chit didn't even

33

wait to find out which of us would make her a better offer."

Ashe swallowed a sharp retort along with a mouthful of buttered eggs. If he admitted that Lissa had been conquered by his offer of food, not by his charms, and that he had let her get away with it, he'd be a laughingstock. Teague was no scandalmonger, but the story was too good to resist.

What was more, knowing Ashe had no further interest in Lissa, Lord Quentin would be encouraged to pursue her, to persecute her with his attentions. Nor, when it came to the test, was he likely to take no for an answer.

"Miss Findlay was delightful company," Ashe said noncommittally.

"You came to an arrangement, then?"

"What, you still have an eye on her?"

"She has that untouched, virginal look I admire."

"Well, nothing lasts forever."

"No," Teague agreed with regret. "Expect it will be gone by the time you discard her, but let me know when the moment comes, will you?"

"By all means. Ah, Daphne, good morning!" Ashe rose to his feet as his widowed sister floated into the room.

At twenty-nine, a year older than Ashe, Daphne Lady Orton was still a beauty. The white satin lining her violet-plumed lilac bonnet showed off the glossy raven curls framing her unlined face, and a snug violet spencer over the

34

high-waisted, beruffled lilac walking dress displayed her elegant figure to advantage.

"Very fetching, my dear," Ashe said appreciatively. "You are in looks today, as always."

"Thank you, Rob," she said in her soft, light, rather fluttery voice, "you always know how to make one feel better, but I assure you I have hardly slept a wink for worrying . . . Oh, Lord Quentin, good morning! I hope I have not kept you waiting long?"

"No more than a minute or two, Lady Orton." Bowing as low as his high collar points and ridiculously tight coat permitted, Teague raised her hand to his lips in a gesture of studied grace. "And such a vision of loveliness would more than compensate for a wait of a thousand years."

To Ashe's amusement, Daphne swallowed this extravagant twaddle with a complacent smile. Turning her head, she said, "Colin, . . . Where are you hiding? Colin, come in here and make your bow to Lord Quentin and your uncle."

"Don't want to," responded a fretful voice from the hallway.

"Please, darling! Oh, Rob, I am in such a worry. Since Miss Prescott gave her notice — it was too bad of her mother to fall ill when I need her so! — I have interviewed a dozen governesses and they are all quite impossible. I am at my wits' end, for I cannot always be taking Colin about with me."

"Hear, hear," muttered Teague.

"The excitement is not good for the child." To

do her justice, Daphne possessed none of the sort of vanity which might suggest to her that a ten-year-old son at her side was too revealing of her own age.

"London is no place for a small boy," Ashe pointed out, not for the first time, "even with a good governess. I wish you will send him to Mama and Nurse Bessemer. Country air will do him a world of good."

"But Mama is too frail and Nurse too old to take proper care of him. No, I cannot send him to Ashmead. Colin, darling, do come in. Just think, you shall have a nice ride in the barouche with Lord Quentin."

"Don't want to."

Ashe, the remains of his breakfast rapidly congealing on his plate, put his foot down. "Colin, obey your mama at once," he ordered.

Feet dragging, Colin appeared. The young Viscount Orton was a pale, skinny boy, with mousy hair and a sulky expression. He was about the same age as Lissa Findlay's brothers, Ashe thought, but what a difference!

His nephew, with every advantage of birth and wealth, was a sickly, discontented brat. They — Michael and Peter, wasn't it? — had displayed even in Ashe's brief meeting with them a natural courtesy, a sturdy independence, and an admirable unselfishness. Hungry as they were, they had saved a scrap of their unexpected treat for their sister. The little one had even apologized for eating more than his share of the bounty purchased with his own penny.

A pain in his "pudding-house," poor child. Ashe felt a pang of sympathy in his own . . . stomach. Surely not in his heart? His heart had nothing to do with the case.

"Good morning, Uncle Robert." Colin bowed to him listlessly, then turned to his mother. "Mama, must I go with you? It is very dull at the dressmaker's."

"You may sit and look at the pictures of pretty ladies in the pattern-books, darling."

Ashe discovered a sudden sympathy with his nephew.

"Don't *want* to! Anyway, they're none of them as pretty as you."

"Darling child!" Daphne swooped upon her son with a kiss. "But I cannot leave you at home with no governess, my love. Come, make your bow to Lord Quentin and let us be off."

Colin glowered at Teague, his mouth set in a mutinous pout.

"Well, never mind that," Teague said with uneasy joviality. "By all means, let us be on our way."

But Colin caught his uncle's eye and at last performed a grudging obeisance.

"Tell you what," said Ashe impulsively, "I'll take you to the park this afternoon, old chap."

The boy's face lit up, making Ashe at once glad he had made the offer and guilty that he did not spend more time with his nephew. But he knew the visit to the park would be hedged about with restrictions. No running with hoop or hobby-horse lest Colin grow breathless or overheated. No playing with chance-met children lest he catch an infection. No feeding the ducks lest he go too near the water, fall in, and take a chill.

Which left a sedate stroll as the only possible activity. Ashe might have defied the prohibitions but that he knew all too well how easily Colin succumbed to every ailment under the sun. A healthy country life was what he needed.

Yet however indecisive and persuadable on every other question, on that point Daphne stood firm. She would not entrust her precious son to the dowager Lady Ashe and old Nanny Bessemer, nor to any mere hired governess, however competent, except under her own eye. And one might as well expect Daphne to fly as to rusticate.

At last left in peace with his breakfast, Ashe discovered he had lost his appetite. He drank a second cup of coffee while he read the political news, then repaired to his study to write some letters.

After staring at a blank sheet of paper for some minutes, Ashe decided he was as much in need of fresh air and exercise as Colin. He would ride out to Hampstead Heath for a gallop this morning, instead of going to his club as planned. Sending for his horse and his valet, he went up to his chamber and changed into riding clothes.

Attired in boots and buckskins, he turned at the door as he left. "Oh, by the way, Mills, will you clean out the middle drawer of my dressing table? Burn the letters. The rest you may dispose of as you choose."

"Very good, my lord."

"Except the most recent acquisition. The handkerchief must be returned to its owner."

"Will you take it now, my lord? Or shall I send a footman to deliver it?"

"No, no, no hurry. Let it stay where it is for the present."

And he went out to try to gallop the unfamiliar restlessness from his bones.

Three

"The last two jam tarts are mostly crumbs," Peter observed, setting out the scanty remains of the basketful on the rickety table.

"I don't mind," said Michael eagerly. "They taste just as good."

"It will make them easier to divide into three," his brother pointed out with some severity.

Michael's face fell. "Not the jammy bits." After a momentary struggle with himself, he said in a rush of generosity, "Lissa, you can have my share of the jammy bits."

Lissa hugged him. "Thank you, pet, but you and Peter may have the tarts. I'm not very hungry."

The day after her supper with Lord Ashe, she had awoken ravenous. Recognizing that her unwonted indulgence had roused an unsatisfiable craving for food, she had sternly disciplined herself to eat next to nothing all day. By the following day the gnawing pangs of hunger had faded. In fact she seemed to have altogether lost her appetite, and she ate only as much as she thought necessary to keep up her strength.

If she fell ill, they would be in dire straits indeed.

Lord Ashe's provisions had lasted longer than she expected, but the last morsels were even now disappearing into the mouths of her two growing brothers. And she did not dare try the same trick again. His lordship had made plain the risk she had taken, she thought with a shiver. How unbelievably lucky she had been to fall in with so kind and generous a libertine!

"It's off to market again tomorrow," she said cheerfully, trying to forget the thinness of her purse.

"Lissa, won't you let me try to make some money?" Peter pleaded. "Lots of boys my age do."

"What of your studies? And I need you to take care of Michael while I am at the theatre."

"I can take care of myself," Michael said stoutly.

"No, you can't," said Peter. "You're too young."

"I'm not!"

"You are, too. But Lissa, listen, I can't study the whole day, and I can find jobs in the streets where I can keep him by me."

"The street boys are thieves and beggars."

"Not all of them," he argued. "Some are quite respectable — well, honest at least. And people will trust me because I'm clean and decently dressed and speak properly. I can hold horses, and only the other day a hawker offered me a pocket full of nuts to watch her barrow for a few minutes. I said no, because I knew you would not like it, but truly, Lissa, I'd come to no harm."

"Nor me neither," said Michael.

The harm Lissa feared was nothing that could be explained to small boys. She was afraid they would associate with the unfortunate children running wild in the streets and absorb their values, losing sight of the principles instilled by their upbringing. The harsh, rigidly judgmental aspects of those principles she had somehow, against all odds, succeeded in softening. Her brothers were all she would wish them to be, but as they grew older her influence was bound to wane. She did not want it replaced by the influence of ragamuffins and guttersnipes.

"We shall see," she temporized. "For the moment, I have enough money to go marketing tomorrow. But now I must go to rehearsal. Peter, did you bring up enough water from the pump to wash these dishes?"

"Yes, plenty. Lissa, I have a splendid idea! We don't need all these pots — I am sure I can sell them."

"I expect you could," Lissa said regretfully, "but they belong to the Piazza Coffee House. They only lent them. In fact, when they are clean you had best pack them all into the basket and return them right away. It's in Covent Garden. Just give Lord Ashe's name."

When she came home from the rehearsal, Lissa found the boys in alt.

"They gave us *money*," shouted Michael,

racing down the stairs to meet her. "A whole crown!"

"Two half-crowns," Peter confirmed, standing at the top, holding out his hand to show her the two shiny silver coins.

"Five shillings? Who?" Lissa enquired, bewildered and not a little mistrustful. "What for? No, let me take off my bonnet and boots and sit down before you tell me. My feet are tired."

Michael fetched her slippers and Peter moved two of their three wobbly chairs so that she could sit with her feet raised on one of them. They were too excited about their sudden riches, though, to wait to tell their story.

"The man at the Piazza Coffee House gave it to us," Peter informed her.

"We went across the bridge, like you said," Michael put in.

"*As* I said."

"*As* you said. We saw lots of boats, Lissa. I want to be a waterman when I grow up."

"Yesterday you wanted to be an ostler," Peter said scornfully.

"I expect you will change your mind several times before you are grown, Michael. That's much better than being too obstinate ever to admit you might be mistaken. So you crossed the bridge, and then along the Strand and up Southampton Street."

"It was easy," Peter said.

"It was an awfully long way," Michael contradicted.

"I mean it was easy to *find* the way, sapskull, with Lissa's instructions."

"Don't call me sapskull!"

"No, don't, Peter. Your statement was not clear, and even if it had been, you know a gentleman does not call another hurtful names."

Peter flushed. "Sorry. Anyway," he continued hastily, "we went to the kitchen and gave them the basket and said the crocks had been lent to Lord Ashe."

"And the man went away."

"And we were afraid he might think we had stolen the stuff."

"But then another man came and gave Peter the money!" Michael exclaimed.

"A tip?" Lissa asked doubtfully. "It is far too much."

"Not a tip." Peter frowned. "He didn't look very pleased. He said it was a refund of the deposit. What's a deposit, Lissa?"

She explained. "But I'm sure five shillings is more than the lot was worth," she said. "No doubt they overcharged Lord Ashe, thinking he would not notice and would not take the trouble to return the things. That must be why the man was annoyed at having to refund the deposit."

"Who cares if he was cross?" said Michael. "We're rich!"

"I'm afraid not," said Lissa, casting a regretful glance at the two half-crowns before her on the table. "The money is Lord Ashe's."

Peter heaved a sigh. "I thought it might be," he

said philosophically.

"Oh." Michael bit his wobbling lower lip. "You mean we can't keep it? But the man gave it to *us*."

"Only because it was you who took the basket back, pet. It was Lord Ashe who paid the deposit in the first place, you see."

"But if he paid a whole crown," Peter argued, brightening, "just to borrow some old pots, and not even caring if they were taken back, then he must have lots of money. He's not poor like us. He doesn't need it and won't even miss it."

It was true. Lissa stared temptation in the face — and after a brief battle she won. To yield to the all-too-plausible argument would set her brothers precisely the example she feared.

"That would be dishonest, Peter," she said gently. "Indeed, it would be just as much stealing as if you picked a gentleman's pocket of his handkerchief, however little he might miss it." She missed hers, though, and she castigated herself again for so carelessly leaving it at the coffee house. She had not cared to tell the boys to ask after it. "You must take the money to Lord Ashe tomorrow, if it is fine."

"I suppose so." Peter made a determined effort to be cheerful. "I daresay he may give us a tip. Do you not think so, Lissa?"

"Very likely."

"Is it far?" Michael asked with deep foreboding.

Lissa retrieved Lord Ashe's card from her hiding place. "39, Dover Street, Mayfair," she read, trying to recollect the map of London she had studied before coming to the great city. "Quite a way, I think, but there are lots of parks, so you may take a nuncheon and stop for a rest and a picnic."

"Is it across the river?" Michael wanted to know next.

"Yes, you will cross Westminster Bridge, if I am not mistaken."

"We'll stop on the bridge so you can look at the boats," Peter promised.

"I shall ask at the theatre tonight for precise directions. Someone is bound to know."

So next morning Lissa saw her brothers off, with a bit of bread and cheese and the two half-crowns in their pockets. Wistfully she watched them walk down the narrow, dirty street. At the corner, looking very small, they turned to wave, and she waved back.

She would have liked to go with them, perhaps to catch at least a glimpse of Lord Ashe, but she knew she must not. In the first place, she needed to save her energy for her exertions at the theatre, which she found more and more tiring. In the second place, she had an unsettling feeling that it would be unwise to see Lord Ashe again. He might take it as encouragement to pursue her, and that she could not bear.

"Who was that, Halsey?" Ashe enquired, descending the stairs as the butler closed the front door.

"A pair of young lads, my lord." He stared with a puzzled frown at something in his hand. "Very odd, my lord. They gave me some money to give your lordship."

"Not messengers from someone who lost to me at cards? I cannot recall that I hold anyone's vowels at present."

"Only five shillings, my lord." Halsey handed over two coins.

"Not a gaming debt, then."

"For the pots, they said, my lord."

"Pots!" Distinctly odd, but so insignificant an amount was hardly worth investigating. Ashe started to shrug, then a thought struck him. "Two young lads?"

"Small boys, my lord. Respectable-looking," he added as his master dashed past him towards the front door, "but lads that age are always hungry. I took the liberty of sending them down to the kitchens my lord."

"Good man!"

Striding down the front steps, Ashe ignored his groom, curricle, and high-bred pair awaiting him in the street and continued down the area steps. The two boys at the bottom, the elder about to knock on the kitchen door, turned at the sound of his boots on the flags.

Ashe had only seen Lissa's brothers by the dim light of a tallow candle, in their night attire, and at the time he had been more interested in their sister. These two, soberly clad in black short-coats and low-crowned hats, might be nothing to do with her. Was he making a fool of himself? "Peter Findlay?" he said uncertainly. "Michael?"

"Good afternoon, my lord." The elder raised his hat and bowed, nudging his little brother, who followed suit.

"Which of you is which?"

"I'm Peter, sir, he's Michael. Did the man give you the money?"

"He did. I should like an explanation. Come with me."

Michael hung back. "Please, sir, the man said we can have something to eat."

Ashe smiled at him. "So you shall, but upstairs, while you tell me all about it."

"In your house?"

"In my house." On the way up, he called to his groom, "Tool them about for half an hour, Burr. I'll join you presently."

"Is that your curricle, sir?" Peter asked.

"Yes. So you know a curricle from a phaeton, do you?"

"Oh, yes, Lissa said I ought . . ." He pulled himself up short, then went on with an air of inspiration, "She says if I want to earn tips holding gentlemen's horses, I ought to know what vehicle they are driving."

"But she won't . . . ," Michael started to protest.

"Yours is a capital rig, sir," his brother drowned him out. "I daresay your team is very fast?"

"They have a fair turn of speed," Ashe agreed gravely, wondering what the boys had been about to say. He did not want to alarm them by probing. "Refreshments in the breakfast room, Halsey," he said, as they approached the butler, still standing at the open door. "Substantial refreshments."

"At once, my lord," said Halsey, but he looked — insofar as a first-rate butler is capable of such a look — as if he thought Ashe had gone out of his mind.

Perhaps he had.

He went to the head of the table and invited the young Findlays to be seated on either side of him. "Now, if you please, tell me about the money," he requested.

This they were perfectly willing to do, in great detail. By the time a footman arrived with a laden tray, Ashe had learnt all about the boats on the Thames and how Michael was going to be a waterman when he grew up.

"Unless I change my mind," the child said seriously. "Lissa says it's all right to change your mind."

"By tomorrow, he'll probably want to be a baker," Peter observed to Ashe, man-to-man.

Over cold meat, bread and butter, plum pie, and tall glasses of milk — the children had excellent table manners, he noted — with a mug of ale for Ashe, he heard about the delivery of the basket to the coffee house, and the refunded deposit.

"So that's it!"

"I thought we were going to be rich," Michael mourned, his face adorned with a milk moustache. "But Lissa said it's your money 'cause you paid it."

"I own I had forgotten all about it. It was exceedingly kind of you to bring it to me." He would have liked to return half-a-crown to each of them, but to do so would negate their efforts. It might also cross Miss Findlay's pride. Perhaps a shilling each when they left would be a proper and acceptable tip.

"It was our pleasure," said Peter a trifle pompously.

"It was a *long* way," Michael contradicted.

Ashe was struck by a stroke of genius. "I'll tell you what, suppose I drive you home in the curricle? Then you can hold the horses, Peter, and earn sixpence while I go in to speak to your sister."

Peter shook his head. "She won't let me work for money. Besides, she'll be at rehearsal."

"All afternoon?" Ashe found himself ridiculously disappointed. What did it matter if he never saw the chit again? She had rejected his advances in no uncertain manner.

"All afternoon. I say, sir, do you think you might be able to persuade her to let me try to make some money? If it's not beneath her dignity, I don't see why she should think it's beneath mine, when I don't. Perhaps if you told her . . ."

"I cannot imagine Miss Findlay would pay the

least heed to anything I might tell her."

"But you're her friend, aren't you?"

"Ah, hm." Ashe found himself unexpectedly at a loss for words. Friendship was not precisely the relationship he had had in mind for Lissa Findlay. But the boy was looking at him anxiously. "Yes," he said, "I hope she considers me her friend. However, the point is moot as she is out this afternoon."

"You could take us home anyway, sir," Michael pointed out hopefully.

"I could indeed." Perhaps on the way to Lambeth he would find an opportunity to satisfy his growing curiosity about the Findlays. "I will. Have you had enough to eat?"

Michael felt his stomach and heaved a regretful sigh. "Yes, thank you, my lord. I haven't got room for a single 'nother bite."

"Nor have I, thank you, sir," Peter agreed, then hissed across the table, "Michael, wipe your face."

Michael hastily removed his temporary moustache with a napkin. At that moment, the door opened and Colin appeared.

"Uncle Robert, Halsey said . . ." He stopped dead. "Who are those boys?"

"Master Peter Findlay and Master Michael Findlay," Ashe said calmly, while he thought, *Oh the deuce what* is *Daphne going to say?* "Peter, Michael," he continued as the brothers slipped down from their chairs and bowed, staring, "this is my nephew, Lord Orton."

51

"How do you do," the Findlays chorused. Michael added with interest, "Are you really a lord, even though you're just a boy?"

"Yes, I'm a viscount, because my father's dead. What are you doing here?"

"They are just leaving," Ashe said hastily.

"Where are you going?"

"Home, my lord," Peter told him.

Colin frowned. "Boys don't call boys 'my lord,' do they, Uncle?"

"It depends upon the circumstances."

"Well, I don't want you to call me 'my lord.' "

"What shall I call you, then?" Peter asked.

"Just Colin, and I'll call you Peter and Michael. Where is your home? Is it far away?"

"A *long* way," said Michael. "Miles and miles. Lord Ashe is going to drive us in his curricle."

Ashe was the recipient of an accusing scowl. "You never take *me* in the curricle."

"Why don't you come, too?" Michael invited.

"A curricle is built for two," Ashe pointed out.

"But I want to go!"

"That's all right," said Peter kindly. "We're just boys and we're all quite thin. We'll squeeze in somehow."

Ashe hadn't the heart to refuse. He would just have to convince Daphne that the Findlay brothers were perfectly respectable, decent, clean, and altogether harmless — and impress upon Colin that he must *never* describe their home to his mama.

On the way, for the first time Ashe could remember, Colin laughed. Surely news of that would appease Daphne, especially as he was unlikely ever to meet his new acquaintances again.

Which would be a pity, Ashe ruminated, the seed of an outrageous idea taking root in his mind.

Lissa stared at her brothers in dismay. "He brought you all the way home?"

"In his curricle," Peter confirmed. "It's a bang-up rig, Lissa, you should see it."

"And his horses go like the wind," said Michael. "He *sprang* 'em to show us."

"He what?"

"Sprang 'em. Them. It means let them go as fast as they want."

"It sounds dangerous," Lissa said dubiously, hanging her bonnet on its nail.

"Just for a short way," Peter reassured her, "after we crossed the bridge, when there wasn't much traffic."

"I think I'll be an ostler after all, or maybe a gentleman's groom. Lord Ashe's groom sat up behind us on a little seat. It looked like fun."

"You can be my groom, if you want," Peter offered. "When *I* grow up, I shall be a gentleman, shan't I, Lissa?"

"You both will, and I trust you will remember that even boys should behave like gentlemen."

"Colin didn't, did he, Peter? He didn't bow to us when Lord Ashe introduced us, and then he *would* come, and then he complained about getting squashed."

"Who is Colin?" Lissa asked, her mind boggling at the vision of the elegant, dashing Lord Ashe squeezed into his curricle with three boys.

"Lord Ashe's nephew. He wasn't really so bad," Peter said tolerantly. "He's just not used to being with other boys. He did cheer up a bit after that, and he didn't make us call him Lord Orton, even though he's a viscount."

Lissa's mind boggled again. Lord Ashe had brought his noble nephew to a seedy area of Lambeth to call upon the woman he hoped to make his mistress?

She could only be glad she had been out. "I hope you thanked his lordship," she said. "It was excessively kind of him to drive you home."

"We thought he wasn't going to," Michael said, "when Peter told him you wouldn't be at home."

"He knew?"

"He said he wanted to talk to you, so I told him you had a rehearsal this afternoon. So they didn't come in, just set us down right at the door."

Shaking her head, Lissa gave up for the present any attempt to understand Lord Ashe. The best she could do was to remain constantly on guard.

Four

Ashe had hoped to choose his moment to speak to Daphne. It was a lot to expect. Burr was sworn to silence, not that he would dream of revealing his master's business to a soul. But Halsey and the footman had undoubtedly already discussed, in the housekeeper's room and the servants' hall respectively, his lordship's friendly reception of two small boys.

Ashe had impressed upon Colin that he must not describe the Findlays' home surroundings. "People cannot help being poor," he said sternly, "and to spread tales about their shabbiness is thoroughly ungentlemanly. Positively vulgar, in fact."

He considered adding a prohibition on mentioning the curricle ride at all, in the hope that Daphne would not hear about it from the servants. To do so would be to lead his nephew into the murky waters of deceit, he decided. And she was bound to find out one way or another, sooner or later.

Sooner, and by way of her dresser, he discovered when she entered the drawing room that evening looking reproachful.

The setting sun, slanting between pale blue

damask curtains, sheened across the crimson satin of her ball dress and struck sparks from the rubies about her white neck.

"You look like an empress," Ashe said sincerely.

"Thank you." Daphne accepted his admiration as her due, preened a little, but was not to be diverted. Sinking gracefully onto a blue-brocaded chair, she addressed him with a plaintive air. "Rob, what is this Marlin tells me about your introducing Colin to a pair of street urchins? I was never so shocked in my life, I vow!"

"Hardly street urchins," he protested, finding himself on the defensive, as he had feared. "They are perfectly respectable children, sent to me on an errand."

"Errand boys, if you will. Still, such are scarcely fit acquaintance for Viscount Orton!"

"I had no intention of making them acquainted. Colin came in while I was talking to them, and demanded to know who they were."

"You might have sent him away, I suppose, or them! If you meant to give Colin a ride in your curricle — which I cannot like! It is a monstrous unsafe vehicle for a child — then why did you take up those ragamuffins as well?"

"Peter and Michael Findlay are not ragamuffins," Ashe said with what patience he could muster. "They had done me a favor, and I had already promised to drive them home. Colin insisted upon joining us."

"You could have refused him. He always does

what you say, as he did with Miss Prescott. La, I don't know what I shall do if I don't find another governess soon! Colin will not mind me unless it suits him, but I cannot leave him all day with only a nursemaid. I wish you would spend more time with him, Rob. You are his guardian, after all."

"I took him for a curricle ride," Ashe reminded her, "and he very much enjoyed it. In fact, he . . ."

At that moment the drawing-room door opened and Halsey announced Lord Quentin Teague. Daphne greeted him with delight, instantly forgetting both her anxiety for her son and her dispute with her brother.

Ashe curbed his annoyance. They were all three engaged to dine with mutual friends before going on to a ball. It was not really the best moment to present his sister with a decidedly controversial suggestion.

He ran her to earth the next afternoon, entertaining callers in the drawing room. Despite her status as a beautiful widow, and her refusal to wear a widow's cap, Daphne had numerous friends among the younger matrons in town for the Season. The rest of her visitors were admirers. These ranged from a mooncalf in a neckerchief with aspirations to be taken for a second Byron, to a greying roué of the Prince Regent's set, reputed to be looking out for a rich third wife.

Surveying them, Ashe decided it was small

wonder if his sister preferred Lord Quentin, also present, to the rest. Foppish and rakish as he was, at least he took neither penchant to extremes.

Ashe set himself to be pleasant to the ladies present, thankful that none were old enough to be on the catch for husbands for their daughters. Gradually the company thinned, until only Lord Quentin remained.

He showed no sign of leaving.

At last Ashe said, "If you don't mind, Teague, I'd like a private word with my sister."

"Of course, my dear fellow, of course. Don't want to outstay my welcome."

"But you were going to come with me to the milliner, Lord Quentin," Daphne reminded him. "You know how much I value your advice. We can talk later, Rob."

"Will you be in tonight?"

"Well, no. I am going with the Burdetts to Lady Cholmondesley's rout. Is the matter so urgent?"

"*You* think so."

"I? You are prodigious mysterious! I cannot imagine what you have in mind. I am all agog, I vow!"

"Suppose I wait for you at Hatchard's Bookshop, Lady Orton," Teague said diplomatically. "The milliner you mentioned is just around the corner, I believe?"

"Oh, yes, that will do very well. I shall not keep you long, I am sure," she added, giving her cicisbeo her hand and her brother a minatory look.

Ashe eyed with disfavor the lingering kiss Lord Quentin deposited on Daphne's hand. The moment the door closed behind Teague, he said, "Why on earth do you keep that fellow hanging about you? I don't trust his intentions. He's a known rake."

"No worse than you, Rob. Everyone knows you have given the Skylark her congé, and you cannot make me believe you have not already found a replacement."

"Teague told you?" Ashe demanded angrily.

"Certainly not," Daphne said, outraged. "He would not dream of discussing such improper relationships with me. He wants to marry me."

"My apologies, my dear. Have you considered accepting his offer? Would you wish to have Lord Quentin for a husband?"

"Oh yes, I am convinced we should suit very well. We enjoy just the same sort of things, you see. He cannot abide the country, except for occasional house parties, naturally, and he never bores me with talk of books or politics or horses. Only he does not wish to be a papa to poor Colin, and of course I cannot abandon my darling son, or let him be sent away to a horrid school."

"Ah yes, Colin." Ashe had to agree that the boy was too sickly to thrive on the harsh regimen of Eton or Harrow. He forebore to mention that he would never permit his ward to be brought up by a Bond Street beau like Teague.

"By the time he is grown, I shall be an old woman!" Daphne wailed.

"Hardly that. You will be in your prime. Without childbearing, females tend to keep their youth," Ashe observed with callous indelicacy, "and after all, Lord Quentin is a third son with no need to breed an heir. Anyway, there is nothing I can do about that. I can, however, relieve you of your immediate difficulty."

"Whatever do you mean, Rob?"

"I have found you a governess."

"A governess! How do you know she will suit? It is quite impossible to find someone both kind and firm, like Miss Prescott. Goodness knows, I have tried. Who is she?"

Ashe's nonchalance was entirely assumed. He was on tenterhooks. "Her name is Findlay, Miss Findlay."

"I don't care about her name," Daphne cried. "Whose governess is she? Has she good references? How did you come to hear of her?"

"As a matter of fact, I have met her. I . . . er . . . She isn't a governess at present."

"Then what is she?" Daphne queried impatiently.

He would have concealed the truth if he could, but the facts were bound to emerge in the end. "An actress."

"An actress? My dear brother, are you feeling quite well? Your wits have gone a-begging, I vow. An actress!"

"She has not been long on the stage. I believe

she would be perfect for Colin."

"But how is it you are acquainted with her? Rob, she is not your . . . ?"

"Good gad, Daphne, no! You cannot really suppose I should introduce my *chère amie* to my own sister, install her under my own roof! I invited Miss Findlay to dine with me after a performance." Ashe held up his hand to stop the question obviously hovering on the tip of her tongue. His face burning, he admitted, "Your assumption as to my intentions is perfectly correct."

"She accepted?"

"She accepted supper. She refused the offer of my protection."

"You did not offer enough. Why else should she dine with you?"

"She was hungry, and she hoped to be able to take some scraps home to the children."

Daphne pounced. "Ha, children! I knew it."

"Precisely what I thought, my dear, but they are much too old to be her offspring. The boys are her brothers."

"Boys? Oh Rob, not those two common boys you let Colin consort with?"

"The very same boys, and uncommonly well brought up they are. I have no doubt of Miss Findlay's ability to . . ."

"Peter and Michael?" Colin erupted from behind a window curtain, his thin cheeks pink with excitement. "Uncle Robert, will Peter and Michael come to live here?"

"Gracious heaven," Daphne exclaimed, "how you startled me."

"Colin, a gentleman does not hide and listen to other people's conversation," Ashe said sternly. His mind raced, trying to remember just what he and Daphne had said. Surely they had used euphemistic language incomprehensible to a ten-year-old?

"Indeed, darling, it was very wrong in you!"

"But you knew I was on the window seat, Mama," said Colin, injured. "You sent for me to come down and make my bow to your callers."

Daphne bit her lip. "I had forgot," she said guiltily.

"Please, Mama, may Peter and Michael come to live here? I don't care about Miss Findlay being an actress. I know I shall like her if she is their sister. They are very *gentlemanly* boys, are they not, Uncle?"

"Very." Ashe took pity on his flustered sister. "But this is a matter for your mother and me to discuss, old chap. Off you go, and not a word of this to anyone or Peter and Michael will certainly never join you in the schoolroom."

"I haven't got anyone to tell. Gentlemen do not confide in nursemaids and footmen," Colin explained with a sad kind of dignity. He trailed to the door, turning as he reached it for a final passionate entreaty: "Let them come, Mama, *please!*"

As the door shut behind him, Daphne said pettishly, "It is most unfair of you to recruit my own

62

son against me."

"Come now! I had no notion he was here."

"But you introduced him to those boys."

"With no ulterior motive. It was seeing his pleasure in their company which gave me the idea of employing Miss Findlay as his governess."

"An actress! She cannot possibly have the proper qualifications."

"I understand she would have sought a position as a governess had she not been under the necessity of providing a home for her brothers. Besides, what qualifications do you require, besides sympathetic discipline?"

Daphne looked blank.

Ashe laughed. "You did not expect your admirable Miss Prescott to teach Greek and Latin and mathematics! Come to think of it, I daresay I ought to look about for a tutor for Colin."

"He is not strong enough to spend all day conning his books!"

"No, two or three hours a day will suffice, and I agree with you that he needs a woman to provide more constant care than you have inclination for."

"I love him," she protested weakly.

"I know, my dear, but a fashionable female has many demands upon her time."

"Oh heavens, the time!" Daphne started up. "Lord Quentin will think I have deserted him, and depend upon it, someone else will have bought that divine hat. I wish I had purchased it when I saw it this morning."

Ashe attempted to recall her to the subject at hand. "I believe what Colin needs most of all is companions his own age, and I am quite prepared to give the Findlay boys a home."

"Really, Rob, I cannot spare the time to discuss it now. Besides, I am heartily tired of arguing."

"Say you will at least grant Miss Findlay an interview, then I shall leave you in peace."

"Oh, very well! Pray ring the bell and have the landau brought round. I must go and put on a bonnet."

She swept out. Torn between annoyance, amusement, and triumph, Ashe obediently rang the bell.

In her drab cloak and bonnet, Lissa crossed the Green Room without a single gentleman sparing her a second glance. She wondered again what Lord Ashe had seen in her to merit soliciting her favors.

She was glad he had not renewed his proposition, she told herself. Rejecting him had not been as easy as it ought to be for a virtuous young lady. She had no energy for another struggle.

Tired and dispirited, she trudged down the steps. As she reached the street, a closed carriage drew forward and stopped directly in front of her.

The door opened. Lissa moved back.

"Miss Findlay," said an urgent voice. Recognizing it, she felt her heart flip-flop. "Allow me to drive you home."

Lissa retreated a little further. "Lord Ashe!"

He stepped down. By the light of the single dim lantern over the stage door, his face was invisible beneath the brim of his tall beaver. "Don't you trust me? You can, you know. Surely I have proved that! I must talk to you, here if you insist but we shall be more comfortable in the carriage."

Her feet ached, a light but chilly rain had begun to fall, and the dark, dirty streets roamed by footpads and drunkards lay before her. With a murmur of defeat, she climbed in, avoiding his proffered hand.

As she sank back on the soft, velvet-covered squabs, an overpowering desire for sleep struck her. She fought it, forcing herself to sit bolt upright. Lord Ashe's bulk darkened the doorway momentarily. He took the opposite seat, then leaned forward to spread a fur rug across her knees.

The simple action made tears spring to her eyes.

Crossly she blinked them back. She was too tired to deal with whatever assault on her virtue his lordship had in mind this time. Not that she feared physical assault. He had indeed proved himself too much the gentleman to use force to overcome her scruples. What she feared was the battering of arguments against her frail defenses,

65

warnings of the inevitability of her fall, perhaps reproaches for the effects of her obduracy on her brothers.

The carriage turned out of the alley and rolled past the ornate, brightly lit front portico of the theatre. Lord Ashe leaned forward, an earnest regard fixed on Lissa.

"You're burned to the socket," he said roughly, and she realized she had slumped back against the cushions again. "Perhaps my business had best wait till morning."

Enveloped in darkness once more, she gave a weary sigh. Apprehension had driven away the urgent need for sleep. If she arranged to meet him tomorrow, she would spend a wakeful night in dread of the morning. Besides, she was reluctant to encourage him by actually making an appointment to see him.

"I had rather hear now whatever you have to say."

"As you wish." His voice was eager. "I have succeeded in persuading my sister, Lady Orton, to consider you for the position of governess to her son."

A flame of hope leapt in Lissa's heart. Then she recovered from her startlement and her mind began to work again. "Her ladyship would never hire an actress as governess. I cannot conceal my present employment."

"I told her. She's willing to give you an interview."

"Truly? But she does not know about my

brothers. How could I expect her to give two un-known boys a home?"

"Peter and Michael may be your strongest card, since Colin is prodigious eager to have them as playmates. As for giving them a home, no difficulty there. The home is mine. Daphne is a widow and resides with me."

So that was his stratagem! Under his roof, Lissa would be at his mercy, unable to evade his pursuit. No doubt he was aware that she was at-tracted to him and hoped proximity would turn the trick. Or he might even stoop to threaten her with dismissal if she continued to reject him. Once she had left the Coburg troupe, she would never be able to return. There were too many would-be actresses ready to leap at the most me-nial position in the theatre.

Out on the street with the boys, penniless, she would have no apparent choice but a sordid, hand-to-mouth life of sin. Lord Ashe was counting on her preferring the comfort of his protection.

She did have another choice, which in such straits she might be forced to turn to. She had no intention of voluntarily putting herself in such a desperate case as to make it appear the lesser of two evils. In any case, Lord Ashe was unaware of that possibility. As far as he knew, she thought with a flash of anger, once in his power her alter-natives would be submission or destitution.

"Bring the boys with you to the interview," suggested the baron. "When she sees their excellent manners for herself, she cannot fail to approve them as companions for her son."

Lissa's fury flickered out as had her hope. By his own lights, Lord Ashe was doing his best for her and her little family.

"There will be no interview," she said sadly. "I cannot accept Lady Orton's kind offer. Please convey my regrets to her."

To her relief, the carriage stopped at that moment. She jumped out and had her key in the lock of the lodging-house door before his voice followed her.

"Lissa, wait! Tell me why not."

If he had called her Miss Findlay, she might have hesitated. The implied intimacy of her nickname confirmed her suspicions.

A moment later she was safe inside, the door locked behind her. Turning a deaf ear to his knock, she leaned against the door, gathering her strength for the long flights of stairs ahead.

Beyond that, at present, she could not see.

Five

The fair, dandified gentleman was watching her again. Having dropped his card without reading it, Lissa did not know his name. She did not want to. The desire in his prominent blue eyes revolted her.

Somehow the equally evident desire in Lord Ashe's brown eyes had never made her feel the same repulsion — which just showed how wise she was to avoid him.

The past few days, avoiding him had taken no effort. She had seen nothing of him since refusing to fall in with his plans for her future. Nicole and Minette condoled with her on failing to hook such an eminently attractive fish. Without actually saying so, Lissa let them believe he had simply found her charms inadequate.

The new program was as long as the old, but the evening's performance ended at last. In the long, low-ceilinged dressing room, Lissa changed into her puritan-plain dress and cloak. She was too tired to join in the chatter of the other girls, but she waited to join the flock hurrying through the dim corridor and bursting into the brightly lit Green Room. Among so many Birds of Paradise, surely one little brown wren might evade the blond gentleman's eye.

He was lying in wait.

"So there you are, my sweet," he said jovially. "I missed you t'other day, looked to see you tricked out in finery like the rest. You and Ashe didn't suit, eh?"

"No, sir," Lissa said tersely.

"Should have come straight to me."

"I fear I mislaid your card, sir."

The unwisdom of this response dawned on her too late, as he waved an airy hand, accepting her apology.

"No matter. Teague's the name, Lord Quentin Teague. Daresay we can come to an agreement, you and I. Let's go and get a bite of supper."

The very word made Lissa's mouth water, remembrance of veal and fish, asparagus and green peas, making her light headed with hunger. She was dreadfully tempted.

But after the fricasseed chicken had come the *puits d'amour.* Lord Quentin was not likely to be easily deterred from plumbing the depths of the well, and she knew now the futility of pitting her small strength against a determined seducer. For that lesson she must be ever grateful to Lord Ashe.

Her hesitation brought a knowing smile to Lord Quentin's homely face. "Ah, you want a little something as earnest of my intentions." He felt in his breast pocket and brought forth a bracelet of red stones set in gold, far too flashy to be anything but tawdry paste and gilt. This he

70

dangled from one finger before her nose.

Lissa drew back, dismayed. "No, indeed, my lord, you mistake me. Pray forgive me, I am very tired and want nothing but to seek my . . . rest."

"That time of the month, is it?" he said philosophically. "Ah well, anticipation sharpens the appetite. Sweet dreams, my pretty."

He was gone before Lissa could summon up the energy to disillusion him.

The next evening Lord Quentin did not appear at the theatre. Lissa dared hope he had found someone else, but the following night he joined the audience just before the grand finale.

This time she must make it quite plain to him that she would never accept his protection. Outside the Green Room door she paused, nerving herself to withstand his wrath.

"Miss Findlay!" The call came from behind her.

She turned to face the stage manager.

"Miss Findlay, I've been wanting a word with you. You are going to have to put a bit more dash into your dancing, or I'm sorry to say I'll be looking out for a replacement."

"I-I shall do my best," she stammered, wondering where she was to find the extra energy.

"I'm sorry," he repeated, shrugging his shoulders, "but the company cannot afford to carry anyone who isn't pulling his weight. Try to get more rest instead of gadding about." With a friendly nod, he went on his way.

Gadding about! Scarcely aware of what she

was doing, Lissa went through into the Green Room, visions of the boys' increasingly wan faces floating before her eyes.

Nicole and Minette pounced on her, their painted faces anxious. "Trouble, duck?" asked Minette.

"He . . . he is not quite satisfied with my dancing."

"We was afraid you'd got turned off," said Nicole, relieved. "Still and all, you oughta be putting something away 'gainst a rainy day. You don't want to keep Lord Quentin on tenterhooks too long, hoping for summat better."

"I am not . . . No, you are right, I must tell him. . . . Oh, if only Lord Ashe . . . !"

"Too late, duck, you had your chance with him."

"But it's not too late. At least, I pray it is not. He asked me to be his nephew's governess, you see, in his own house. I know it is only a ruse to have me at his mercy, but oh, I had far rather him than Lord Quentin."

The girls were gaping at her.

"*Governess?*" Nicole choked out.

Lissa nodded.

Minette shook her head. "You got it all wrong, duck. A gentleman don't set up his convenient in his own house, with his family and all, not a real gentleman like Lord Ashe."

Before Lissa could question this statement, Lord Quentin approached. "All right and tight now, Miss Findlay?" he enquired.

Flustered, fumbling for words, Lissa blurted out, "No!"

Nicole and Minette exchanged a swift glance. "She ain't quite right yet, m'lord," Nicole hastily announced.

"Give her another day," advised Minette.

Lord Quentin frowned. "Oh very well," he grumbled petulantly, "but I'm otherwise engaged tomorrow. I shall be back the day after, though, so don't go accepting *carte blanche* from anyone else." He turned on his heel and pushed his way through the throng.

"There you are, Lissa," said Nicole, "you got two days to find out what Lord Ashe is up to. Make the best of 'em."

Minette wished her good luck, and the two went off about their own business.

Lissa lingered a few minutes, until she was sure Lord Quentin must have left the theatre. Trudging homeward through the mild spring night, she wondered whether Minette could possibly be right.

She knew herself to be woefully ignorant of the ways of the world. Was a governess safe from the attentions of the master of the house? Had Lord Ashe truly accepted her innocence and made his proposal in good faith? Or was her mistrust justified?

On the point of accepting the risk even before Minette spoke, she now saw her way clearer. At the very least, the boys would eat well for a while. The alternative, even if she kept her place in the theatre, was to watch them sink further into malnourishment, perhaps fall sick, even die. What was her virtue beside that?

Still, she would not give up without a fight. And there were always the pearls.

Reaching home, Lissa plodded up the stairs, chewed a dry crust, and slumped onto her pallet, beneath the thin coverlet. As she sank into sleep, somehow she could not help being happy at the prospect of seeing Lord Ashe again.

Then suddenly she was wide awake again. She had failed to take into consideration that more than a sennight had passed since he invited her to an interview with his sister. Since then she had had no word from him. Perhaps he was too deeply offended by her refusal to renew the offer.

Or perhaps Lady Orton had found a satisfactory governess by now. Even if she had not, it was still her decision, not Lord Ashe's, as to whether to hire Lissa. She might very well have agreed to the interview just to please her brother, with no real intention of considering an actress for the post.

There was no sense in worrying about what she could not change, Lissa told herself. Unless morning brought a new perspective, she would stand by her decision. What had she to lose but the few remaining shreds of her pride?

With a sigh, Ashe gave up trying to hide behind the *Times*, folded it, and set it beside his half-emptied plate. He was about to rise when his butler came into the breakfast room.

"Halsey, what the deuce is going on above stairs?"

"I was just coming to inform your lordship that her ladyship urgently desires your presence." In response to Ashe's raised eyebrows, he coughed deferentially and continued, "I understand, my lord, that Lady Orton is having a disagreement with the latest governess as to whether she is resigning or being dismissed."

Ashe groaned. "What's he done now?"

"I believe, my lord, that Master Colin, on being pressed to eat his breakfast, threw it at the unfortunate woman. A boiled egg, my lord, *lightly* boiled, and bread-and-milk."

A quarter of an hour later, Ashe reseated himself at the table with a fresh plate of food. The governess, promised a quarter's wages, was packing. Daphne, with her abigail's aid, was trying to decide which bonnet to wear with her new walking dress. Colin, after a forced and begrudged apology, sat down sulkily beside his uncle.

"A lightly boiled egg and a bowl of bread-and-milk for Master Colin," Ashe ordered the butler.

"I'm not hungry."

"You will eat your breakfast."

"Then I shall be *sick*."

Ashe nodded to the butler, who withdrew. "If you persist in not eating, Colin, you will fall ill. It would serve you right, but it would very much distress your mama, so I will not have it."

Colin sat in mutinous silence. Ashe applied himself to his plate and his newspaper, doing his best to ignore the memory of a small boy with a hunger pain in his "pudding-house." Miss Findlay had rejected his help, and that was the end of the matter.

"I want Peter and Michael." Colin's lower lip trembled. "Why can't they come and play, Uncle Robert, even if Miss Findlay isn't a proper governess?"

Ashe was saved at least temporarily from difficult, if not impossible explanations by Halsey's return with a tray. The butler set down an egg cup and a bowl before Colin, then turned to his master to present a folded sheet of rather grubby paper.

"Just delivered, my lord. By the two young lads . . ."

Springing to his feet, Ashe exclaimed, "Are they gone?"

"No, my lord. They wished to await an answer, and I ventured to invite them to wait in the hall, not the kitchen, seeing as last time your lordship — ah — desired to speak to them."

"Show them in." Ashe sat down, feeling rather foolish. Had he jumped to the wrong conclusion, he would have made a proper cake of himself. That explained why his heart beat rather fast as he unfolded the letter.

"Who is it, Uncle?" Colin asked with bated breath, glancing back and forth from Ashe to the door. "Is it . . . ? It's not . . . Peter!" he squealed, and launched himself at the bowing boys, skidding to a stop before them. "Michael!"

Ashe could not see his nephew's face, but he heard the beam in his voice. Peter was grinning. Michael stepped aside and peered rather anxiously past Colin at the table.

"Gosh, do you have an egg for breakfast?"

"You can have it," said Colin generously.

"Colin, I said you are to eat your egg, and I meant it. Come and sit down." As Michael's face fell, Ashe added hastily, "Halsey will bring Peter and Michael as many eggs as they would like."

Michael's grey eyes rounded. "Six," he said. "Ten. Two dozen. Lots and lots."

"Two," Peter told him sternly, "and we haven't made our bows properly yet. Good morning, my lord."

"Good morning, my lord," said Michael, obediently bowing again. "I can eat more than two eggs."

"There are sausages and bacon and kidneys on the sideboard."

"Kidneys?" The child blanched.

"You won't make him eat them, will you?" his brother asked forebodingly. "They make him sick."

"Good Lord no! Take what you want. Fresh muffins, Halsey, and we'd better have a jug of milk."

"Very good, my lord."

The boys settled and chattering away — Colin absentmindedly eating as he talked — Ashe at last turned his eyes to the letter. It was brief, impersonal:

My lord, If the position of governess to your nephew is still available on the same terms, I wish to apply. Your ob'd't servant, Melissa Findlay.

Ashe had a very good idea of why she had refused before. The initial impulse which had made him call out to her, even run after her and bang on her door, had quickly given way to pique. How dared she assume he was so debauched as to set up a mistress under his own roof?

He had half a mind to tell her she was too late.

No, he could not do it. And not just because of his nephew's happy face, or Peter's manful efforts not to speak with his mouth full, or Michael's frank gobbling. Ashe was afraid Lissa — Miss Findlay — had been driven to change her mind by desperation, and he could not bear to think of her desperate.

"Peter, is your sister rehearsing this morning?"

"No, sir, not till afternoon."

"Then pray excuse me, gentlemen. Colin, I am going to have a word with your mama. You may take your friends up to the schoolroom when you have all finished eating."

"Really and truly? Oh, famous, Uncle Robert!"

"Thank you, sir," said Peter, "but we have to take an answer back to Lissa."

"You shall have your answer presently."

"It's a long way home," Michael pointedly reminded him.

"How fortunate that my horses are in need of exercise," said Ashe with a smile.

He went upstairs and was admitted to his sister's pink and white boudoir. Daphne, in a wrap frothy with lace, sat at her dressing table while her abigail removed curling papers from her black locks.

"It is too tiresome, Rob," said Daphne tranquilly, "none of my hats is quite the right shade of green. Green is such a difficult color to match, I vow. I shall have to purchase a new bonnet."

"I'm sure you will look quite delightfully in old or new, my dear. We must talk about Colin. Have you any engagements this morning?"

"No, nothing in particular. Marlin, you may finish my hair later. I am quite at my wits' end, Rob. That odious woman had not the least notion how to deal with Colin."

Ashe paused until the door closed behind the tall, raw-boned dresser, then said, "I have heard from Miss Findlay. She is willing to take on the job of attempting to 'deal with' Colin."

"Your actress?"

"Not mine, nor anyone's," Ashe said emphatically.

"Oh, very well, I am ready to try anything, I declare. I shall see her, and if she is as ladylike as you promise, and her brothers as gentlemanly, she may come for a month's trial."

"Fair enough." He let out the breath he had not realized he was holding. "The boys you may see as soon as you are dressed. They brought Miss Findlay's letter and I have sent them up to the schoolroom with Colin."

"Rob, that is too bad of you! I wished to meet them before I allowed Colin to associate with them."

"Just go and see them all together. You will find Colin a changed creature in their company."

Daphne pouted, but again conceded. "Since they are here already . . . You had best send a footman for Miss Findlay right away. I have calls to pay later."

"And a bonnet to purchase. Rather than risk any delay, my dear, I shall go and fetch Miss Findlay myself."

Though she looked at him rather doubtfully, as if suspicion once more raised its head, all she said was, "Yes, I had almost forgot the bonnet, and I do wish to wear my new gown to drive in the Park with Lord Quentin this afternoon. Thank you, Rob. Pray ring for Marlin before you go."

Complying, Ashe wondered whether Teague was going to prove a fly in the ointment. With any luck the fellow had forgotten Lissa by now. However, he knew her profession and assumed her lack of chastity. He could, if he so chose, create a grand scandal.

True, he was by no means a devotee of scandalous gossip. What was more, he had no interest in Colin. Should he by chance discover that Lissa was the boy's governess, he might be persuaded to hold his tongue for Daphne's sake. He did, after all, claim to be fond of her.

Ashe ordered his curricle and informed Peter and Michael, still eating, that he was going to fetch their sister.

"Good," said Michael. "Lissa likes eggs, too."

Had sheer hunger changed her mind?

In the late spring sunshine, the kitchen gardens of Lambeth sprouted in orderly green rows, a pleasing sight. The contrast with the dingy rows of invading tenements was the more dismaying. The blue sky above brought little cheer to the narrow streets, yards and alleys. Ragged children played in the dust, and streams of filth ran down the gutters.

Miss Findlay's street was one of the more respectable. Nonetheless, Ashe had his groom hold his horses rather than entrusting them to one of the hopeful urchins who ran up when he stopped. The hunched crone who opened the door to his knock eyed him grimly and announced that she did not permit gentleman callers.

"I am glad to hear it, ma'am," Ashe said with his most engaging smile. "Will you be so good as to inform Miss Findlay that . . . er . . . Ashe has come to convey her to his sister's?"

The woman turned her head and shouted, "Billy, run up an' fetch Miss Findlay. Tell 'er Mr. Ashe is 'ere from 'is sister. Won't you step in, sir, an' wait in the 'all?"

Catching a whiff of stale cabbage, mingled with less identifiable odors, Ashe said hurriedly, "Thank you, I shall wait in my carriage."

How had a sensitive creature like Lissa Findlay survived in that pestiferous hole? Would she come, if only to escape it, or would she change her mind again?

Six

Lissa did not keep him waiting. Though she knew a moment of panic when she heard Lord Ashe had come himself to fetch her, she hastily flung a shawl about her shoulders and hurried down. She could always refuse the situation if it were offered her, she told herself.

Lord Ashe jumped down from his curricle as she stepped into the street.

"Good morning, Miss Findlay. My sister is expecting you. I'm glad you changed your mind."

Paradoxically, the warmth of his smile both sent a frisson of trepidation down her spine and set her at ease. "I am not certain I am doing the right thing," she confessed as he handed her up into the carriage.

"You have nothing to fear from me," he assured her, pressing her hand lightly then instantly letting it go. "But I know you would not let fear deter you from doing what is best for your brothers. The first time we met, you gave me proof of your willingness to throw your heart over."

"To what?" she asked, alarmed. Had he so mistaken her as to believe she had given him her heart and so meant to let him enjoy her favors?

Swinging up beside her and taking the reins

from the groom, he laughed. "I beg your pardon, a hunting term, referring to the courage to tackle a difficult jump."

"Oh, yes, I remember!" A distant memory: herself a small girl on a small, grey, Welsh Mountain pony; an elderly groom urging her to throw her heart over; the triumph of flying over the low pole; and cantering around to see that Papa was watching, applauding from the paddock rail.

Lissa's throat hurt from the effort of holding back tears. Lord Ashe was looking at her oddly, eyebrows raised but concern in his dark eyes.

"I must have heard the phrase somewhere," she said weakly.

"Do you ride?"

"N-no." She had not ridden in seven or eight years, so it was not really a fib, though why should she cavil at one minor taradiddle when she was living a lie? She must strive harder to banish the memories which made her life of deception so much more difficult.

The groom sprang up behind, and Lord Ashe forebore to question Lissa further. She sensed, though, that he was not satisfied with her responses.

To distract him, to make him forget his curiosity, she commented upon the fine day and the flourishing market gardens on either side of the high road. In truth, it was a pleasure to leave the mean streets behind. For some time, she had lacked the energy to walk farther than she needed.

Lord Ashe, half his attention on the busy traffic, responded amiably to her remarks. When Lissa, exclaiming at the splendid view from Westminster Bridge, mentioned Mr. Wordsworth's beautiful description of the scene, he quoted the first few lines.

" 'Earth has not anything to show more fair:
Dull would he be of soul who could pass by
A sight so touching in its majesty.'

"You enjoy poetry, Miss Findlay?"

"Yes. No!" Bother! An actress was unlikely to be acquainted with non-dramatic poetry, yet a governess ought to be familiar at least with the major poets. Oh what a tangled web! she thought, wishing William Wordsworth's name had never passed her lips.

"Some poets better than others?" His tone was grave, but the glance he turned on her showed a glint of laughter in his eyes.

"Yes," she said, grateful yet uneasy.

"My sister does not expect you to instruct Colin in the academic subjects, Latin and Greek and such," he continued, "so much as to provide sympathetic discipline."

"Oh, but I . . . that is, I should be happy to read poetry and other English books with him, as I do with Peter and Michael."

"Of course. Your brothers are to be Colin's companions in study as well as in play."

Though nothing could please her more, she was too uncertain to rejoice. Lord Ashe seemed to consider his sister's approval a foregone conclusion, but as the curricle rolled through the smart streets of St. James's and crossed Piccadilly, Lissa grew more and more apprehensive.

Even if Lady Orton succumbed to her brother's influence far enough to hire an unknown ex-actress, she might well resent his interference. The lady of the house could make a governess's life miserable in a host of petty ways. Or she might attack Lissa through Peter and Michael. The boys were good-natured and well behaved, but no angels. Suppose her ladyship insisted on their being punished for every minor infraction, perhaps even blamed them for her own son's misbehavior?

There was another worry: Lissa was by no means sure she could manage young Lord Orton. From what her brothers said, the child was more in need of discipline than sympathy, whereas Peter and Michael had needed her loving kindness to soften a harsh discipline.

"You are very silent," Lord Ashe observed, drawing rein before a gracious brick house with stone pediments and pilasters. "Daphne is no dragon, I promise you."

"What if she does not like me?" Lissa said in a small voice.

"That is a bridge we shall cross if and when we come to it."

His use of *we* was at once comforting and disturbing. She had never before met anyone who so confused her emotions, but she had no time to analyse the feeling as he handed her down from the curricle.

Five stories from basement to garret, 39 Dover Street was large for a town house, with two wide, sparkling clean sash windows on either side of the fanlighted front door. Surely there was room enough for three young boys to romp on a rainy day without excessively disturbing the other inhabitants. Altogether the environs were vastly more healthful for growing lads than the grim, grimy streets of Lambeth.

Lissa prayed Lady Orton would offer her the position. For her brothers' sake, she was prepared to endure Lord Ashe's attempts on her virtue — if any. This morning his demeanor was thoroughly gentlemanly and unexceptionable.

Perhaps she had grown too thin and wan to attract him. The thought ought to have come as pure relief, but she could not deny a shade of chagrin.

He ushered her into the house with the merest touch on her elbow. Her shiver was surely due to coming in out of the sun into the vestibule, floored with coldly gleaming green-veined marble, lit by a domed skylight far above. She pulled her shawl more closely about her as a haughty, black-clad butler approached from the nether regions.

"Her ladyship is in the front parlor, my lord.

Her ladyship desires your lordship's presence while she interviews Miss Findlay." With a stiffly regal nod he acknowledged Lissa's presence.

"Thank you, Halsey. Bring tea and biscuits to the parlor, if you please."

A flash of startlement crossed the butler's broad, impassive face. Supplying refreshments to an applicant for a post in the household was obviously unheard of. "Very good, my lord," he said woodenly.

"I brought Miss Findlay away before her breakfast," Lord Ashe condescended to explain, mendaciously, "and mine was much interrupted, you may recall."

"Indeed, my lord."

"The boys are in the schoolroom?"

"So I believe, my lord."

"Excellent. Come, Miss Findlay."

Lissa was far too nervous to note the furnishings of the parlor, though she received an impression of elegance combined with comfort. She could not suppress a gasp of surprise as a very pretty girl turned from the window and came towards them. Capless, dressed in emerald green in the height of fashion, with the new, wider skirts and a profusion of bows and rouleaux, Lord Ashe's sister looked scarcely twenty.

"I thought . . . From what the boys said, I thought Lord Orton was near Peter's age."

"He is. Daphne, may I present Miss Findlay? She finds it impossible to believe you are old enough to be Colin's mama."

Lissa lowered her gaze and curtsied, flushing. A personal remark was impertinent, however flattering, and hardly likely to endear her to Lady Orton. Besides, a peek showed that her ladyship, close to, was clearly at least in her mid-twenties, so she would take it as insincere flattery.

But Lady Orton smiled complacently. "You are too kind, Miss Findlay," she said in a soft, sweet voice. "I was certain worry over Colin must have given me a dozen grey hairs by now. But gracious! you do not look at all like an actress, such a poor little dab of a thing. Are you old enough to be a governess? Do you think Colin will mind you?"

Sustaining with fortitude the blow to her already minimal vanity, Lissa told her, "I am nineteen, my lady. As for how Lord Orton and I shall deal together, I can but try."

"You will not be over strict with him? Colin's health is not robust, I fear."

"I believe strictness should be tempered with kindness," Lissa said with more emphasis than she had intended.

"Oh, yes, what Colin needs is kindness and attention."

"And companions his own age," put in Lord Ashe firmly.

"Yes, indeed. I have met your brothers, Miss Findlay. They seem amazingly well-bred."

Lissa felt her cheeks redden again. "You see us

in reduced circumstances, ma'am. My brothers are of . . . respectable birth."

"And you also, I can tell." Lady Orton seemed to have dismissed the unfortunate, not to say disgraceful, connection with the stage. "I trust you are able to start immediately? Poor Colin so hates waiting about in the shops, and I simply must go out to buy a bonnet to match this dress. I shall have to wear that old thing this morning." She waved at a chair where reposed a charming Leghorn hat with three white ostrich plumes.

"Immediately, ma'am?" Lissa asked, taken aback. "You mean this instant? You mean you wish to engage me?"

"To be sure. At least for a month's trial. You cannot conceivably be of less use than the last half dozen who came to me with splendid references. As for 'this instant,' I have a few minutes before I need depart. Pray come and be seated, and I shall tell you all about my darling child." She moved towards an amber velvet sofa.

"I . . . I must fetch my things, ma'am, and give my landlady notice."

"Write a note," proposed Lord Ashe, who appeared vastly amused by his sister's precipitate decision, "and I shall send for your belongings."

Thinking of her mother's pearls under the floorboards, Lissa shook her head. "Thank you, sir, but I prefer to go myself later, whenever it is convenient for Lady Orton." Ought she to refer to "her ladyship"? Her still proud spirit balked at such an admission of servitude, but she was, after all, accepting a position as a servant, however superior.

Lord Ashe gave her a thoughtful look; the viscountess merely said, "Yes, go later, pray. I shall take Colin to pay one or two calls later. Oh, and you will have to discuss your salary with my brother, who is Colin's guardian."

"Indeed, ma'am, I cannot accept a salary when my brothers are to be given a home." She spoke to Lady Orton but turned to Lord Ashe, suddenly afraid she had misunderstood, or the offer of a home for Peter and Michael had been withdrawn.

"Fustian!" he said roughly. "I ought to offer your boys a salary for acting as my nephew's companions and models, for he has not half their manners. I daresay you would refuse it, however, so I shall merely provide a little pocket money and decent clothes."

"Clothes? We cannot accept clothes!"

"I shall not propose to dress you, Miss Findlay, but Lord Orton's constant companions must be properly attired." His manner became businesslike. "That is not negotiable. As for you, you shall have the same as I paid your predecessors. Is that satisfactory?"

More than generous, considering her lack of credentials, yet his sudden coolness set Lissa at a distance, employer to employee — for which she ought to be still more grateful. "Yes, sir," she acquiesced quietly.

"Apply to Voss, my secretary. I shall instruct

him to pay you a month in advance. My carriage is at your disposal to take you to Lambeth when you are ready. Just tell Halsey or one of the footmen to have it brought round." He turned to his sister. "I shall leave you to expound your requirements, Daphne. Do not, I beg you, place too many restrictions on the child."

"He *is* sickly, Rob."

"I know, my dear, but he will never grow stronger without reasonable exercise."

Lord Ashe's patient tone suggested this was no new debate. Whether it would have continued along well-worn grooves Lissa did not discover, for the door opened and Halsey announced, "Lord Quentin Teague, my lady."

Aghast, Lissa shrank back. Lord Ashe looked dismayed. Lord Quentin, catching sight of her, looked both thunderstruck and thunderous.

"What the deuce . . . ?" he started.

"Lord Quentin!" Picking up the Leghorn hat as she passed, Lady Orton floated gracefully to meet him, her other hand held out in welcome. "I have found a new governess for Colin. I am in great hopes that Miss Findlay will suit him exactly."

Bowing over her hand, Lord Quentin made a gargling sound, produced perhaps by a variety of emotions combined with an excessively high collar.

"How kind of you to come so quickly, Lord Quentin. You know I rely upon your judgement." Lady Orton glanced back at Lissa and, setting the hat on her head, tranquilly announced as she tied the ribbons, "I am going to purchase a bonnet now, Miss Findlay. Lord Quentin always advises me. We shall talk later."

"And I'll have a word with *you* later, Ashe!" The dandy's eyes popped belligerently in his crimson, apoplectic face.

"Later, by all means." Lord Ashe sounded almost as tranquil as his sister, but there was a warning note in his voice as he added, "Nothing need be said until then, I believe."

"Certainly not!" With exaggerated solicitude Lord Quentin ushered the oblivious Lady Orton towards the door.

"Come along, Miss Findlay, if you please," said Lord Ashe in a peremptory tone. "I see it is left to me to present you to my nephew."

Lissa hesitated. She wanted to discuss this ominous event, or rather, to beg him for reassurance that all was not spoilt. But he waited impatiently, holding the door. She hurried after the others.

Lord Quentin and Lady Orton were already stepping through the front door, her ladyship smiling up at her escort as she pulled on her gloves. They were obviously on the friendliest terms. No doubt he could persuade the easily influenced lady that hiring an ex-actress as governess was unthinkable. He might even tell her Lissa was her brother's mistress.

Lissa looked up pleadingly at Lord Ashe. "What . . . ?"

"The schoolroom is on the second floor, Miss

Findlay," he interrupted her, indicating with a slight motion of his head the butler, closing the front door, and a maroon-liveried footman just arriving with a tray. To the latter he said, "Bring that up to the schoolroom, William."

"At once, my lord." The footman removed himself towards the back stairs.

As Lissa and Lord Ashe mounted the main staircase, she held her tongue, very much aware now of the butler crossing the hall below. The servants could make her life very uncomfortable if they discovered her disreputable past. Should they gossip about it, they could even make their employers' lives uncomfortable among the *ton*, though not half so uncomfortable as Lord Quentin might.

Lord Ashe's thoughts ran on the same lines. "My groom will not talk," he said, leading the way up the narrower flight to the second floor. "Your brothers are discreet, are they not? They have not mentioned your past profession to Colin, I believe."

"They have learnt that some things are best not spoken of. It is Lord Quentin who concerns me."

"You may leave Teague to me. He will not spread gossip which could harm Daphne, since he professes to love her."

"To love her!" Lissa exclaimed, astonished.

"To wish to marry her, at least," he said dryly.

"But it was his pursuit which drove me to reconsider your offer. Of the post of governess," she clarified hurriedly. "Why does he go looking for a . . . a mistress if he is in love with Lady Orton?"

"What a green child you are! Teague sees no conflict between the pursuit of my sister and the pursuit of ladybirds, a not uncommon attitude." Lord Ashe glanced back to frown down at Lissa. "He was harassing you?"

"He guessed from my clothes that you had not . . . not . . ."

"Taken you into keeping? This is the very devil! I wager he suspects I mean to set you up in my own house under my sister's very eyes."

Do you? Lissa longed to ask, but did not quite dare. "I fear so," she murmured.

At the top of the stairs, he stopped and turned, still frowning. "We shall have to be very discreet," he said abruptly, then swung round and headed for a door towards the front of the house.

So he did intend to make further attempts upon her virtue. Her heart sinking, Lissa followed him into the schoolroom.

Seven

"Lissa, look at me!" Michael shouted joyfully. Eyes shining, he rode a gaily caparisoned rocking horse with all the verve of a knight charging into battle.

The horse galloped away in the corner of a spacious, airy room overlooking the street. Daffodil yellow curtains gave an impression of sunshine though the day was too far advanced for the sun to strike the three large windows, which faced slightly north of east. A cheerful room, Lissa thought, ideal for children, especially with the thick carpet on the floor to deaden the sounds of their play.

Michael's mount's bright paint suggested that its owner had rarely ridden it. Lissa's heart went out to a child so frail he took little pleasure in so splendid a toy.

"Very fine," she said with a smile. "But you must dismount and make your bow to Lord Ashe."

"I already did. He gave us breakfast, Lissa, a simply *bang up* breakfast. I had *two* eggs, and . . ."

"Tell me later, pet. First you stand. You know that is the rule whenever a grown-up enters the room you are in."

"I thought that was one of *his* rules," Michael explained, sliding down from the wooden saddle.

Lissa darted a glance at Lord Ashe, but he did not ask to whom the "his" referred. Eyebrows raised, he was looking towards the scarred deal table behind which Peter had already risen to his feet. Beside Peter, a thin, sickly boy was just beginning to stand up, a mutinous pout on his sallow face.

"I don't see why I should stand up when it's only my uncle and a governess."

Lord Ashe opened his mouth but Peter forestalled him.

"Your uncle's a grown-up," he said, "and you're just a boy. And a gentleman always stands up for a lady. My sister's a lady. Don't you want to be a gentleman?"

Grinning, Lord Ashe glanced to Lissa. "You have no need of another champion, I see. I'll be off. If you run into any difficulty my sister cannot solve, come to me."

"I trust I shall have no reason to approach you, sir," Lissa said primly.

His mouth quirked. "We shall see. Colin, let me remind you that you requested Miss Findlay as your governess."

"Only because I want Peter and Michael here."

"Well, we shan't stay if you're not nice to Lissa," said Michael.

"Not for a minute," Peter confirmed.

Colin's mouth drooped. "I *will* be nice," he cried.

"Of course you will." Lissa moved hastily towards him. "Boys, you must make allowances for Lord Orton. He is not accustomed to having friends, but he will soon learn how to go on."

"I let Michael ride my rocking horse," Colin said hopefully.

"So you did. Michael, you may remount now. Does your steed have a name?"

"I call him Apollyon," said Michael, "because he's very fierce."

Lissa thought a better name could be found than that of the king of the monstrous locust-horses in *Revelation*. She said nothing for the moment, however, not wishing to draw Lord Ashe's attention to what was a distinctly odd choice for a small boy.

"I used to call him Dapple," said Colin, "but I'm too big for him now. I let Peter look at my book, too, Miss Findlay." He pointed at the volume lying open on the table before them, displaying a vivid-colored picture of a knight in full panoply. "He says he hasn't got any picture books at all."

"I wasn't allowed," Peter explained, "but I may now, mayn't I, Lissa? It's not one of the Reasonable Rules?"

Lissa was dismayed to discover how revealing her brothers' most innocent remarks seemed to turn out. "No, no, picture books are quite acceptable," she hastily assured Peter, casting a nervous glance back at Lord Ashe.

He was gone. While she was engaged with the boys, he had slipped away, closing the door so quietly she had not heard him leave. How much he had overheard she had no idea.

Fortunately, young Lord Orton saw nothing odd in his new playfellows' words. In fact he showed a disposition to believe that Peter, at least, could do no wrong. Whether he would extend the same indulgence to Lissa remained to be seen.

"I say, old fellow." Lord Quentin, arriving early to escort Daphne to the evening's entertainment, caught Ashe in the hall on his way to dine with friends at his club. "A word with you."

Sighing, Ashe led the way into the front parlor. He had hoped to postpone for a few days the inevitable explanations, but he should have known he could not evade Teague for long. The man positively haunted the house.

Inclined to be brusque, Ashe decided he'd brush through better if he did the pretty. After all, Teague was concerned for Daphne's well-being. "Take a chair," he invited, lounging against the mantelpiece. "A glass of Madeira?"

"Thank you, no." With a distinctly uneasy air, Teague took a turn about the room, fiddling with his quizzing glass. His overtight nether garments forced a birdlike strut. In his mushroom-colored coat and pink-and-green watered-silk waistcoat, he looked to Ashe's sardonic eye rather like a pouter pigeon. "Deuced bad *ton!*" he blurted at last.

Ashe constrained himself to mildness. "I shan't pretend not to know what you are talking about, but perhaps you would be more specific?"

"Installing your opera dancer, your *fille de joie,* under the same roof as your sister, devil take it! *Damned* bad *ton!*"

"Ah, but I haven't. Do sit down, there's a good chap. You're making me dizzy. Miss Findlay may have been an opera dancer, but she was never *my* opera dancer, you see. What is more, she is no *fille de joie.* I have every confidence in her innocence."

"Damme if she didn't as good as agree to accept my protection."

After a momentary shock, which he hoped he had concealed, Ashe guessed Lissa must have been trying to evade Teague without making him angry with an outright rejection. "As good as?" he queried.

"Said she wasn't well. Feminine troubles, you know. Another day or two . . ."

"In that day or two she took steps to assure herself of a respectable future. I repeat, she is not, and never has been, my mistress."

"If you say so," Teague conceded, his voice full of doubt, "of course I must accept your word. You have no proof of her past, though, and even if you did, to foist an opera dancer on Lady Orton in the guise of a governess is the outside of enough."

"My sister knows Miss Findlay was an actress. No one else will, if you don't spread the news abroad."

"As though I should! Make Lady Orton the laughingstock of the *beau monde*. I want to marry her, remember. You're telling me she offered the chit the post knowing she was an actress?"

"Daphne is ready to seize any straw. You should be glad she has found someone to take care of Colin."

"If it works out," Teague said gloomily. "What can an opera dancer know of bringing up difficult children that half a dozen experienced governesses don't?"

Ashe debated whether to mention Miss Findlay's brothers. An unnecessary complication for the moment, he decided, now that he had soothed Teague's initial ire. They could hardly be kept hidden for long, but he would cross that bridge when he came to it.

"We must hope her tenure will be longer than the last several," he said smoothly.

"Aye, but she'll have to go, mind, if you seduce her, now you've got her under your thumb."

"Deuced bad *ton*, seducing one's dependents!"

"Not near as bad," Teague protested, "as a kept mistress under your own roof. That's why most governesses are pudding-faced or past praying for. I know any number of fellows . . ."

"Not you, I trust?" Ashe snapped.

"No governesses in my household, I do assure you. There's the odd toothsome maidservant, of course. Always make proper provision for 'em and there's no cause for complaint, I say." Catching the kindling antipathy in Ashe's eye, Teague hastily added, "Naturally I wouldn't try anything with another man's servants. Miss Findlay's safe from me as long as she's in your employ."

They both turned with relief as Daphne came in, a beautiful sight in green-trimmed pink crepe over a green sarcenet slip. After an exchange of compliments, the matched pair departed, leaving Ashe to stride across Piccadilly and down St. James's Street to Boodle's.

He found he had a great deal on his mind. Teague, though allowing himself to be quieted, had raised some valid points. Convinced as Ashe was of Lissa's virtue, obvious as her respectable upbringing must be to discerning eyes, he knew next to nothing of her past. She was deucedly secretive about it. He had a nagging sense of something smoky in the background.

He realized he did not even know whether she was responsible for her brothers' excellent conduct. Perhaps they had had another teacher. Was she really competent to take charge of Colin?

If not, he would have no excuse to retain her in his household.

Of course, that would reopen the way to an altogether different sort of relationship. A twinge in his loins told him he had by no means given up hope of taking the delectable Lissa Findlay to his bed.

Reaching Boodle's Club, he was absorbed into its atmosphere of politics and cards, and he spared not another thought for Lissa until he strolled homeward through the dark streets. Slightly bosky, he wanted a woman, but as yet he had found no replacement for the Skylark. Until he had found a new *chère amie*, he decided, he had best see as little as possible of Miss Findlay.

In the week after Lissa and her brothers removed to Dover Street, she caught scarce a glimpse of Lord Ashe.

The boys reported to her his daily brief visits to the schoolroom. These always took place after luncheon, when they were quietly reading and she had retired to her chamber to put up her feet for an hour to restore her flagging energy.

Her room was tiny but pleasant, with white walls and ceiling, blue gingham curtains at the windows, and a matching counterpane on the narrow bed. The chest of drawers had seen better days and the seat of the single chair was patched, but Lissa had no complaints. After Lambeth, it was heaven.

Lounging back against two plump, feather-filled pillows, she reveled in the comfort and the lingering lavender scent of the bed linens.

She could postpone her rest one day to see Lord Ashe, but she was afraid that would simply play into his hands. Having brought her to his house, he appeared to be making a deliberate effort to avoid her, and the only purpose she could

103

guess at was to tantalize her. Instead of counting on constant nearness to win her over, he had changed tactics, unless he had always planned matters thus. In any case, he must hope to pique her interest by assumed indifference.

If it was assumed. More likely he had come to his senses on seeing her, drab, wan, and careworn, next to his beautiful sister amid elegant surroundings — yet it was after that he had spoken of being discreet.

That was it! He was being discreet, lulling Lady Orton's suspicions before he attempted any familiarities with her son's governess.

For Lissa, this was a breathing space, no more.

Very soon, she would feel no need of repose in the middle of the day. Already good food and proper rest were reviving her vitality, making her feel slightly guilty for deserting her charges. Not that they were far off. Her bedchamber adjoined the night nursery, which was next door to the schoolroom.

She heard footsteps, the firm, vigorous tread of booted feet, on the landing outside her door. Lord Ashe had come for his regular visit.

Lissa sat up and swung her legs off the bed, then caught herself up. With a deliberate effort she lay back again, forcing herself to relax. She would not run after him, must not let him think she courted his notice.

All the attention she wanted from him was his nod of greeting when their paths crossed in the front hall or on the pavement outside the house, his polite "good morning" or "good afternoon." He tipped his hat, she sketched a curtsy, and they went their separate ways, their eyes never meeting.

Discretion or indifference?

Lady Orton's neglect of her son's governess was easier to explain. As long as Colin was well and happy and caused no trouble, she saw no need to discuss his requirements with Miss Findlay. She sent for him daily, to the drawing room when she had callers or to her dressing room before dinner. Lissa was prepared to believe her ladyship loved the boy dearly. It was just that her mind and her time were occupied with more important matters such as clothes, shopping, and an endless round of entertainments.

Though sad for Colin, Lissa did not blame Lady Orton for her frivolity. Such was the way of the Fashionable World. Lord Ashe, she gathered from the nurserymaid, spent a good deal of his time playing cards at his club, dancing at balls, and attending sporting events. That his morals were less than perfect she was all too well aware.

In short, however kind and generous, he was a shallow fribble like the greater part of the aristocracy. Lissa was sorry but unsurprised.

From the schoolroom came a sudden burst of laughter, three boyish trebles and a deeper chuckle which brought an involuntary smile to her lips. She heard the click of the schoolroom door closing, and then receding footsteps.

At least Lord Ashe took the trouble to check

frequently on his nephew's welfare. Since she heard no complaints, Lissa assumed both he and Lady Orton were pleased with Colin's improved behavior and obvious contentment.

Rising, she tidied her hair and donned her grey worsted summer pelisse. With a moue of distaste she reached for her bonnet, wishing it had been practical to bring away more than one. Not that the other two were any more modish, but the chipstraw hat would be much more suitable to the present fine weather.

Given half a chance, she suspected she might develop quite an interest in pretty clothes, if not to quite the same extent as Lady Orton.

As always before leaving her chamber, she glanced out of the window. Looking over the small back garden and the mews, she had a view of the large gardens of Lansdowne House and Devonshire House. It was almost like being back in the country.

She crossed the landing, where lingered a faint, spicy, masculine scent of Imperial water, and entered the schoolroom. The boys all jumped to their feet.

"Let us go to Green Park while the sun is shining," she said with a smile.

"Oh yes, do let's!" Colin cried. "Look, Uncle Robert has brought me a new whipping top."

"And a hoop and a hobbyhorse," Michael said excitedly, rushing to retrieve the toys from where they leaned against the wall. "We can take turns."

Peter was pensive. "Lissa, I wasn't sure what to do. Lord Ashe knows Colin can't run about much, as boys do with a hoop or a hobbyhorse. Do you think he really brought them for me and Michael? We oughtn't to accept them, ought we?"

"If he presented them as gifts for Colin, it was not for you to reject them, whatever you guessed his purpose to be. But you are right that you ought not to accept gifts from Lord Ashe, except on your birthdays perhaps. I am glad you considered the question." She hugged him.

He wriggled indignantly from her embrace. "I'm too old for that stuff," he said. "I'm too old, really, for hoops and hobbyhorses, but I daresay we shall have fun all the same."

It was past time Peter learned to ride a real horse, Lissa thought wistfully. Too much to hope for. She was proud of him for making the best of things.

They walked the few hundred yards along Piccadilly to Green Park. Lissa made them carry the new toys, for the wide street was busy as ever, thronged with drays and gigs, stagecoaches, tilburys, phaetons, curricles, even farm wagons. A hoop rolling out into the roadway would scare any number of horses.

The hilly greensward of the Green Park attracted few riders and no carriages, reason enough for its popularity with nurses, governesses, and their charges. The milch-cows pastured there were accustomed to playing children. Lissa had seen one struck by a falling kite, standing patiently with no more than a reproachful moo as its attendant milkmaid disentangled the kite string from its horns.

Lissa had formed the habit of buying a cup of milk for each of the boys whenever they came to the park. Fresh drawn from the cow, it was a very different substance from the thin, bluish fluid sold by street vendors.

Today, with luncheon not long past, she would wait until just before they went home. Besides, she had noticed that when Colin drank milk at the beginning of an outing rather than the end, he wheezed terribly at the slightest exertion. If he had not had any, he was able to run about for several minutes at a time before discomfort slowed him down.

In fact, she had a good mind not to let Colin drink milk at all for a day or two, to see if it made any difference.

The fresh milk could do Peter and Michael nothing but good, though they hardly needed any supplement to the excellent fare provided by Lord Ashe's kitchen. Michael, especially, no longer thought about food in every spare minute.

The first time Lissa brought the boys to the park, he had been most reluctant to throw to the ducks on the reservoir the stale bread Colin had begged from Cook.

"I'll just keep some in my pocket in case I'm hungry later," he had said.

108

"But it's *old*," Colin pointed out in astonishment. "You can have new bread when we get home, or cakes."

"Cakes?" asked Michael, round-eyed.

"Yes, cakes. What kind do you like best? I'll tell Cook to make some."

"I don't know. We didn't never used to have cakes."

"I'll tell Cook to make lots of different kinds so you can try them all," Colin had said importantly.

By now Michael was accustomed to feeding perfectly good crusts to the mallards and swans. He and Peter dashed back and forth, making sure each received its fair share, while Colin kept quite still, enticing the boldest to eat from his hand.

That ritual over, they moved on. Lissa let Colin run about and roll down hillocks with her brothers, but kept a careful eye on him. The slightest cough, the least sign of shortness of breath and she called him to her. To reconcile him to strolling or sitting beside her, she was careful always to prepare a supply of riddles and conundrums and other word games. Not only did he enjoy solving them, he tried them on Peter and Michael on the walk home.

How quickly the house on Dover Street had come to feel like home, Lissa mused, pausing on the pavement to look up at the now familiar façade. The garret in Lambeth had always been a place to be endured. The thought of ever having to return to that dreadful half-life made her shudder.

She followed the chattering boys into the vestibule and up the stairs.

On the table in the schoolroom a note awaited her. Lord Ashe requested her presence in the library that evening after dinner.

Lissa's breath caught in her throat. Had Lady Orton judged her unsatisfactory and asked her brother to dismiss her? Or was the safe haven about to prove itself a comfortable trap?

Eight

The boys were tucked up in bed. Lissa wondered if it was the last time her brothers' heads would rest on those plump, soft pillows. She kissed them good-night — Colin too — then drew the window curtains against the lingering evening light and repaired to the schoolroom.

It was too early to go down to the library. Lord Ashe dined at the fashionable hour of eight, and though the only guest was Lord Quentin, who was to escort Lady Orton to Covent Garden, they would be at table for some time yet. Lissa had already changed into her brown silk before joining the boys for supper. She picked up some mending.

After setting two stitches in Peter's torn shirt cuff, she put it down again. Her hands were not steady enough to do a neat job.

She would prepare the next day's lesson, just as if she was not to be dismissed, or driven away by an indecent proposal. She took up Colin's beautifully illustrated child's history of England. It was like one she had owned once, so much easier to learn from than the dull tome Peter had had to contend with. But even with a colored picture of Drake playing bowls and another of

Spanish galleons under full sail, she could not concentrate on the routing of the Armada.

She might as well go and await her fate downstairs. This could be her only chance to see the library. It should be interesting, for in the days when she had access to a large collection of books she had been too young by far to appreciate it.

As she pattered down the stairs, she recalled that Lord Ashe knew Wordsworth's works, so he probably had a reasonable collection even though he was a rake and a fribble.

On the threshold she paused with a gasp. The candles had not yet been lit but the fading light from the west-facing windows showed row after row of books, from floor to ceiling, on three walls. The sight brought back strong memories of Papa's library, of sitting on his lap while he read *Puss in Boots* and *Sleeping Beauty* to her. How she missed him, even after eight years!

She forced herself to concentrate on the present. Lord Ashe's collection, limited by the space of a town house, must be smaller than Papa's, but still there were hundreds, perhaps thousands of books. She had not the faintest notion where to start looking.

Dinner dragged on interminably. Daphne and Teague had spent the past half hour discussing whether she ought to carry her pierced ivory fan or the chicken-skin painted with a Chinese scene. They were to be called for by friends, so

Ashe could not even point out that they were going to miss the beginning of *Don Giovanni*. Not that it would have hurried them; they went because it was the thing to do, not for the music.

Cracking another walnut, Ashe had just decided to claim an appointment at his club and leave them *tête-à-tête* when Halsey came in.

"Lord Prewing's carriage is at the door, my lady."

"You are right, Lord Quentin," said Daphne with her enchanting laugh, "the Chinese fan will be best. Good night, Rob dear."

"Enjoy the opera," Ashe said ironically as she glided out on Teague's arm, ivory satin skirts rustling.

The butler returned after seeing them out. "Will there be anything else, my lord?"

"Light the candles in the library, please, and convey my request to Miss Findlay to join me."

"Miss Findlay is already there, my lord, so I took the liberty of sending William to light the candles for her."

"Very good." Ashe picked up his scarce-touched brandy glass. "Has she taken tea already?"

Halsey looked uncharacteristically flustered. "Miss has never ordered tea in the evening, my lord, and in the absence of instructions . . ."

Ashe nodded his understanding, but frowned. What other ordinary perquisites of her position had Lissa deprived herself of through diffidence, or ignorance? "Possibly she does not care for it.

Bring the tea tray to the library, in any case."

Leaving the brandy on the table, he crossed the hall. He was oddly ill at ease, uncertain how to handle the situation, for his relationship with Lissa Findlay was far from straightforward. Did she see him as an employer, a would-be lover, a well-meaning friend, or some blend of the three?

He was not even sure how he regarded himself, he thought wryly, pushing open the door.

"Miss Findlay?"

She started, turning from the long library table where she had been gazing down at the papers thereon.

"Lord Ashe! You took me by surprise." She curtsied, color flooding her face, then swiftly ebbing.

"I beg your pardon, ma'am." He noted with interest that her gown was of silk. It was incredibly badly cut, though, baggy-bodiced and limp-hemmed, and of a singularly ugly brown which suited her not at all. Her dark brown hair was scraped back under a plain white cap, but wisps had escaped to caress her smooth brow and neck.

"I hope you don't mind . . ." She gestured at the table. "I did not like to take any books off the shelves."

"What is it?" Stepping forward, he saw his plans spread out for all the world to see. He had forgotten leaving them there after a last look before the meeting tomorrow morning. Acutely embarrassed, he straightened them and started to roll them up. "Just something I play at in my spare time."

"*You* designed that bridge?" she asked in astonishment, then blushed again. "I beg your pardon, I do not mean to pry."

"Not at all, not at all. It's . . . er . . . it's just that most of my acquaintance would consider it an odd sort of occupation for a peer. Daphne thinks I'm crackbrained and begs me not to let anyone find out."

"I think it is admirable. Will you not show me?"

Devil take it, the chit was trying to set him at ease! All the same, she seemed genuinely interested, and it was pleasant to have someone to appreciate his work. Trying to conceal his eagerness, he unrolled the large sheets.

Far from being concerned only with the shape of the arches and parapet and the overall style of his bridge, Miss Findlay proved fascinated by the technical details. For some time the talk was all of spans, piers, piles and abutments, of timber, masonry and mortar. She even asked intelligent questions about the force of river currents and the weight of traffic loads.

"I'm not sure of my calculations," Ashe confessed. "Thomas Telford, the president of the new Institute of Civil Engineers, has agreed to check the plans tomorrow. If all is well, I hope to start building this summer."

"Where is it to be erected?"

"At Ashmead, my estate in Gloucestershire.

The River Whitewithy forms one boundary. A new bridge will considerably shorten the distance to Bascombe-on-the-Water, our nearest market, especially from the new village."

"New village?" Miss Findlay queried.

Ashe felt his face redden again. "The old one was badly sited, in an unhealthy hollow, and the cottages were reaching an unrepairable state of dereliction. I could not in good conscience allow my people to go on living in such squalor."

She smiled, the first wholehearted smile she had ever directed at him. His heart flip-flopped, and for a moment he remembered only that he wanted her.

Lissa saw the change in his eyes, from the warmth of rather embarrassed enthusiasm to the heat of desire. She could only surmise that the mention of the squalor of the old village had reminded him of the squalor from which he had removed her, and his purpose in so doing.

Moving away, she made as if to study the elevation of the bridge as she said, with an involuntary tremor in her voice, "You designed the new cottages?"

"How did you guess?" he asked ruefully. "A social solecism even worse than the bridge, should it become known. Pray don't give me away."

"I shan't, but I think it still more admirable than the bridge."

"Confess, you believed me a complete coxcomb, a good-for-nothing wastrel."

She dared a peek at his face. He was grinning,

boyish, no sign now of that frightening passion.

"A coxcomb? Oh no, merely a sad rattle," she retorted.

Lord Ashe laughed. "Well, you have found me out. I admit to allowing an occasional serious thought into my head." He sobered. "Indeed, I asked you to join me tonight for a serious enough purpose."

"W-what purpose?" Lissa moistened suddenly dry lips. Surely he would not joke with her one minute and dismiss her the next, so his "serious purpose" must be seduction. Still, somehow she no longer feared he would threaten her with losing her place if she resisted.

Before he could elucidate, the second footman came in with a tea tray. Lord Ashe directed him to set it on the large rosewood desk at the end of the room.

"And, Jack, bring up a chair for Miss Findlay. Miss Findlay, pray be seated." He moved around to the other side of the desk. "Will you be so good as to pour?"

"Certainly, sir," Lissa murmured. If he was attempting to disarm suspicion, he was certainly setting the scene well.

"Then let us get down to the business of my nephew's education," he said as the footman departed, adding dryly as soon as the door closed, "A vastly respectable beverage, tea. But perhaps you don't care to drink it in the evening?"

"I-I have never had an opportunity to develop the habit."

"Indeed?" His dark eyebrows rose enquiringly, but she said no more and he did not press the question. He took the cup of tea she passed him. "Should you wish to develop the habit, you may order it, you know."

"I would not wish to encroach."

"Nothing of the sort. In this household a governess is regarded as a lady, not just another servant. Miss Prescott frequently dined with my sister and me when we had no guests. In your case," he said with a wry smile, "I think it wise to allow the invitation to come from Daphne. It will, I'm sure, as soon as she is convinced you are here to stay."

"Then I am not to be dismissed?" Lissa asked tentatively, reassured enough to sip at her tea.

"Good gad no! Whatever put that idea into your head? I have never seen Colin happier, and his manners are no end improved, by your teaching or by the example of your brothers, or a bit of each. Believe me, you'd have heard from Daphne long since were it not so."

"He behaves better because he is no longer bored and discontented." She did not want to take more credit than was her due. "Miss Prescott taught him well, I collect, but he has been sadly isolated."

"Chiefly because of his health. What I want to consult you about is whether you think him strong enough to take up serious studies for a few hours a day. If so, I'll have Voss look about for a tutor. School is beyond Colin, I fear, but to let him grow up an ignoramus would be to fail in my duty as his guardian. He will have an estate to manage, his place to take in Society and his seat in the House of Lords."

So it was no vague fondness which led the baron to take an interest in his young nephew. He took his responsibility for the boy seriously. Lissa was discovering unsuspected depths in Lord Ashe's character this evening.

"I am certain two or three hours a day would not hurt him. It is excitement and overexertion which make him ill. His brain is not at all weak — indeed, I should not be at all surprised if he is almost as clever as . . . oh!" She clapped her hand to her mouth.

"About to boast of your brothers' prowess, Miss Findlay?" Lord Ashe drawled, smiling.

"I do not consider Michael's mental abilities anything beyond the ordinary," Lissa protested, "though perhaps he is too young to judge."

"But Peter?"

"It is not my place to claim that Peter is more intelligent than Lord Orton."

"But such is your opinion. I am glad you don't think my nephew lacking in wits."

"Oh no! Why, he learned the Greek alphabet in no time and has already begun to . . . oh!" Again she cut herself short, dismayed at the way his informal friendliness made her tongue run away.

"To?" He waited.

After all, if he did not hear from the boys, he

119

would from the new tutor. "To get a few words by heart. You see, Peter studies his Greek every day, and Michael is beginning to learn, so Colin wanted to join in."

"Peter taught Colin the alphabet?"

"No." She sighed. "I did. I read Greek."

"Good gad!" Ashe was astounded. Though aware that there was some mystery about her, he had never dreamt it included so masculine and intellectual an accomplishment.

And young Peter was studying Greek? Ashe had been slightly taken aback by the way the Findlay boys treated Colin as an equal, more an honorary brother than a superior scion of the nobility. He would have expected their sister to teach them a proper deference towards their betters. But Peter had not only the manners but the instincts of a gentleman, including a lack of subservience, and he was studying the Classics.

Who the deuce were the Findlays?

Ashe found he was staring at Miss Findlay like the veriest gapeseed, and the poor girl looked deucedly apprehensive. "No need of a tutor, then!" he remarked cheerfully. "Colin will learn better from you, I don't doubt."

"But I know no Latin," she confessed warily. "I expect you wish him to study Latin."

"It is usual," Ashe admitted. Greek but no Latin? More and more intriguing. "What of mathematics?"

"Nothing beyond elementary arithmetic, just enough to keep household accounts."

"Then I must find a tutor. Needless to say, he shall teach Peter and Michael as well."

Miss Findlay leaned forward eagerly. "Truly? You meant it? I should like it of all things."

"I trust they will feel the same way!"

"Peter will be pleased as Punch. We have never read anything but the New Testament and the early church fathers, and he is dying for something new."

"What," Ashe exclaimed, "no Homer, no Sophocles or Aeschylus or Aristophanes, no Herodotus, no Plutarch, no Plato?"

She bit her lip. "I have heard of Plato. Have you read all those?"

"Not since my schooldays, I confess, but they are all here in the library. Peter — and you — must borrow whatever you wish."

"May we?" Her face lit up. "English books too?"

"Whatever you wish," he assured her, warmed by her pleasure. He had not considered that poverty might have deprived her mind of nourishment, as well as her body.

"Are there any medical books?"

"Not recent publications. I have not purchased any. Why? Does Peter wish to become a physician?"

"Good gracious, no, he will have . . . I mean, no, it is just that I had hoped for some advice. You see, I have observed that Colin has more difficulty breathing when he has recently drunk milk, and I wondered whether the same has been observed in other people. Should you object — do you think Lady Orton would object — if I tried what a few days without milk will do?"

"By all means try it," Ashe said a trifle doubtfully, "though I understood the doctor advised plenty of milk to build up his strength."

"He cannot gain strength if he is too breathless to take proper exercise," Miss Findlay argued earnestly. "If I find not drinking milk helps him, I shall try if junkets or cheese suit him better, which have the same nourishment in a different form. Or perhaps plenty of milk to drink in the morning, when he is going to sit still at his studies for several hours."

"A good notion." Ashe was impressed. "I can see you have thought deeply on the subject. It is kind in you to take such an interest in my nephew's health."

"Kind?" She looked surprised. "How can I not take an interest when it affects him so deeply and he is in my charge? Besides, I am already very fond of Colin. I cannot claim," she added with painful honesty, "to love him as much as I do my brothers."

"Blood is thicker than water."

"Yes, but . . . Yes. But I am sure my affection for Colin will grow when we have been together longer. After all, I have known Peter and Michael forever."

"True. Are they happy here?"

"Can you doubt it?"

"I'm referring not to a comparison with your

attic in Lambeth," Ashe said impatiently, "but to . . . before."

"B-before?"

Her obvious alarm made him moderate his tone. "Come, Miss Findlay, you cannot expect me to believe you and your boys were bred to such a life. Indeed, I cannot believe you lived it more than a few months without sinking into degradation. What brought an educated, virtuous young *lady* to cavort upon the stage for the delectation of rakes and 'sad rattles' like me?"

His quotation of her view of him brought a fleeting smile to her lips, but she said with anguish, "I cannot tell you!"

"Then it can be no ordinary tale of lost fortune. I must surmise that you were rendered penniless by a close relative's disgraceful conduct."

"No! Not exactly."

"Not exactly disgraceful? Not exactly a close relative? Will you not trust me? Perhaps I can help."

Shaking her head, she bowed it over hands clasped so tight the knuckles showed white. "You cannot help, but I owe you some sort of explanation, I know. We are not truly penniless, only I cannot obtain any funds without revealing our whereabouts. The relative is my . . . stepfather, and his conduct was not what most people would call disgraceful, only so dreadfully harsh I could not bear to let the boys suffer any longer."

"You stole them away from their father!"

She looked up at him, fear in her eyes. "I should not have told you. Pray ask no more!" And springing up, she fled.

Nine

After his violent reaction to her disclosure, Lissa expected Lord Ashe to follow her and press for more details. When he did not, when a sleepless night was succeeded by a perfectly normal morning, she feared he meant to report her to some authority or other as an abductor.

Nothing happened. She began to wish for a chance to explain herself further, but he did not even come as usual to talk to the boys after their luncheon.

Colin was sent for to the drawing room. On his return he reported that his uncle had gone off to Ashmead with Mr. Telford, the engineer.

Lissa assumed that Lord Ashe's preoccupation with his bridge had driven her misdeed from his mind. After all, her predicament was none of his affair, except insofar as it affected Colin. She had no conceivable reason to steal the child away as she had her brothers. Colin was thriving. Why should his uncle upset the apple cart?

His mother, more emotional than logical, was another matter, but by the time three days had passed without a word, Lissa began to feel safe.

Then Lady Orton sent for her.

Lissa hastily tidied her hair. Wisps *would* escape, however carefully she knotted it and hid it beneath the cap she had made as appropriate to her new station in life. Not that her appearance was likely to make any difference to her fate if Lord Ashe had suddenly recalled her confession and written to his sister.

She hurried down to the front parlor.

"Shocking!" exclaimed Lady Orton as Lissa entered.

"Ma'am?" Lissa's dismay faded as she realized her ladyship's head was bent over a periodical, which had aroused her disapproval. Her canary yellow gown, trimmed with white mull flounces, certainly provided no cause for censure, nor did the delightful Leghorn hat on the table at her elbow.

"Oh, Miss Findlay! Pray come here and tell me if you do not think this the horridest thing in creation. I cannot abide this new fashion for toques to be worn with evening dress, can you?"

"I fear I know little of fashion, ma'am."

She looked Lissa up and down. "Dear me, so I see. How odd, I quite thought actresses always dressed to the nines."

"I am a governess, Lady Orton."

"And a singularly ill-dressed governess," said Lady Orton severely. If Lord Ashe had revealed Lissa's "abduction" of her brothers from their guardian, her dowdy appearance had driven the fact from Lady Orton's mind. "Sober colors are no excuse for such shockingly bad design and execution. Did you sew your gown yourself?"

"No, ma'am." Lissa bit her lip to stop a giggle escaping.

"Have you an evening dress? Is it any smarter?"

"It is silk, but no better cut, I believe."

"Oh, dear, Miss Prescott was positively modish in comparison. I had intended to make plain that you are welcome to dine with my brother and me when we are alone, but I shall not be able to swallow a morsel with such a horrid sight in view. You must have a new gown made up."

"I must regretfully decline your kind invitation," Lissa said firmly. "To open my slender purse for a gown, when I have several which are perfectly wearable, would be the height of folly."

"Wearable? Hmm." Lady Orton set down *La Belle Assemblée* and once more looked Lissa up and down. "You are somewhat shorter than I, and as slender as your purse. I have several half-mourning gowns put away somewhere, from when Lord Orton died. They are by no means in the latest fashion, of course, but at least they are well made. Marlin shall alter them to fit you."

Lissa was sure she ought to refuse, but she simply could not bring herself to do so. Her mouth actually watered at the thought of a few elegant gowns — and any gown of Lady Orton's, even half-mourning, was bound to be lovely.

Mr. Exton, her stepfather, for want of a better word, considered vanity akin to the deadly sin of pride, as well as a precursor to envy, covetousness, and lust. Himself full of pride in his lack of covetousness, he had never begrudged the money spent on Lissa's clothes. He just made sure they conformed to his grim notions of modesty and propriety.

Any confidence in her own looks had been sternly suppressed by Mr. Exton and the dissenter school he had sent her to. On the other hand, Lissa had been much in demand for hymn singing, and it was only her voice which had given her any hope of being hired by a theatre. That she had, in scanty stage draperies, attracted the interest of not one but two lords had greatly surprised her.

In Lady Orton's pretty castoffs, might she not herself aspire to being pretty?

If so, the effect on Lord Ashe's already tender susceptibilities was to be feared. In addition, pride rebelled against wearing castoffs. Nonetheless, Lissa heard herself accept. "Thank you, ma'am, you are very generous."

Lady Orton waved away her thanks. "Not at all. I have no use for them and I cannot abide ugliness about me. Do sit down here beside me, and do take off that hideous cap, Miss Findlay, I beg of you. Your wearing a cap when I do not makes me feel monstrous old, for I fear I can give you ten years."

"I thought as a governess I ought to wear one," Lissa said uncertainly, untying the ribbons.

"You are too young," her ladyship affirmed. "La, my dear, Marlin must do something about your hair, also. Simply looking at it scraped back like that gives me the headache, I vow. It is not quite so dark as mine, I fancy."

"No, mine is merely dark brown, while yours is true jet black, and as lustrous as jet." Lissa spoke with honest admiration, hoping her words did not sound like fulsome flattery.

Lady Orton's smile was innocently self-satisfied. "I fancy so. I use a basil wash to make it shine. You must try it. What is it, Halsey?" she asked as the butler stepped in.

"Lord Quentin, my lady." He moved aside to admit her cicisbeo.

Lord Quentin advanced, his smile turning to a frown as he noticed Lissa. She rose and curtsied but, ignoring her, he kissed Lady Orton's hand. "If we are to drive in the park, we ought to be off, dear lady."

"Gracious, is it so late? Miss Findlay and I have been having such a comfortable cose, I did not realize the time. There was something I wanted to ask you, Miss Findlay. What could it have been?"

About her stealing her brothers away from their guardian? Lissa prayed not. "Something about Lord Orton, ma'am?" she proposed cautiously.

"Colin, of course! My brother tells me you believe Colin is strong enough to study Latin with a tutor."

"I believe it will not harm him, and may even help by keeping him quietly occupied."

"Perhaps. You would keep a careful eye on his health?"

"Naturally, Lady Orton. He is somewhat improved of late."

"Rob mentioned something about milk," she said vaguely. "How very clever of you. I am really prodigious glad Rob found you, Miss Findlay. Colin is quite fond of you, I collect, and positively dotes upon your brothers. His manners are vastly better, too, are they not, Lord Quentin? Only yesterday he bowed to you without being reminded."

"He did," Lord Quentin admitted, not visibly impressed. "That is a prodigious fetching gown. I see you took my notion of tassels depending from the collar. Charming! Let us go and display it to the *ton*."

Lady Orton put on her bonnet. "I had Marlin sew matching tassels around the brim. What do you think?"

"Hmm." He stroked his receding chin. "Yes, indeed, a charming conceit, though it would not do to make them any larger. You will undoubtedly set a fashion, my dear Lady Orton."

Beaming, she departed upon his arm, Lissa forgotten.

Lady Orton did not forget to instruct her dresser regarding the half-mourning gowns for Lissa. Disapproving but obedient, Marlin took in and shortened two evening gowns, four morning gowns, and half-a-dozen walking dresses.

The colors ranged from grey-green lavender to bluish slate grey and pale pearl grey, shades quite different from the leaden grey Lissa was accustomed to. The skirts were much narrower and less ornamented than the present fashion dictated. Lissa did not mind.

Nor did she mind when the woman, disparaging her lack of inches, showed her how to pile her hair up on top of her head to lend her height.

The first new gown she wore was a walking dress of what Marlin described as dove-color, a warm, pinkish grey. The close fit of the bodice embarrassed her, though Lord Ashe had not yet returned from Gloucestershire to see the way it outlined her bosom, grown fuller with good food.

Still, she was glad the abigail had softened to the extent of adding a pelisse to her new wardrobe. Of glossy bronze-hued lustring, it matched none but would go with any of the gowns. There was a Leghorn hat, too, trimmed with a curling white ostrich plume.

With the pelisse over her arm, Lissa went to the schoolroom, where the boys were waiting for their outing to the park. She paused on the threshold, ridiculously shy.

"Lawks!" cried Michael, "you're the beautifullest lady I ever did see."

Lissa laughed. "Thank you, pet, but not *lawks*, if you please."

"My mama is more beautiful," said Colin, "but you do look very pretty, Miss Findlay."

"Thanks to your mama's kindness."

"*Very* pretty," Peter confirmed, "and like a proper lady at last. I thought you'd have to wait till I grow up."

"Everything will change when you grow up, Peter dear," Lissa said softly. "Come, let us go to the park before it decides to rain again."

She wore her new pelisse to walk through the streets, but took it off as soon as they reached the park. Far from pouring as it had the past few days and even that morning, the afternoon was hot.

Newly rain-washed, the city air smelled near as fresh as in the country. In the cheerful sunshine, wisps of vapor rose from sparkling wet grass and the still spring-green leaves of the trees and shrubberies.

Lissa enjoyed strolling along the paths while the boys ran up and slithered down delightfully slippery hills. The seats of their breeches were muddy in no time. She apologized mentally to the laundry woman, but did not stop them. The clean air, together with his milkless regimen, definitely agreed with Colin. Almost as tireless today as Peter and Michael, he even had breath to spare for shouts of sheer exuberance.

By the time they turned homeward, Lissa had grown accustomed to the snug fit of her new gown. She was by far too warm to put on the pelisse. As they walked along Piccadilly, no one turned to stare at her, though the boys' decidedly grubby appearance drew some amused glances and a censorious raised nose or two.

On the well-scrubbed doorstep of 39, Dover Street, small boots deposited a dismaying quantity of mud. Lissa was about to tell her charges to go down into the area and through the kitchen, but Jack opened the front door and they dashed in.

"Boys, stop!" she cried. "Shoes off before you take another step."

All three dropped to the marble floor. Lissa hoped no guests would come down the stairs at just the wrong moment.

"My bootlaces are all knotted, Lissa," Michael complained. "They won't come untied."

"Leave it to me, miss," said the footman, kneeling. " 'Twould likely be me as had to clean up if you'd've let 'em go on. There's one done, Master Michael."

Peter and Colin were already in their stocking feet. Peter took a step towards the staircase and was struck with a splendid notion.

"Look!" He slid across the polished marble with a whoop.

Colin promptly followed suit. The domed vestibule resounded with their cries of glee, soon joined by Michael's piping note. As they whizzed about, Lissa could not help smiling, and Jack laughed aloud.

"Times I've wanted to do that!" the young footman admitted.

"But you did not, and they ought not. Peter! Colin!" she called belatedly.

Too late. Michael flew across the floor, lost his precarious balance, and was caught up in the arms of Lord Ashe.

Lissa hurried forward. "I beg your pardon, sir, I should not have let them . . ."

"Don't blame Lissa, my lord," Peter interrupted. "It was my idea. You must punish me."

"I did it too," Colin chimed in. "It was a famous idea. It was *fun*, Uncle Robert."

"Are you going to beat us?" Michael whispered, pale faced, as his captor set him on his feet.

"Beat you?" Lord Ashe's nascent grin gave way to a frown and he sought Lissa's eyes. She remembered telling him of Mr. Exton's harsh treatment. "Good gad, no! As I recall, it was famous fun."

"You used to slide on this floor?" Michael asked disbelievingly. Colin and Peter gathered around.

"Well, once or twice. I spent most of my childhood in the country. The hall at Ashmead is floored with the most splendidly slippery parquet. But you are fortunate that Colin's mama is not at home and receiving visitors. She would have had every right to be annoyed had you disturbed them."

" 'To every thing there is a season, and a time for every purpose under the heaven,' " Peter quoted.

"Exactly."

Lissa intervened. "And now is the time for you

134

all to go upstairs and change your clothes." They scampered away. Turning back to thank Lord Ashe for his forbearance, she saw on his blue Bath-cloth sleeve the print of a small muddy hand. "Oh, no, Michael has dirtied your coat!"

He glanced down. "Mills will easily brush it off when it dries. Colin seems well."

"He is."

"And you look well." He smiled at her.

Blushing, Lissa gabbled something about his sister's kindness and hastily changed the subject. "Was your business in Gloucestershire successful, sir?"

Lord Ashe grimaced. "Telford advised a slightly different site for the bridge, which will involve revising some calculations."

"Will it delay the construction?"

"Not by much, if I just buckle to and get it done."

"Shall you?" Lissa ventured.

He laughed. "I shall. I want it well under way before winter weather complicates matters. Rather the reverse applies to the boys' studies. Voss has found a man who sounds suitable, and I shall interview him this evening, but I am inclined to put off hiring a tutor until the autumn, to allow them a summer of leisure. I am in hopes that Daphne will allow Colin to go down to Ashmead under your aegis."

"Summer in the country would be pleasant, but I doubt Lady Orton would be willing to trust him entirely to my care after so short a time. She stays in town?"

"She remains more or less in residence here, dashing off hither and yon to various house parties. Family life in the country does not suit her."

"And Lady Ashe is not well enough to take charge, I understand?"

"My mother is frail," he acknowledged, "no longer robust enough to contend with boyish high spirits. Not that Colin has shown any sign of high spirits before now."

"Oh dear!" Lissa said guiltily.

"My dear Miss Findlay, I am congratulating you, not blaming you."

"Still, perhaps I had better go and see what they are doing."

As she moved towards the stairs, he called after her, "Don't, I beg of you, put it into their heads to slide down the banisters!"

She glanced back. "Did you . . . ? You did! They will think of it soon enough themselves, I fear!"

Climbing the stairs, she was aware of a curiously warm feeling inside her. Lord Ashe had approved her looks in her new dress without making her feel threatened by his attentions. Nor had he frightened her with any reference to her stepfather. Instead he had treated her as a respectable and respected governess — yet there was more to it than that.

She dared to think that, in his manner as much as his words, he had treated her almost as a friend.

He had joked with her, congratulated her, talked of his work as well as of Colin's welfare. But she had been the first to mention the bridge, she remembered. She must not let herself be misled by his charm. Noblemen did not make friends with governesses.

Nonetheless, the warm feeling remained.

The weather also remained warm, or rather excessively hot, and dry. No breeze stirred the sweltering air. Foul stenches drifted into Mayfair from the slums and the river. Soot from a hundred thousand coal cooking-fires begrimed streets and houses, and dulled the green of grass and foliage in the parks and squares.

After three days of increasingly smoky air, Colin could no longer run more than a step or two before he started wheezing. Soon Lissa had to stop even taking him to the park: the walk was too much for him. Letting Peter and Michael go alone, she stayed at home with Colin. Though she tried to keep him quietly occupied and amused, he forlornly envied his friends' freedom.

Then he developed a dry cough. Coughing fits made breathing difficult even when he kept quite still.

Lissa discovered that frequent sips of warm barley-water at least soothed the cough, so she kept some over a spirit lamp. Lying down made him worse. That evening, Lissa sent her brothers to sleep in her chamber and sat up with Colin in the night nursery, soothing him as he struggled for air.

"Don't tell Mama," he begged. "She will only send for Dr. Hardin . . . and he will bleed me and give me nasty medicine . . . which doesn't do any good. Even Miss Prescott . . . said it's no good for me."

Convinced what was making him ail was the foul city air, Lissa hesitated. She had heard nothing from Lord Ashe, and if he could not overcome his sister's resistance to sending the boy to the country, Lissa was bound to fail. Lady Orton, just returned from a few days in Brighton, had not yet sent for Colin. Lord Ashe had not visited the schoolroom in several days.

Yet Lissa felt herself lamentably young and ignorant. She could hardly rely on Colin's judgment of the efficacy of Dr. Hardin's unpleasant remedies. Perhaps the physician had some new treatment to try. Suppose she did nothing and Colin fell seriously ill?

In the course of the next morning even speech became a struggle for him. By midday Lissa knew she could no longer cope alone. When Peter and Michael left for the park, she sent the nurserymaid with a message to Colin's mama.

The girl returned to say Lady Orton had gone to a picnic at Richmond and was not expected to return much before dinner.

"Then pray go down again and inform Lord Ashe that his nephew is ill."

" 'Is lordship's gone to the 'Ouse of Lords, miss. There's no knowing when 'e'll be back.

'Pends if there's somefing going on 'e's interested in partic'lar, like."

Lissa had not known Lord Ashe took an interest in the business of government. She should have guessed when he spoke of Colin taking his seat in the House of Lords. To interrupt him there seemed impossible; to send a messenger in search of Lady Orton was useless.

Should she take the responsibility for calling in the physician? Suppose he prescribed cupping again? Lissa did not think Colin was strong enough to be deprived of several ounces of blood.

She glanced at him. Leaning against his heap of pillows, he looked far too small and pale to be bled. Hollow-eyed, he gave her a game but pitiful smile and her heart went out to him.

He wheezed a plea. "Not Dr. Hardin, Miss Findlay!"

His fear of the doctor was agitating him, the worst thing for his condition. "No, I shall not send for him," Lissa said. *Not yet*, she said to herself and prayed that Lord Ashe would come home soon.

Peter and Michael returned home first. They entered the night nursery with anxious enquiries as to how Colin felt.

"Not well," Lissa said, setting down the book she had been reading to him.

"We'll cheer you up," Michael told him. "We saw such a funny thing in the park! There was a big dog. He was nice. We played with him,

139

throwing his ball, didn't we, Peter?"

"Until he saw the cows and decided they were more fun to chase than the ball. They galloped all over the place with their tails in the air, and the dairymaids were all shrieking and jumping up and down. Then one sat down in her milk pail and got stuck!"

Colin started to laugh. He doubled up, gasping. His face took on a bluish tinge.

Ten

Ashe had tailored his speech, on the benefits of sanitary housing for the rural poor, to his audience of noble landowners, lamentably thin, since many had already gone into the country. He dwelt on the inefficiency of sickly laborers and the profit to be expected of improvements in their health.

He had no expectation of laws being passed to encourage the replacement of damp, crumbling hovels. The most he hoped for was to cause a few careless landlords to consider where their advantage lay and thus to alleviate the plight of a few unfortunate tenants.

Three of his peers had come up to him afterwards to tell him he had dashed well made them think.

Striding homeward up Dover Street, he had the oddest urge to report his modest success to Miss Findlay. She would appreciate his efforts and applaud his accomplishment, as Daphne would not. But one simply did not seek out a governess for any reason not concerned with her charge.

His encounters with her always turned out much less formal than he intended, which was why he had avoided the schoolroom for the past several days. By now Colin must be feeling neglected. Ashe really ought to go and see him.

He would report on the unsuitability of Voss's candidate for the post of tutor, and confirm Daphne's refusal to let Colin go to Ashmead. And, in passing, he might just mention his speech.

As he entered the house, Halsey hurried to meet him. "My lord," the stout butler said anxiously, taking Ashe's hat and gloves, "I understand Master Colin is unwell."

"More so than usual?"

"The nurserymaid — not an unintelligent girl in her way, my lord — says Miss Findlay is quite worried. Her ladyship being out for the day, Miss requested that your lordship be informed as soon as . . ."

"Thank you, Halsey." Ashe took the stairs two by two.

He paused on the upper landing. Peter's mirthful voice came from the night nursery.

". . . sat down in her milk pail and got stuck!"

Matters could not be too serious. Smiling, Ashe opened the door.

Laughter changed to a horrible choking sound. He saw Miss Findlay leap to her feet and bend over Colin, her hands on his shoulders as he sagged forward, fighting for air.

"Sit up!" she said urgently. "You cannot breathe with your lungs compressed like that. Peter, bring a glass of warm barley-water,

142

quickly. Sit *up,* Colin darling."

Ashe sprang to the other side of the bed. With his greater strength, he forced Colin to sit upright. The child's face was livid, bathed in sweat, terrified.

Miss Findlay, her arm lightly about his heaving shoulders, caught one clutching hand. She talked to him softly, steadily, soothingly, only the faintest tremor in her voice betraying her terror to Ashe.

"Hush, love, keep still. Don't be afraid. You will be better directly. See here, Peter has brought your drink. You know how it relieves your throat. Your uncle will hold it for you while you sip."

Ashe took the glass from Peter's trembling hand and presented it to Colin's blue lips.

"Sip, just a tiny bit, that is right," Miss Findlay's murmured reassurance continued. "Come now, you are easier already, I can tell. Another sip. Don't cry, love, you are a big boy, too big to cry. Sip again. Good! What a brave boy you are. Show your uncle how calm you can be. How proud of you he is!"

"Excessively proud." Ashe took the girl's cue, noting that already the livid tinge was fading from Colin's face as his breath came easier, though he still wheezed dreadfully. "You're a regular prime 'un, old fellow. That's it, another sip and we'll soon have you all to rights."

Colin finished the drink, and Ashe looked round for Peter to refill the glass from the pot on the chest-of-drawers. Both the Findlay boys were gone.

"I'll fill it," he said. "Shall I lay him down?"

"No, just let me rearrange his pillows. Lying down makes things worse."

With the child propped upright on the pillows, Ashe crossed to the chest and poured the warm barley-water. As he returned towards the bed, a small, frightened face peeked around the door.

"Is he going to be all right?" Michael asked fearfully.

"Yes, he's much better already," Ashe said.

"Lissa, Peter's *crying*. He didn't mean to . . . we didn't mean to make Colin ill. We just wanted to cheer him up. We didn't know a funny story would make him ill."

"Of course you did not, love." She sent Ashe a glance of appeal. "I don't want to leave Colin."

"I'll go."

She trusted him to reassure her brothers, he thought, filled with inexplicable elation. Michael trusted him too, slipping his little hand into Ashe's as they left the night nursery together.

"Peter doesn't usually cry," he said, anxious to defend his brother, "even when he's whipped. He's not a milksop."

"I know."

"I shan't cry anymore when I'm big like him. Are you going to whip him?"

"No. Is he not in the schoolroom?" Ashe asked as Michael turned the other way.

"No, in Lissa's room." He pushed open the

144

door. "We slept here last night 'cause Lissa stayed up with Colin. Peter, Colin's going to be all right!"

After a swift, curious glance around the small chamber, Ashe turned his attention to the boy curled up on the narrow bed, his fair head buried in his arms. Peter's shoulders shook with silent sobs. Sitting on the edge of the bed, Ashe wondered what to say. His occasional jaunts with Colin had not taught him how to handle children.

But he had been a child himself. Surely he had once made a similar mistake?

"Peter, Colin is none the worse for his attack, and no one blames you for it."

"It was my f-fault. I m-made him laugh."

"You could not have guessed it would make him ill. Your sister didn't, or she would have stopped you, would she not?"

"Y-es. Is he really all right?" Peter sat up, sniffing and wiping his eyes with the back of his hand.

Ashe handed him a handkerchief. "He is not well, but no worse, I believe, than before."

"Truly? Then I shan't care for any punishment."

"Punishment?" Good gad, but these children expected the worst at the slightest transgression, intended or not! "Why should I punish you when your aim was to raise his spirits?"

"Only God can see into one's heart," Peter explained seriously. "Man judges and chastises

145

actions not intentions."

"True, no doubt, in many cases, but man is quite capable of taking extenuating circumstances into account."

"What's 'tenuating circumstances?" Michael asked.

"Let me tell you a story. Once there was a little boy, somewhere in age between the two of you. His mother was very pleased and proud when he learned anything new, his letters, say, or to jump on his pony. So when he shot his first rabbit, he hurried to show her. Now it just happened that she was taking tea with several visiting ladies at the time. He rushed into the drawing room waving a bloody corpse. One lady fainted, two fell into hysterics, one jumped up on a chair as if it were a live mouse, and one ran away."

Peter snickered. Ashe found it hard not to laugh at the memory, though at the time he had been appalled. He continued, "That's not the end. The one who ran away bumped into a footman bringing in a jug of hot water. It spilt and badly scalded her foot and his hand."

"Gosh!" said Michael.

"What do you think was his punishment?" Ashe asked.

Michael shuddered. "I bet his papa beat him till he couldn't sit down, or even stand up straight, and locked him in his chamber on bread and water for a whole week and made him learn *five hundred* verses."

"Lissa wouldn't," said Peter. "Lissa would say

it was a mistake and you must learn from it, and do something to help the people you upset. Was it you, sir?"

"It was."

"What did your father do?"

"I was obliged to apologize to everyone, of course. Then I had to hold myself available to run errands for the lady until her foot healed. So she wasn't angry with me any longer, and I wasn't angry with her, since her silliness had not earned me a beating. And, believe me, I have never again waved a dead animal around in a lady's drawing room!"

"What about the footman, sir?" Peter wanted to know.

Ashe thought back. His father had not even mentioned the footman's injury, he recalled. It was his and Daphne's governess who pointed out that the man — scarcely more than a boy then — was an innocent victim of his thoughtlessness. Under her prodding, he had himself come up with a way to make amends.

"I helped him with his work until his hand was better. We became good friends, and now Parrish is my butler at Ashmead."

"Good," said Michael with satisfaction.

"What can I do for Colin to show I'm sorry, sir?" asked Peter. "I already help Lissa as much as I can so she can look after him better."

Ashe regarded him reflectively. His blue eyes were red-rimmed from weeping; in rubbing them he had transferred a certain amount of dirt from hands to face; his fair hair was raggedly cut, by his sister no doubt; his wrists protruded from the too-short sleeves of his jacket — damn! Ashe had forgotten to give orders for new clothes for the boys — and there were grass stains on his shirt. He looked a regular ragamuffin, yet Ashe knew him to be responsible beyond his age.

"I must talk to your sister about Colin's health," Ashe said, "but I don't want to do so in his hearing, lest it distress him. Can I trust you to sit quietly with him, reading to him perhaps, while we talk?"

"I'll read about the Knights of the Round Table. That's what he likes best." Peter took a deep breath. "What shall I do if he suddenly gets really bad?"

Was it too much to ask of a child? He could send for the nurserymaid. But he'd as soon trust Peter and the lad was eager to make amends. "You will send Michael for us. We shall be right next door, in the schoolroom. We'll even leave both doors open."

"I'll run very fast," Michael promised.

Ashe recalled Lissa's insistence on calmness. "And you will do your best to reassure Colin and keep him quiet until we arrive."

"You'll come right away?"

"Right away."

"I'll tell him not to be frightened because it happened before and he was all right afterwards. But I hope it doesn't happen."

"If you haven't seen him taken so bad before, I

don't expect it will. Come along, then."

Lissa looked round as Lord Ashe returned with her brothers. Peter was red-eyed, but whatever his lordship had said to him had clearly comforted him.

"Sir, I must speak with you," she said.

"Two minds with a single thought. In the schoolroom? Peter and Michael will take care of Colin."

"I know what to do," Peter assured her. "I'll read to you, Colin, if you like."

"Yes," Colin whispered. "The King . . . Arthur . . . book."

"I'll fetch it," Michael volunteered, and trotted off.

Lissa and Lord Ashe followed. Suddenly exhausted, Lissa dropped onto a chair at the table and propped her head up with one hand. If he berated her for not calling in a doctor, she was going to burst into tears.

She struck first. "Colin is never going to be well in London," she said bluntly. "I am convinced it is the bad city air which makes him ill. His condition has deteriorated shockingly since last we had rain to wash some of the smoke out of the air."

Moving to the window, Lord Ashe looked out at the sunshine which had once cheered Lissa and now seemed to strike with a pitiless glare. He turned, leaning against the windowsill, silhouetted against the brightness so that she could not see his face.

"You think he would be healthy in the country?"

"I believe he would be better. I cannot guarantee he would be cured, but it breaks my heart to see him suffering, and so frightened, just because his mama wants him here." Regardless of the risk to her employment, her indignation boiled over. "Lady Orton left London without him. She has not seen him in several days!"

Ashe was taken aback by such vehemence in one usually diffident. If she had constituted herself Colin's champion after a mere few weeks, no wonder she had taken upon herself the removal of her brothers from their unpleasant situation.

Still, to abstract minors from the care of their lawful guardian, however harsh, was not at all the thing. In fact, it was illegal, and Ashe, in not reporting it, was very likely compounding a felony. Since her disclosure he had been wondering whether he ought to attempt to find out more and do something about it.

Peter doesn't cry, even when he's whipped. Michael's voice rang in his ears. *I shan't cry anymore when I'm big like him.* This was the child who had saved a piece of his penny bun for his hungry sister, when he had a "pain in his pudding-house" from hunger. And Peter, who did not mind any punishment as long as Colin had recovered — they were both clearly used to being beaten for every unintended peccadillo.

Good gad, had the brute beaten *Lissa?*

Ashe decided on the spot that this was the

point in a relatively law-abiding life when he and the law parted company. He would ask no questions, make no effort to discover who the Findlays were, where they came from, what their real name might be.

His long silence alarmed Lissa. She recalled that losing her post would devastate her brothers more than herself, and would not help Colin.

"I beg your pardon, sir," she said, all her diffidence returned. "I did not mean to be impertinent."

"Impertinent?" Shaking his head, he came to pull out a chair and sit down opposite her. "The truth may sometimes sound impertinent, I daresay, but it is nevertheless the truth. Daphne loves her son, I do believe, but she is no more cut out for diligent mothering than for a country life."

"Then he will have to stay here?"

"By no means. I am his legal guardian. I have the authority to take whatever steps I consider advisable."

As he paused in thought, Lissa suppressed a shiver. Mr. Exton had the same authority. His notion of what was advisable in the upbringing of children could scarcely be more different from Lord Ashe's.

She did not know what his lordship had said to comfort Peter and Michael, but she was passionately grateful.

"Perhaps I have been remiss," he said now,

ruefully, "in giving way to Daphne. Yet until now I have had no more than a suspicion that Colin would go on better at Ashmead, which I put down to my own happy childhood there."

"Until now? You believe me, then?"

He smiled. "After your scientific experiment with the milk, Miss Findlay, how can I not?"

"Moving Colin to the country would be another experiment," Lissa pointed out.

"He cannot well be worse off," Ashe said decisively. "That fit terrified me quite as much as him. Is he strong enough to travel?"

"Not a great distance. Not so far as Gloucestershire. And if he has another fit before the morning, I should be as afraid of moving him as of keeping him here."

"Exactly. That's why I propose to leave immediately and to take him to my aunt Busby in Buckinghamshire, not much more than twenty miles off. How soon can you get packed up everything that Colin, you, and your brothers will need for a night?"

Joyful, Lissa jumped up and rang the bell for the nurserymaid. "Half an hour?"

"The carriage will be at the door, ma'am." He rose, looking faintly amused by her enthusiasm. "I'll send off a groom at once with a note to prepare my aunt for our arrival."

"You will come? But oh! Lady Orton will not be back from Richmond so soon!"

"You may leave Daphne to me. There is

nothing to stop her joining us. But if she chooses not to," he added with a grin, "then she is welcome to berate me at a distance as much as she may please!"

Eleven

Lord Ashe carried his nephew down to the luxurious traveling carriage. Depositing him within, he turned to hand Lissa up.

"I had several pillows put in," he said. "You will know how to arrange him most comfortably. I shall ride to leave you more space."

"Peter may very well sit beside the coachman," she protested.

"No need." He glanced at Peter and Michael, who had gone forward to inspect the team. "To tell the truth," he went on in a conspiratorial whisper, "I had far rather ride in this weather than be cooped up in the carriage. I shall check with you frequently to make sure all goes well. Come along, boys!"

Peter and Michael scrambled in and they set off.

Lissa half hoped Colin's breathing would ease as soon as they left the city streets. It was too much to expect. As they passed the Tyburn turnpike and rolled through the little village of Shepherd's Bush, slowly so as not to jolt him, he continued to wheeze.

Yet, propped against his pillows, he watched the passing scenery through the windows and took a lively interest in the sights pointed out by Peter and Michael. A lightning-blasted oak, a pair of magpies (one for sorrow, two for joy) on a fence, a tavern called The Bat and Ball, a bright-painted canal boat passing under a bridge: Colin did not speak but he looked, and his eyes were brighter than Lissa had seen them in days.

Thanks to Lord Ashe's thoughtfulness, she had two flasks of barley-water from which Colin sipped regularly. When his lordship appeared at the window to report that they would shortly stop to change horses, Lissa told him her patient had not had a coughing fit in over an hour.

"He is tired, though. How much farther have we to go?"

"We are about halfway. I rode ahead to hire a private parlor at the Target Inn, so he may rest for a while."

"You think of everything, sir."

"Not I, but I try. For you, tea; for the boys, lemonade and cakes."

"What kind?" asked Michael, by now a connoisseur of cakes.

"Wait and see!" said Lissa.

"I'm going to be a pastry cook when I grow up."

Lord Ashe laughed, and rode forward to speak to the coachman. Lissa watched him. She had not seen him on horseback before, or only a glimpse from the schoolroom window high above the street. He looked splendid, she thought, his tall, broad-shouldered figure straight yet at ease in the saddle of the black gelding.

How her view of him had changed since she had felt his gaze on her from the box above the stage! Even then, when he was a stranger, his character unknown to her, she had felt the tug of attraction. Now she knew him, how could she help but love him?

It was just as well they were separating, she decided sadly. When he left her in the country and went back to town, she could stop wondering what she would do were he once more to offer her *carte blanche*. She would no longer have to fight the temptation to accept, to enjoy a few months of love before he tired of her. It would be her only chance to experience the sweetness of a man's embrace, for by the time Michael was old enough to be safe from Mr. Exton she would be well and truly on the shelf.

The carriage slowed, turned sharply, and pulled up in the courtyard of a bustling hostelry. Lord Ashe came to carry Colin in.

When they left the inn, an hour later, Colin was definitely breathing less laboriously. He was even comfortable enough to dose off. Peter and Michael quietly played a game suggested by Lord Ashe which involved each choosing a particular color of horse and counting a cricket run for each one spotted on the busy Oxford Road. A matched pair counted as four, or a boundary hit, Lissa gathered, and a matched team was a six. It kept them occupied.

Unoccupied, Lissa started to worry about their reception by Mrs. Busby. Doubtless Lord Ashe would not tell his aunt that Lissa had been an actress. Still, a governess of a mere nineteen summers was more suitable for nursery children than for a ten-year-old boy. Add two brothers and Mrs. Busby might well consider the whole business decidedly queer.

She was not likely to turn her sister's son and grandson away, and in any case it was in Lord Ashe's hands. Trusting him, Lissa let herself succumb to weariness after a sleepless night. She drowsed off.

The sway of the carriage around a sharp turn roused her. Her first thought, as always, was for her brothers. In a dim, green light Peter sat opposite her, a look of conscious nobility on his face. Michael had fallen fast asleep slumped against his shoulder.

"My arm's gone to sleep," he whispered. "I didn't move him in case he woke up and disturbed you and Colin."

"Thank you!" she said, turning to Colin.

He was just beginning to stir. For the first time in days, Lissa could not hear his respiration. She leant towards him, holding her own breath. The soft susurration of normal breathing was music to her ears.

As he rubbed his eyes, she glanced beyond him through the window. The dimness was explained: the side of the carriage brushed a verdant hedge. So narrow was the lane that leaves grazed the opposite window, too.

"We have left the turnpike," Lissa said. "We must be nearly there. Wake Michael, Peter — gently. However did he manage to get his face dirty in here?" She felt in her reticule for a handkerchief.

"Where are we, Miss Findlay?" Colin asked sleepily.

"Nearly at your great-aunt's."

"I can talk! Peter, I can talk! I was getting very tired of listening all the time."

The boys chattered while Lissa spat on a corner of her handkerchief and cleaned Michael's smudged cheek.

"What is your great-aunt like?" Peter enquired. "Do you know her?"

"Yes, she came to London once when I was little, to stay in Dover Street. She's very fat and she doesn't like boys."

"Not even *good* boys?" Michael asked.

"Not *any* boys."

Lissa's sense of foreboding returned.

The hedges vanished and the carriage rumbled up a hill with the smooth, grey trunks of beeches on either side. The sun shining through the leaves far overhead cast a dappled greenish-gold light. Though spring was nearly past, clumps of fragile pink-tinged windflowers still bloomed beneath the trees.

Despite her anxiety, Lissa's heart could not but rise at the beauty of the scene. Colin was so much better they would be able to leave for

Gloucestershire on the morrow, she told herself. One night at Mrs. Busby's was survivable. What was more, she had forgotten that, as a mere governess, she probably would not have to meet the lady, and although Colin must make his bow, the others need not.

A high red-brick wall appeared, marching between the trees towards the road. They came to a small brick lodge and the carriage turned in between octagonal gateposts and wrought-iron gates, standing open.

" 'Is lordship said you was on the way," the lodgekeeper called to their coachman with a wave. The gates clanged shut behind the carriage as it moved on.

Ashe had not so much forgotten as refused to recollect how his aunt still made him feel like a grubby and ill-mannered small boy. As he paused on the threshold of her immaculately tidy sitting room, her raised lorgnette stripped him of dignity and sophistication before she so much as uttered a word.

"Pray excuse my dirt, ma'am."

"If you had stopped to wash and change out of your riding clothes, you would not need to beg my pardon." Her biting tone and cold eyes, magnified by the lenses, belied the inanimation of her round, dew-lapped face. Massively inert, she half sat, half reclined upon a well-padded sofa, her equally inert, overfed pug sprawled on her vast black satin lap, a box of bonbons at her elbow.

Mrs. Busby was a widow, her late husband having not so much died as faded away. Ashe was not alone in nursing a sneaking fantasy that she had somehow absorbed the unfortunate Mr. Busby's substance, like a praying mantis consuming its mate.

"I have ridden ahead but the carriage is not many minutes behind me, aunt." Though Ashe heard the note of grovelling apology in his own voice, he was powerless to change it. "My note was brief, so . . ."

"Very brief."

"I wrote in haste, ma'am. So I wanted to explain before Colin arrives."

"I cannot conceive of any explanation which will justify foisting a sick boy on my household." Lowering the lorgnette, she reached for a sweetmeat. She did not invite her nephew to be seated, nor even to advance further into the room. "Indeed, it seems to me highly inadvisable to remove an ailing child from his home."

"That's just it, ma'am. The nature of Colin's illness made removing him from the city not merely advisable but imperative." He embarked upon a tangled account of symptoms, attempted treatments, and Miss Findlay's discoveries.

"You are babbling, Robert! How long do you intend to make my house the site for your medical experiments?"

"We shall not impose upon you for more than one night. Colin is so much improved that I trust he will be quite fit enough by tomorrow to make his bow to you before we go on to Ashmead."

"Make his bow to me?" said Mrs. Busby in horror. "I assure you I can well dispense with that civility. A pert boy, as I recall, spoilt by his mother just as your mother spoilt you."

Since the criticism came from the dowager Lady Ashe's own sister, her son forebore to flare up in her defense. In fact, his chief feeling was relief. If Mrs. Busby had no intention of seeing Colin, there was no need whatever to mention Colin's two young companions. The manor was quite large enough to make a chance encounter unlikely, especially as she seldom left her apartments on the ground floor.

"As you wish, aunt," he said meekly.

"I still fail to comprehend why you brought the boy here. I shall speak to the governess. Perhaps she will be able to provide a round tale. Send her to me — *after* she has removed her travel dirt. You may go."

Bowing, Ashe went. He was sorry to have involved Miss Findlay in an interview with his aunt, but he was not about to argue.

"Whew!" he whistled silently, wiping his forehead as he closed the door behind him.

The butler, waiting and no doubt listening in the hallway, gave him a sympathetic glance. "Three adjoining chambers are being prepared, my lord," he said in a low voice, "as your lordship's note to *me* requested. One for Lord Orton, one for his governess, and one for his young companions, and a small sitting room nearby."

"Thank you, Benton." Ashe slipped him a guinea. "No need to mention the other two boys to your mistress."

"None at all, my lord," the butler agreed blandly. "Allow me to show you to your rooms. Your lordship will require hot water, no doubt."

"And plenty of it, but I shan't be able to change until my carriage arrives."

"Naturally, my lord. May I venture to suggest that madam is unlikely to require your presence again in the immediate future?"

"Doubtless." Ashe groaned. "However, I cannot allow Miss Findlay to face the drag . . . my aunt alone."

Benton nodded gravely. "Your lordship will find a decanter of Madeira in the dressing room," he promised, opening a door.

"Dutch courage? You're a good fellow, Benton! Let me know immediately when the carriage comes."

"Certainly, my lord. Perhaps the two . . . ah . . . young gentlemen will not object to continuing round to the stables and ascending by the back stairs?"

"Sheer genius! I have no doubt they will be delighted," Ashe exclaimed, and dished out another guinea.

The carriage emerged from the beech wood, rolled down an avenue of elms, and came to a halt before a large house of mellow red brick half hidden by Virginia creeper. The front door stood open, though the heat of the day was past.

Before the coachman's "Whoa, there!" had faded, a footman in green livery dashed down the steps, followed at a more stately but still hurried pace by the butler. The carriage door was flung open, the step let down. A trifle overwhelmed by the enthusiastic welcome, Lissa gathered her reticule and her shawl and prepared to descend.

The butler appeared in the doorway, blocking her way. With a regal nod, he said in a low voice, "Lord Ashe's compliments, miss, and he requests that the young gentlemen remain in the carriage as far as the stables."

Lissa frowned. Did Mrs. Busby dislike boys so much she would not even let them enter by the front door? "Lord Orton is very tired," she said. "I should like to get him to bed at once."

"Of course, miss. I should say, the *other* young gentlemen."

No better pleased, Lissa assumed her brothers were to be treated as servants. However, she was in no position to protest. She was comforted by the thought that the order must surely have originated with the lady of the house, not Lord Ashe. At least the butler had referred to them as gentlemen.

"Very well. I shall explain to them." She turned her head to speak to Peter.

Her chagrin must have been plain, for the butler said quickly in a still lower voice, "I should explain, miss, that it's by way of being a conspiracy. His lordship desires to keep the young gentlemen's presence unobserved by the mistress. Thomas here is to go with them and smuggle them up the back way."

Thoroughly puzzled, Lissa gave up trying to understand. "Very well," she repeated. "Peter, Michael, Lord Ashe has arranged for the footman to smuggle you into the house from the stables, so don't ge" t down yet."

"What's *smuggle?*" asked Michael.

"An adventure," Lissa told him, and she stepped down.

Before she could turn to assist Colin, Lord Ashe burst out of the house and leapt down the steps, another footman following at a trot.

"Miss Findlay!" He cast a hunted glance over his shoulder. "Has Benton explained?"

"Not exactly," she said tartly.

"Oh. Well, I'll tell you later. I'll carry Colin in."

"I can walk," Colin announced, "but I'd rather be smuggled. It's not fair. Why can't I have an adventure, too?"

Lord Ashe exchanged a long-suffering look with the butler, then shrugged. "No reason, I daresay. As you wish." He moved back. "Miss Findlay, permit me to escort you into the house, by the *front* door."

"Yes, thank you, but just a minute. Colin, you may walk from the stables into the house, but you are not to attempt the stairs. I expect Thomas will carry you." She smiled at the footman.

He blushed. "To be sure, miss, it won't be no trouble."

Benton succeeded in looking as if he was raising his eyes to heaven without visibly moving a muscle. "You go along, too," he directed the second footman, apparently doubting Thomas's ability to control three children intent on adventure.

Lord Ashe stuck his head into the carriage. "Smugglers have to be *very quiet*," he hissed at the boys.

They nodded solemnly, their eyes agleam with excitement. The footmen jumped up behind and the carriage proceeded on its way.

Mounting the front steps at Lissa's side, Lord Ashe ruefully remarked, "You must imagine you've come to a madhouse."

"Have I not?" she asked in mock disappointment. "What a sad take-in! I quite thought I was to observe the inmates for nothing, instead of paying my shilling at the Bethlem Hospital."

"You shall hear all," he promised, "but not until we are safely above stairs. My aunt lives wholly on the ground floor these days."

Benton conducted them to a small room up two pair of stairs. It appeared to have been hurriedly converted from a rarely used bedchamber into a sitting room. The bed, swathed in holland dust sheets, had been pushed against the wall, and the chest of drawers and washstand were likewise swathed. An ill-matched assortment of small, easily portable chairs stood in a circle about a folding card table. Even in the warm evening light, the effect was bleak.

The butler looked about in distress. "I fear this is the best that could be arranged on such short notice, my lord."

"Will it do?" Lord Ashe asked Lissa. "It's just until tomorrow, so that you and the boys have somewhere to sit."

"It will do very well," Lissa assured him.

"Your chamber is directly opposite, miss." Benton pointed out the door. "There is a connecting door to Lord Orton's, and the young gentlemen just beyond. The baggage will be brought up directly."

"Thank you, Benton. I am sure we shall all be quite comfortable."

The butler bowed himself out and Lissa turned to Lord Ashe.

"Won't you sit down?" he suggested.

She had enough experience with children to recognize a delaying tactic when she saw one. "I have been sitting for hours, and well-sprung as your carriage is, I am glad to stand for a while. Besides, I must go and settle the children in a moment. Do tell me, pray, why they are being *smuggled* into the house?"

"Because, Miss Findlay, I am a pusillanimous poltroon," he said wryly, "in fact an arrant coward."

"You?" she exclaimed, startled.

"I confess, my aunt has a way of making me quake in my boots. Oh, it's easy for you to laugh.

166

Wait until you meet her."

"Meet her! I cannot suppose Mrs. Busby has any desire to meet her great-nephew's governess."

"I'm afraid she does, and it's my fault. You may curse me from here to kingdom come if you wish. The fact is, Aunt Busby cut up rough over my bringing Colin here and I made a hash of explaining why his illness made it necessary. She expects better of you."

"Well, I daresay I shall be able to make it plain," Lissa agreed, her lips twitching again. "Especially as the blame for our coming to her house rather than elsewhere is entirely yours, since I did not know of her existence."

"Don't laugh at me, you wretch!" he said, half laughing himself. "You do see, I trust, that having been raked over the coals for introducing one boy into her house, and a relative at that, I was reluctant to admit to two more."

"I am only surprised that the notion of coming here ever crossed your mind."

"A moment of madness. There, this is your chance to wonder at a lunatic without paying your shilling."

"Another time, sir. If I am not mistaken, that noise in the passage is the boys being quiet!" She moved towards the door.

He stopped her with a hand on her arm. "My aunt wishes to see you as soon as you have . . . er . . . tidied yourself, Miss Findlay, not that you appear to have collected any travel dirt." His swift, anxious gaze ran over her from head to toe.

Though entirely passionless, his scrutiny together with his touch on her sleeve made her pulse quicken. She took another step towards the door. "I must see to the boys first," she said firmly.

"Yes, of course. I had my hair combed with a joint-stool for appearing in riding dress, so now the bags have arrived I shall go and change before I escort you down. Never fear, I shan't let you enter the dragon's lair alone!"

His words of reassurance were the reverse of reassuring, Lissa thought as she crossed the passage to Colin's room, whence came the sound of boyish voices. A protector who avowed himself daunted by his aunt — she might do better on her own!

Yet how gratifying that he had owned his cowardice to her, as though she were truly a trusted friend. Calling his aunt a dragon was another sign, for a gentleman did not criticize his relatives to just anyone.

Though the dragon awaited her below stairs, she was smiling as she pushed open the chamber door.

Michael ran to her. "Lissa, Peter says I can't be a smuggler when I grow up!"

Laughing, she kissed him. What Mrs. Busby missed, not liking boys!

Twelve

"What are *you* doing here, Robert?" Mrs. Busby snapped as Lord Ashe ushered Lissa into her sitting room. "I do not recall requiring your presence."

His lordship looked positively abashed. "I just came to make Miss Findlay known to you, Aunt."

"Get on with it, then!"

"Colin's governess, ma'am, Miss Findlay. My aunt, Mrs. Busby."

Lissa curtsied. "How do you do, ma'am."

"Come here, girl." The dragon raised a lorgnette, breathing not fire but icy disapproval as Lissa moved forward. "How old are you?"

"Nineteen, ma'am."

"You are by far too young to have any authority over a boy as old as Colin. Daphne has always indulged him abominably, permitting the most obnoxious behavior. Without doubt she employed you because she knew you to be incapable of disciplining him."

Since the censure was aimed more at Lady Orton than herself, Lissa had no difficulty disregarding it. She was glad, though, that she had taken the time to put on an old gown and scrape back her hair under a cap again.

"Lord Orton does mind me, ma'am," she said, "although I prefer to try to teach self-discipline. He profits greatly, I believe, from the example of . . . Lord Ashe."

"Ha!" snorted Mrs. Busby.

Lissa did not dare glance back at Lord Ashe. She had only just avoided giving away her brothers' involvement in Colin's life, but the substitute all too obviously failed to impress. She concentrated on keeping her face straight and her voice grave as she attempted to protect her would-be protector. "His lordship exerts a beneficial influence over Lord Orton, I assure you, ma'am."

"No one so wanting in conduct can possibly exert a beneficial influence."

"Oh, come now, Aunt!" Lord Ashe protested weakly.

"If you must stay, then hold your tongue. And stop looming there like a monument. Sit down, sit down. Miss Findlay, you may be seated. I trust you are able to enlighten me as to my nephew's reasons for this incursion?"

Clearly and concisely Lissa described the course of Colin's illness and her deductions. "I may be wrong, ma'am," she allowed, "but already he is much improved. At any rate, after his paroxysm it seemed to me of the first importance to remove him from London immediately. Lord Ashe agreed. Since our goal is Ashmead, and your house lies in the way thither, he hoped for your indulgence for one night."

"Hoped? Counted on!" Mrs. Busby glared at him. "Small chance I had to refuse. Still, what's done is done, and I shall not turn my sister's only grandchild from my door."

"Thank you, Aunt."

"When do you mean to abandon your profligate ways and provide her with more grandchildren? Legitimate ones."

Lissa simply could not resist peeping at his lordship. His face was crimson.

"Please, Aunt, spare Miss Findlay's blushes if you will not spare mine!"

"Bah! The governess of a growing boy cannot afford to be missish. She must teach him not to follow your example in libertinism, at least! Well, girl?"

"I shall do my best, ma'am," Lissa said primly.

"A fruitless endeavor. Men are all alike. They run riot unless you keep the whip hand, and I could tell at a glance that you are too feeble for that. I trust you are capable of controlling Colin until you leave in the morning. I will not have noise and mischief in my house."

"I shall keep him quiet, ma'am."

"See that you do," Mrs. Busby said with a wave of dismissal. "You have missed dinner, Robert. I keep no town hours here. Benton will find you something to eat and you may join me for tea."

Lord Ashe followed Lissa out into the hall. "Whew!" he said, thoroughly discomfited. "What an abject creature you must think me,

Miss Findlay. Why she has the power to put me in such a quake, I cannot conceive."

"I would venture to guess that Mrs. Busby acquired her ascendancy when you were a child. It is not easy to eradicate early impressions." Witness the loving natures her brothers had somehow preserved through the years of pitiless severity.

He looked startled, then thoughtful. "You may be right. My aunt used to come to Ashmead to run the household whenever my mother was brought to . . . was confined. Daphne and I used to creep about like mice for fear of her wrath. However good we were, our little brothers and sisters were always stillborn or died soon after birth."

"Mrs. Busby told you it was your fault?" Lissa demanded, absolutely furious. What a dreadful burden of guilt to lay on any child, as bad as anything Mr. Exton had ever done!

"Not exactly," Lord Ashe assured her hastily. "She just warned us that if we misbehaved it would make Mama ill."

"That is bad enough." Lissa allowed Mrs. Busby the benefit of the doubt. "I daresay she did not realize you might imagine a connection with the loss of the babies. But that would be quite enough to explain why she so easily discomposes you, I expect."

He gave her an odd look. Flustered, Lissa was afraid he must consider her shockingly immodest, even impertinent, to declare her views of his behavior, and with such unwarranted confidence. She was about to apologize when Benton approached them.

"My lord, at what hour do you wish to dine?"

Lord Ashe turned to Lissa. "May I join you at nursery supper?" he requested.

"Of course, sir, if you wish."

He turned back to the butler, who said with a suspicion of a grin, "Supper will be served immediately, my lord. I am given to understand that the young gentlemen are ravenous."

"Cakes and lemonade don't last long at that age. As a matter of fact, I'm sharp-set, too, after riding all afternoon. Let us dine! Come, Miss Findlay, permit me to escort you."

He offered his arm. Lissa laid her fingertips on his sleeve in the approved style, but, more tired than hungry, she found herself glad of his support up the stairs. If she leaned more heavily than was perfectly proper, his lordship made no attempt to take advantage of their closeness.

At the top she let go. He smiled at her and said, "A good meal will restore you, and I count upon it to fortify me for tonight's ordeal. How I envy your escape from drinking tea with my aunt! Though I must say *you* did not seem intimidated by her strictures."

"She has no power over me or mine. At worst she could turn us out of the house, but in that case I am persuaded we may rely upon you to find us shelter in an inn."

"You may indeed, though I trust we have

avoided such a fate. Come to think of it, her power over me has no greater extent! The worst she can do is write a distressing account of my shortcomings to my mother." He paused thoughtfully. "Which she will anyway, regardless of anything I do or fail to do."

Reaching the makeshift sitting room, they dropped the subject.

Peter and Colin were squabbling over a game of draughts, Michael drawing on his slate with colored chalks Lissa had brought. Lord Ashe went straight to sort out the squabble, leaving Lissa free to admire Michael's ship — and his lordship's kindly firmness.

What a contrast with how Mr. Exton would have repressed them! Lord Ashe had a wonderful way with children. Sooner or later he would want to set up his own nursery, to settle down and marry. Too soon, no doubt, long before Lissa was free to take up her rightful position in the world and enter the ranks of eligible maidens. By which time, she reminded herself, she would in any case be at her last prayers.

The prospect of a future as an old maid had not much troubled her before she came to know Robert Ashe.

The footmen brought up laden trays. It was an odd meal, the product of a kitchen used to feeding a greedy old woman with a taste for sweets, now called upon to provide at short notice both nursery food and a gentleman's dinner. Lord Ashe had to make do with such kickshaws as fricasseed veal and minced chicken patties instead of a good, hearty roast, while the boys ate too much of the puddings and jellies. At least there was plenty.

Soon after eating, Lissa put the tired boys to bed. After tucking them in with a kiss she was ready to retire to her own bed, but she went across to the sitting room to wish Lord Ashe good night. He was gone.

She sat down for a moment, in case he had just stepped out. The next thing she knew, he was standing over her, holding a candle. The candle flame danced in his eyes.

"Miss Findlay, you have liberated me!"

"What?" she asked sleepily.

"I have just taken tea with my aunt. Instead of cowering as usual before her usual diatribe, I told her about my speech this morning. She called me a sapskull, admittedly, both for my views and for believing I could change anyone's mind, but she did seem to regard me as a serious adult for the first time in my life!"

Lissa smiled up at him. "Congratulations! But you liberated yourself. What speech?"

"I'll tell you tomorrow. Come, you cannot sleep there or you will be lamentably stiff in the morning." He reached out his hand.

Taking his hand, she rose. Her gaze met his and held. The flames in his eyes changed from dancing elation to a steady flare of desire. His clasp tightened as he pulled her towards him.

Then he let her go and stepped back.

"I should like to be on the road reasonably early tomorrow." His voice was studiously matter-of-fact. "Can you and the boys be ready by nine if you are called at eight?"

Lissa tried to think. "Quarter to eight?"

"Quarter to, it is. Good. Aunt Busby does not rise till ten!"

Her hand still warm from Lord Ashe's clasp, Lissa fell asleep the moment her head touched the pillow. Nor did she find time for reflection next day, with three children to care for during a journey of nearly sixty miles. Yet when at last, after a last stop for refreshments, all three boys drowsed off, her thoughts turned not back to the evening before, but ahead.

Though Lord Ashe had joined them in the carriage at intervals throughout the day, for the last stage he rode ahead to warn the household of their coming. At least one welcoming face would greet them on their arrival.

What Lady Ashe would think of the invasion of her peace remained to be seen.

Keeping the boys quiet for a single night was one thing; they could not be suppressed indefinitely, not without using Mr. Exton's methods. Ashmead belonged to Lord Ashe, but it was his mother's home. She was bound to have some control over who was permitted to take up residence.

Presumably she would not go so far as to turn her only grandson away. His companions and his governess were another matter. As Daphne's mother and Colin's grandmother, she would surely have considerable influence on the choice of a governess once he was living with her. Suppose she decided Peter and Michael were too disruptive, or Lissa was incompetent?

Lissa had had nothing to fear from the abominable Mrs. Busby. Lady Ashe was altogether a different kettle of fish. And they were sisters.

How alike were they? Lissa racked her brains to remember what Lord Ashe had said about his mother. The impression Lissa retained was that Lady Ashe was a semi-invalid who viewed with disfavor the high spirits of children. The same might be said of Mrs. Busby, too obese to move easily and dead set against boys — of any age.

Despite her worries, a small smile curved Lissa's mouth. The last thing she had expected was to see the worldly, competent Lord Ashe routed by a stout old lady.

Somehow that small sign of weakness, of fallibility, made her love him all the more. It was just as well that once she was installed at Ashmead and he returned to London she would see little of him — always assuming he persuaded his mother to let her stay.

At worst, she would be here for a few days, for want of anyone else to care for Colin. Curious to see the countryside surrounding her new home, however temporary, Lissa gazed out of the window as the carriage turned off the high-road.

Though the summer days were at their longest, the sun had just set behind a hill, leaving feathery wisps of pink cloud floating in the blue. The hill was a smooth green mound, its turf cropped short by recently sheared sheep. Tall trees dotted the slope, which was separated from the lane by a drystone wall. In the strip of grass at the base of the wall, Lissa saw red campion and ox-eye daisies and yarrow.

The air felt soft and smelled sweet. Here, if anywhere, Colin would achieve health and strength.

Lissa turned her head to contemplate the boy, stirring in his sleep as the carriage jolted over a pothole. Though he was pale after the long day's journey, he breathed freely. He would soon have roses in his cheeks, she vowed, if only she and her brothers were allowed to stay.

The carriage rolled through a pretty hamlet of slate-roofed cottages built of honey-colored stone. The stone was unweathered, Lissa observed with interest. This must be Lord Ashe's new village. She leant forward to see better — until she realized she herself was observed with interest by the women standing gossiping on doorsteps.

Sinking back against the squabs she wondered if they knew who she was, travelling in their landlord's crested carriage. The messenger he had sent off yesterday afternoon should have arrived hours ago at Ashmead, and the servants there were bound to have relatives in the village. News would spread fast that young Lord Orton was coming to live with his grandmother. The villagers would guess the face at the window must be his governess.

Lissa just hoped they would not, in a few days' time, observe with equal interest the governess in ignominious retreat after being dismissed.

Thirteen

"It sounds to me like an abduction!"

Quailing, Lissa stopped dead on the threshold of the candlelit drawing room. Surely Lord Ashe had not told his mother that she had run off with Peter and Michael from her stepfather's house!

By candlelight Lady Ashe was still lovely and, like her daughter, younger-looking than what must be her age though her black hair was streaked with silver. Despite her words, she was smiling teasingly at her son.

"Abduction?" he said. "Not a bit of it, Mama. I'm Colin's legal guardian, after all. I have bowed to Daphne's whims for longer than I ought."

"Well, my dear, you are past the age for boyish scrapes. You had best tell me all about it." She caught sight of Lissa. "Oh, you must be Colin's governess?"

"Yes, ma'am." Lissa curtsied. "Lord Ashe said I should come down as soon as the boys were settled."

Lord Ashe rose. "Come in, Miss Findlay," he invited with a smile. "I rely upon you to persuade my mother that I am not run mad. Miss Findlay is much better qualified than I, Mama, to explain why we are here."

"I shall try, sir." Lissa advanced and curtsied again.

Lady Ashe, as slight and fragile-looking as Mrs. Busby was massive, regarded Lissa with a slight frown. "You are very young to have charge of Lord Orton," she said. She cast a quick, doubtful glance at her son, whose eyes were on Lissa. "And rather too pretty to be a governess."

"Needs must when the devil drives, Mama — if you will pardon the expression. Miss Findlay has two young brothers to support."

"Indeed! Dare I guess that the young friends you brought with Colin are Miss Findlay's brothers?"

"They are, and Colin has been happier since they joined him than I've ever known him."

"Indeed," Lady Ashe repeated, but this time more thoughtfully than disapprovingly.

"I believe Lady Orton is satisfied with my care of Col- . . . Lord Orton, ma'am," Lissa said quickly.

"Then I await with interest your explanation of why my son has seen fit to remove you and your charge from Lady Orton's authority without her prior consent." Again she glanced at Lord Ashe, still standing. "You had best be seated, Miss Findlay," she said dryly.

Wearily, Lissa took a nearby chair, and Lord Ashe resumed his seat. With his supportive interpolations, she described the course of Colin's illness, her reasoning, his acute attack, and his improvement once they left the city behind.

Her ladyship bestowed an approving look on her son. "It does sound as if you were justified in rushing the boy away, Rob. I have always said the country is healthier for children. But, whatever my wishes, you know my physician will not permit me to supervise a nursery."

"You will not have to stir a finger, Mama. Miss Findlay is truly competent despite her age and beaut . . . and brothers," he substituted weakly, and hurriedly continued. "I've no more business in the House, so I shall stay for a while to make sure all goes smoothly. When I leave I shall keep you apprised of my movements so that you may summon me back in case of need — which I don't anticipate."

"I shall try to keep the boys out of your way, ma'am," Lissa said. "There is surely enough room in the house and outside to avoid disturbing you, though I cannot promise they will always be quiet and angelic."

"Good heavens, no, how unnatural that would be!" Lady Ashe said with a laugh. "You must not suppose I share my sister's dislike of boyish high spirits. It is just that I have a weak heart, alas, and must not exert myself to oversee them. Well, Robert, we shall see how it goes — always supposing Daphne does not rush down to Ashmead and dismiss Miss Findlay on the spot."

"I prophesy that she will not arrive for at least a week. She is invited to Woburn Abbey for a few days for a grand summer fête. She and Teague have talked of nothing else but what to wear for it this fortnight! The Duke of Bedford will certainly take precedence over her son, especially as she knows in her heart Colin will be well cared for."

"No doubt. Sir Quentin Teague? I must talk to you about that gentleman, my dear. Miss Findlay, that will be all for now, thank you."

Lissa found her way back to the nursery wing with a new worry on her mind. She had been too anxious for Colin's health to consider Lady Orton's reaction to her part in stealing him away. It was all very well for Lord Ashe to tell her to leave his sister to him, but Lady Orton had no control over him. All she could do was reproach him.

She could dismiss Lissa, and all the world would hold her justified.

At least Lord Ashe would be here to reason with her. Lissa had assumed he meant to go straight back to town, but of course he would not wish to waste the journey. As well as preparations for building his bridge, he doubtless had other estate business to occupy him.

She ought to be dismayed that she was not to be relieved at once of his disturbing presence, yet her heart refused to sink. After their journey together, she was more in love than ever. Though he was no less unattainable than before, she could not but be glad when he was near.

If he was right, she had a week before Lady Orton arrived, a week in comfortable and beautiful surroundings with every day bringing a hope of seeing him. She would try to put aside her worries and enjoy it.

Next morning, in view of Lady Ashe's comment on her looks, Lissa decided it was advisable to pull back her hair and wear a cap again. She even put on one of her old gowns, but quickly took it off again, wondering how she could have borne to go about clad in such appalling clothes.

Her chamber, more spacious than her room in Dover Street, overlooked the stables and walled vegetable gardens. All the walls were of the golden Cotswold stone, as was the house itself, the low, rambling manor she had glimpsed in the dusk last night. Beyond the gardens rose a sheep-dotted green hill crowned with a spinney.

The country was very different from the arable district in Suffolk where she had spent her childhood, she thought, striving to forget the grimy collieries of Leicestershire. This was much prettier, even under a thin haze of cloud. Also much better for rambling boys, without endless muddy ploughland or fields of growing crops to be avoided.

She must check with Lord Ashe as to whether there were any places she ought not to take the boys. It was *not* just an excuse to see him, she assured herself. He might have coverts with birds not to be disturbed, or neighbors who objected to trespassers.

A dog barked in the stableyard below. Tears rose to Lissa's eyes as she remembered Folly, the gun-shy spaniel which had been her and Peter's pet. Mr. Exton disapproved of animals in the house, of useless animals anywhere. Banished to the stables, Folly had disappeared, never to be seen again, less than a week after they took up residence with him.

Lord Ashe would surely let the boys have a dog to call their own, outside if not in. But she must wait to ask until she was sure she and her brothers were not to be sent away, or Peter's heart would be broken again.

Turning from the window, Lissa cast a last glance in the looking glass. She tucked an escaping curl under the cap, picked up her old shawl, and went to join the boys.

The table in the vast day nursery was already set for breakfast. At one end sat a hunched crone whose apple-cheeks and bright eyes belied her wrinkled face and white, wispy hair.

"Miss Findlay, may I present Nanny Bessemer?" said Colin in his grandest manner. "She was Mama's nurse, and Uncle Robert's."

"How do you do, Mrs. Bessemer," Lissa said apprehensively. Lord Ashe had mentioned the old woman, but indicated that she had retired years ago. If she took against Lissa and started to interfere, she could make her job difficult, or even impossible.

"How do, miss. Why, you're nowt but a child yoursel'! Sit you down, dearie. Now you needn't fear I'm bent on meddling, for I'm not up to much nowadays, and that's the truth. Find

185

mesel' nodding off at all hours. But me eyes is good as ever they was. I can mend torn shirts and I can gi' you a hand making sure Master Colin and his fine young friends wash behin' their ears and such."

"Thank you, Nanny," said Lissa with a smile, while the boys protested that they always washed behind their ears without being told.

Breakfast came, carried in by a footman and the nurserymaid, arrived from London late last night with the luggage. Lissa was glad to see the obliging young girl, and she was delighted to see Colin start on a boiled egg as if he were famished.

As soon as Michael's first, urgent pangs of hunger were assuaged, he demanded, "Lissa, why have you got that horrid thing on your head again?"

"Because it is the proper dress for a governess. I only took it off because Lord Orton's mama wished me to. Lady Ashe will certainly expect me to wear it."

"I'll tell Grandmama you're prettier without a cap, Miss Findlay," Colin volunteered.

"Pray do not! I have no objection to it, I assure you."

"When Mama comes, she will tell you to take it off again."

"In that case, I shall leave it to Lady Ashe and Lady Orton to come to an agreement and inform me of their decision. In the meantime, you are not to mention it to your grandmama, Lord Orton."

"Lord Orton!" Peter exclaimed. "Won't Colin's grandmama let you call him Colin any longer?"

"She did not say so, precisely, but she spoke to me of him as Lord Orton, so that is how I shall address him."

Colin pouted. "I don't like being called Lord Orton."

"You might call the lad Master Colin, miss," Nanny Bessemer suggested. "Her la'ship likes things done proper but she's no ogre."

"That's better," Colin said sadly, "but I was going to ask if I can call you Lissa, like Peter and Michael do."

" 'If I *may . . . as* Peter and Michael do,' " Lissa corrected automatically, thinking. "Suppose I call you Master Colin and you call me Miss Lissa? If Lady Ashe dislikes it, we shall change."

They soon had an opportunity to discover the dowager's opinion. The footman who came to clear the table brought a message: Miss Findlay, her charge, and her brothers were summoned to Lady Ashe's sitting room.

Nanny was a great help, wiping the milk moustache from Michael's upper lip and egg yolk from his chin, and slicking down his unruly hair, while Lissa made sure the older boys were clean and tidy. She tied the ribbon of her cap more firmly under her chin and draped the shawl around her shoulders to conceal as much as possible of Lady Orton's elegant gown and her own figure.

187

"All ready? Come along, then. On your best behavior, boys!"

As they descended the stairs to her ladyship's ground floor apartments, situated in the wing farthest from the nurseries, Michael asked anxiously, "Does your grandmama like boys, Colin?"

"Mostly," Colin assured him.

Lady Ashe, in a pink, beruffled dressing gown, reclined on a sofa in a sitting room full of roses. Every table held a vase, and a huge bouquet filled the fireplace, hiding the empty grate. Lissa prayed the boys would not knock any over. All possible surfaces were covered with exquisitely embroidered flowers, she noted.

Curtsying, she murmured, "Good morning, ma'am."

"Good morning, Grandmama."

"Good morning, my lady," Peter and Michael chorused, and all three bowed in unison. Lissa was proud of them.

"Good morning." Lady Ashe held out her hand to her grandson. "Colin, dear child, come and kiss me. How do you feel this morning?"

"Right as a trivet, Grandmama. Much better than in London. I was *dreadfully* ill, but Miss Lissa made me better."

"Miss *Lissa?*"

"She said I may. Peter and Michael call her Lissa 'cause she's their sister, but I have to say Miss 'cause she's my governess."

"I see. If Miss Findlay permits it, I daresay

188

there is no harm. Will you present your friends to me?"

Colin made a masterly job of the introductions. Peter bowed again and said politely, "How do you do, ma'am."

Michael burst out, "Are you Lord Ashe's mama?"

Lissa cringed as Lady Ashe raised her eyebrows in an expression strongly reminiscent of her son at his most sardonic. "I am," her ladyship acknowledged.

"When he was a little boy, did you faint or have hysterics when he came into your drawing room with a dead rabbit, all bloody?"

Appalled, Lissa reached for her little brother, not sure whether to clamp her hand across his mouth or bundle him straight out of the room. To her astonishment, Lady Ashe laughed.

"Neither, my dear. I told him to deliver the corpse to the kitchen for Cook to dress for dinner."

"Gosh, really? When I'm old enough, I'll shoot a rabbit for your dinner if you like. But I *shan't* bring it into your drawing room."

"Thank you. You are a little young for a gun, but how would you like to go fishing? The tackle Lord Ashe used as a boy must be about somewhere, and I believe there were poles and nets for his cousins, too, enough for the three of you."

Peter and Colin swung round to Lissa, faces alight with hope.

"May we?" Colin begged.

"Would it be bad for Colin?" asked Peter, earning an approving look from Lady Ashe.

"I doubt it. Fresh air without too much exertion — it sounds perfect. Thank you, ma'am."

Lady Ashe nodded graciously. She asked Colin about his lessons, raising her eyebrows again slightly when he said he didn't mind having a tutor, come autumn, as Peter and Michael were to study with him. Standing by the door, Lissa watched her face carefully, anxious not to let the boys tire her. She seemed to enjoy their chatter, however.

They were telling her about the King Arthur book when a tall, severe-looking woman came in. Lady Ashe introduced her as her cousin and companion, Miss Barbican.

A moment's swift thought told Lissa that though a hired companion and a governess were roughly equal in status, a cousin — even a poor relation — was superior. She curtsied as Peter bowed, quickly copied by Colin and Michael. Again Lady Ashe looked upon Peter with approval.

Miss Barbican gave them a stiff, frosty nod. "You must not let the children weary you, Maria," she said to Lady Ashe.

"They do not, Jane, I assure you. Colin's young friends appear to be well-behaved boys, Miss Findlay is in charge, and Robert keeps an eye on them all, so I have no need to exert myself. It will be delightful to have young people about the place again, I vow."

Lissa dared hope her ladyship might even help to persuade Lady Orton to let Colin stay at Ashmead under his governess's care.

Lord Ashe awaited Lissa and the boys in the schoolroom. "How did it go?" he asked.

"Uncle Robert, Grandmama said we may go fishing!"

"And did Miss Findlay say you may go fishing?"

"Yes, we asked, didn't we, Miss Lissa?"

"You did," Lissa agreed with a smile. "Lady Ashe thought your fishing tackle must still be about, sir?"

He directed the boys to look in a cupboard in the corner. They dived in with cries of excitement, excavating rods, fishing nets and butterfly nets, cricket bats and balls, shuttlecocks and battledores, and other outdoor paraphernalia.

"How did it go?" Lord Ashe repeated to Lissa.

"Very well. Unlike Mrs. Busby, Lady Ashe appears to have an affinity with small boys."

"She was always an indulgent mother to me. I'm afraid Daphne rather got the short end of the stick," he mused. "She was never permitted to fish or play cricket with me. You know: Boys will be boys, but girls must be young ladies, which explains, I daresay, why her interests now are so limited." He flushed, as if suddenly realizing he ought not to criticize his sister to Lissa. "Were you brought up on that principle?"

"Oh no. Until I was eleven . . ." She hesitated,

trying to foresee whether she was about to give away any dangerous secrets. "We had lots of neighbors with both boys and girls about my age, and Papa encouraged me to try whatever I wished."

"Whereas your stepfather, I collect, did not even allow boys to be boys," Lord Ashe said grimly. Lissa flinched, dreading questions. He touched her sleeve. "Never fear, I don't mean to probe."

"Thank you," she whispered, and turned with relief to stop a squabble over who was to get the best fishing pole. "You shall take turns. Master Colin first, because all these things were his uncle's, then Peter because he is the eldest."

"I don't mind," Michael said bravely, obviously minding a great deal.

"You shall be first with something else," Lissa promised, hugging him.

He pulled away. "Don't do that. I'm too old for that baby stuff."

"Already?" said Lissa with a pang of dismay.

"No, you're not," Peter said at once. "Not till you're eleven."

Colin flung his arms around her waist. "You can hug me. I'm only ten."

"Me, too, just this once," said Peter loftily, joining in.

Michael changed his mind. "You can hug me *any* time, Lissa," he cried.

Laughing, Lissa embraced all three.

"What about me?" Lord Ashe asked in a plaintive voice.

Lissa sternly suppressed a quiver of longing. She cast a reproachful glance at him over the boys' heads, as Colin said, "You're *much* too old, Uncle Robert."

"Not too old, I hope, to take you fishing."

"No!"

"Will you really?"

Deserting Lissa, they flung themselves on Lord Ashe.

"You will come with us, Miss Findlay! I cannot possibly control all three at once."

"I am sure you can, sir." Lissa badly wanted to go, but common caution told her she must not spend too much time in his company. Not only was the frisson she felt when he suggested hugging her a danger signal, but Lady Ashe would legitimately view such conduct with disfavor, perhaps with suspicion. "I must see all our clothes and books sorted out and properly disposed, so that we can begin lessons tomorrow."

"Lessons!" Colin protested. "We are not to have a tutor till the autumn."

"You don't want to forget everything you know, do you?" said Peter. "The tutor will think you're a slowtop."

"Just an hour a day," Lissa promised. "That will be plenty, especially as I do not wish to tax Master Colin's strength when he was so recently ill."

"I suppose Colin is well enough to go fishing?" Lord Ashe's question brought a horrified pause as the boys saw their treat withdrawn.

"I'm *excessively* well!" Colin cried.

"All the same," said Lord Ashe blandly, "I cannot think it wise for Miss Findlay to entrust you entirely to me on this first outing, when she is the one who knows how to deal with your attacks."

So Lissa went, too.

Fourteen

Lady Orton arrived, Sir Quentin in tow, a day before her brother expected her. Magnificent in a royal blue carriage dress and beplumed bonnet, she swept into the schoolroom just as Colin was about to go down for his daily tea with his grandmother.

Colin ran to her — stopping on the way for a hasty bow — and kissed her. "Mama, it is *such* fun here, you cannot imagine! Are you coming to live at Ashmead?" he asked eagerly.

"Live at Ashmead? Good gracious, darling, I should go into a decline."

"But I can breathe properly here. I don't want to live in London. Couldn't I live here with Miss Lissa and Peter and Michael? And Grandmama and Uncle Robert, too, of course. And Nanny. And Curly."

"Curly?"

"Curly's a terrier. Uncle Robert's lent her to us, but if we go on living here he'll *give* her. And you could come to see me *very, very* often?"

"I am very, very cross with Uncle Robert." A cloud that was nearly a frown passed across her lovely face.

"I am so sorry, Lady Orton," Lissa said apprehensively. "We left in a great hurry and there was no way to notify you beforehand."

"My dear Miss Findlay, no blame attaches to you. I would not expect you to hold out against my brother's orders."

"But I did not try," Lissa confessed. "It was my belief that Master Colin's health would improve in the country which induced Lord Ashe to remove him to Ashmead."

"Well, it appears you were right," Lady Ashe acknowledged, regarding her son with a sunny smile. "I do believe you have grown an inch, my love, in just a week, and your cheeks are quite rosy."

"I can play cricket, Mama, and climb trees, and run quite a long way. Not as far as Peter and Michael."

"Almost," said Michael encouragingly. "Your legs are longer than mine."

"Colin was very ill in London, my lady," Peter put in. "We thought . . . we were afraid he was going to die."

"Darling, was it so dreadful?" Lady Orton hugged Colin. "The note your uncle left me said you had a bad attack, but the servants told me the doctor was not called in."

"Dr. Hardin never did me any good. I was frightened, Mama. If it wasn't for Miss Lissa I'd be dead now, and you would have to wear black like when Papa died. I don't want to go back to London."

"We shall see, darling. I must consult your

grandmama and Miss Findlay and Uncle Robert — after I have rung a peal over his head."

"Ring away," said Lord Ashe, sauntering into the room. "My head is at your disposal, Daphne. I am ready to own myself at fault, provided you realize Miss Findlay had no say in the matter."

"I know that. I am really quite cross with you, Rob. You might at least have stayed at Aunt Busby's so that I could see Colin before you brought him all the way to Ashmead."

Lord Ashe's eyes, brimful of laughter, met Lissa's. "My dear Daphne, you cannot suppose Aunt Busby would have permitted us to remain in her house a moment longer than absolutely necessary to Colin's health. Indeed, she regarded his sickness as one more affront to her sensibilities."

"Was she perfectly horrid to you? Poor Rob! And to you, Colin darling?"

"No, Mama, for I did not see her. We ran away in the morning before she woke up."

Lady Orton's laugh chimed like silver bells, and that was the extent of the peal she rang over her erring brother's impenitent head.

If her ladyship consulted her mother and Lord Ashe about Colin's remaining at Ashmead, Lissa knew nothing of it. To her it appeared that Lady Orton accepted the removal as a *fait accompli* and ceased to fret over it.

She and Lord Quentin stayed for several days. They called on neighbors, which led to a flurry of social activities in the district. They shopped in Bascombe-on-the-Water, which led to Lissa's acquisition of a bonnet and yards of ribbon, lace, and bugle trimming, discovered on arriving home to be shockingly commonplace. They strolled in the rose garden, which led to Lady Orton tearing a flounce on a thorn. They were introduced by Colin to Curly, which led to muddy footprints on Lord Quentin's pantaloons.

They remembered an invitation to a house party in Hampshire and dashed off. Colin moped for half an hour, then dashed off to the stables for the daily riding lesson.

Lord Ashe had purchased ponies for all three boys. When Lissa protested, he said learning to ride was part of Colin's education, which they had agreed Peter and Michael were to share.

"If they cannot ride with him, do you imagine he will have the least interest in riding? You ought to learn, too. They will enjoy it more with you than with a groom when I cannot take them out."

"No," Lissa said resolutely. "They will have to make do with a groom. I have no habit, and you must see that it would be grossly improper in me to accept an article of clothing from a gentleman."

He accepted her adamant refusal. She had given in over the fishing expedition, but she would not be beholden to him for providing a mount, still less a riding dress. What would Lady Ashe think if her son spent money on a horse for the governess? Moreover, Lissa recalled having told him she did not ride, and to feign complete ignorance of the requisite skills once in the saddle was beyond her acting capabilities.

She had too much to hide from him already, enmeshed as she was in a life of deception. For the boys' sake she could not regret it, but she had not bargained for the strain of constantly keeping up her guard.

In spite of that strain, in spite of her fruitless love for Lord Ashe, Lissa delighted in summer at Ashmead. Not for years had she known such comfort and content.

A good part of her pleasure came from seeing her brothers rejoicing in every day. Though brought up in the country, Peter and Michael had not been allowed to enjoy the many pleasures offered to small boys by woods, fields and streams. They had never played hide-and-seek among the trees, hunted butterflies and beetles, or paddled in clear, cool running water with minnows tickling their toes. They loved every minute spent outdoors.

So did Colin, and Lissa's pleasure in his happiness was tinged with self-congratulation. His strength increased daily. He wheezed only when he tried to run uphill, or after sneezing fits brought on by certain flowers. Lissa soon worked out which plants he must avoid and taught him to recognize them.

Lady Ashe, who saw Colin every day, noted the improvement in his health and sent for Lissa one morning to thank her.

"As you are aware, Miss Findlay," she said, "I was most dubious as to your suitability for the post of governess to my grandson. Your youth, your looks, your brothers, all created an unfavorable appearance. However, I cannot deny that your brothers are ideal companions for the child, and your care of him has been exemplary."

"Thank you, ma'am. I am very fond of Master Colin."

"And he of you, I collect. So, your youth and the boys turn out not to be disadvantages. About your looks I am less certain."

"Ma'am?" Lissa resisted an urge to tug on her cap.

"I understand you spend a good deal of time with my son."

Willing herself not to blush, Lissa said firmly, "Lord Ashe spends a good deal of time with the boys, ma'am. He is a devoted uncle and, I believe, enjoys their company. But it is only natural that he generally wishes me to be present to take over the responsibility when he needs or chooses to turn his attention to other matters."

"Hmm, perhaps. I hardly imagine, though, that the boys are interested in the design of cottages. Did not Lord Ashe show you over one of his cottages?"

"He did, ma'am. I own that I was more interested than the boys, but Lord Ashe wished to impress upon Lord Orton, while he is young enough to be impressed, the value of sanitary housing for . . ."

Lady Ashe waved her to silence. "Yes, yes, I have heard his sermons upon the subject! Lord Orton's estate, however, stands in no need of a new bridge, yet I hear that you frequently go to inspect the progress of the construction."

"Very frequently!" Lissa smiled. "Can you imagine, ma'am, anything more calculated to appeal to small boys than a great structure gradually arising from all that mud and bustle? I assure you, when we go there, it takes all my care to stop them joining in."

Her ladyship admitted the justice of this observation, though she did not appear entirely reassured about the effect of Lissa's looks upon her son.

For her part, Lissa had wondered at Lord Ashe's continued presence at Ashmead. She had expected him to leave, to return to London, to go visiting, like his sister, or to join the social scene in Brighton.

If she was tempted to believe he remained for her sake, a moment's reflection sufficed to disabuse her of that notion. The construction of the bridge was enough to explain his staying. What with overseeing that, the general business of the estate, entertaining and being entertained by the neighbors, and the time he spent with the boys, he was constantly busy.

Lissa came to realize how deeply he loved Ashmead. This was his true home, his sojourns in London a mere hiatus.

He did go away for a few days now and then, to visit particular friends. In August, in turn, he and Lady Ashe invited a few friends and relatives to stay for a week. Lady Orton returned to Ashmead for the occasion, Sir Quentin as ever at her side. Colin was made much of in the drawing room each afternoon, but otherwise the nursery party was unaffected, except for seeing little of Lord Ashe while his guests stayed.

They left, and life went back to normal — to what, Lissa cautioned herself, it was all too easy to regard as normal. How she wished this existence might go on forever!

Autumn was coming. As sure as the swallows turned south, the *Haut Monde* would turn towards London. Lord Ashe would resume his seat in the House of Lords; Lady Orton would repair to town for the Little Season; Lissa's boys must go back to their serious studies.

With Colin looking so healthy now, his mother might think him fit to return to London. Lord Ashe might not wish to hire a tutor to reside at Ashmead when his services would be required only a few hours a day. Lissa no longer lived in constant fear of dismissal, but the uncertainty of their future abode unsettled her.

She dreaded the prospect of seeing Colin ailing again, his lungs under assault by the foul city air. As she had foretold to Lord Ashe, her affection for the boy had grown with familiarity. If he would never be quite as dear to her as Peter and Michael, the slight difference was largely due to her brothers' utter dependence on her.

The country was better for them, too, though having survived the months in Lambeth they would doubtless continue to thrive in Dover Street. For herself, Lissa was torn.

Would life at Ashmead continue to content her if she only saw Lord Ashe occasionally, on rare, brief visits? Could she bear the close quarters of Dover Street, where he was always nearby yet his occupations had no room for three boys and a governess?

Because here at Ashmead, whatever she had told Lady Ashe, as often as not the boys ran off to play while she and Lord Ashe talked endlessly. Here, he was her friend.

Autumn was coming. In the orchard, pears and plums were ready for harvest and apples ripening fast. In the fields, the brambles sagged beneath the weight of their glossy fruit. One sunny afternoon, Lissa took the boys blackberrying.

Purple-fingered and purple-mouthed — and in Michael's case purple-shirted — they wandered with their cans along hedgerows wreathed with old man's beard, garlanded with the scarlet, orange and green fruit of the bryony. Curly bounced alongside, with many a side excursion after smells.

Finding a good spot, they settled down to serious picking. Lissa took off her obstructive bonnet and hung it on a branch of a hedge-maple.

"Look at these, they're enormous," shouted Colin.

"Mine are supergigantenormous." That was Peter.

"Not as big as mine."

"Ripeness and sweetness are more important than size," Lissa pointed out.

"Lissa, I can't reach that bunch. They're big *and* ripe."

"They do look good. Bother!" Lissa stretched in vain. "I should have brought a crooked walking stick."

"Allow me." Lord Ashe was climbing a nearby stile, his horse already tied to a side post.

"Uncle Robert, I've picked lots and lots."

"Not as many as I have," Peter claimed. "Michael has hardly any because he keeps eating them."

"Eating's what they're for, aren't they, Lissa?"

"Yes, pet, but do not eat too many or you will have a tummy-ache."

Lord Ashe smiled at Michael, an oddly sympathetic smile. "They taste even better with sugar and cream, not to mention in pies and jellies. Wait just a minute while I pull down that sprig for Peter, then I'll help you fill your can."

Lissa moved back as he approached, laughing when half Peter's "supergigantenormous" cluster ended up in his lordship's mouth.

With Lord Ashe's aid, Michael's can was soon full, as were the other three. Lissa had brought a couple of spares, but the boys had

had enough of picking.

"Curly ran off ages ago," said Peter, waving at the wood at the bottom of the field, its trees already touched with bronze and yellow. "Listen, she's barking. May we go and see what she's doing, Lissa?"

"Yes, go along with you, but listen in case I call. If I'm not here when you come back, I'll be picking in the next field. Thank you for your assistance, sir," she said, as the boys ran off.

"Let me help you fill those two, since I have every intention of helping to consume the pies and jellies. We've pretty well stripped this side of the hedge. Shall we try the other side?"

His horse sidled out of the way as he gave her his hand to climb the stile. Because of the staining berry juice, both had taken off their gloves. The touch of his warm, strong fingers sent a trembling shock up her arm that spread in a warm glow throughout her body. Eyes lowered, she prayed he would not notice how she was affected.

Nothing could be more dangerous than revealing that she loved him, a peril she had somehow so far avoided. Though by now she felt quite safe in his company, the discovery might encourage him to resume his pursuit, to attempt again to seduce her. More likely it would simply embarrass him. In his discomfort, he would not want her to remain in his household.

With the good references she felt she had earned, she was confident of obtaining another position, even one where she could take Peter and Michael. But she did not want another position!

She wanted to be near him, however painful it was.

Lost in thought, she picked for several minutes in silence. Lord Ashe was silent too, industriously filling his can a few yards from her. Here in the shade on the east side of the hedge the air was crisply autumnal. Soon Lissa would have to go back to wearing her old, dowdy, woollen dresses, but for the moment stooping and stretching after the best berries kept her warm enough.

As she reached in among the brambles after a succulent cluster, thorns caught her sleeve. She set down the can in her other hand and leaned forward to unhook the delicate muslin. One of the waving canes dangling from above grabbed her hair.

"Oh *bother!*"

Lord Ashe looked round and grinned. "Hold hard, your champion is coming to the rescue. Don't pull, Miss Findlay! You will only make it worse."

Lissa obediently held still as a strand of hair came loose from its pins and tickled her cheek.

He freed her sleeve first. Incautiously she raised her hand to her hair.

"Ouch!" She sucked her pricked finger.

"Do keep still or we shall have to hunt in the attics for a wig for you to wear. Good Lord, how did you manage to get so entangled?"

His closeness, the feel of his fingers in her hair, took away her breath. She tingled all over, from the top of her head to the soles of her feet. Closing her eyes, she fought to retain her composure.

"I shall have to take out your hairpins, I fear," Lord Ashe apologized in an unsteady voice.

Her hair cascaded about her ears, all but the locks caught in the thorns. The tugging and wrenching that followed brought tears to her eyes.

"Ouch!"

"Am I hurting you? Nearly done. There. Don't move or you'll get stuck again!"

His hands on her shoulders, he turned her to face him as he guided her clear of the brambles. His indrawn breath was all the warning Lissa had before his arms went around her and his lips met hers.

Startled, her heart pounding wildly, she gave herself up to the sweetness for an immeasurable time.

Then sanity swept back. She would not, must not become his mistress when she yearned without hope for so much more. Frantically she beat upon his chest.

He released her at once and stepped back, his face flushed, his breath coming fast. His eyes closed as if to shut out the sight of her.

"I'm sorry. The temptation was irresistible."

"You should have resisted!" she cried, turning away. "Now I cannot stay here. I shall have to seek another position at once."

"No! Why should you suffer for my misbehavior, you and your brothers?"

"They ... *We* would suffer more if I yielded my virtue."

"Miss Findlay, I no longer have designs upon your virtue, I swear it. You must believe me. That was a momentary aberration." His voice shook. "I can control myself. I *will* control myself."

"It will not do, sir. You know it."

"But what of Colin? He needs you. You cannot abandon him. I shall go. If it will ease your fears and persuade you to remain at Ashmead, I shall remove to town at once. When it's absolutely necessary for me to come down, I shall stay out of your way and never seek to see you."

Head bowed, hands clasped tight, Lissa stood silent, unable to utter a word. Never to see him, knowing she was the cause of his exile from his beloved home! Yet, for the boys' sake, what could she do but accept his sacrifice?

Fifteen

Lord Ashe departed the next morning. He told the boys he was going to find them a tutor. Colin and Michael groaned, but Peter was excited, looking forward to delving into the mysteries of Latin. If he had no other prospects, he might have made his way as a scholar, Lissa thought, trying to enter into his enthusiasm.

She had not seen Lord Ashe since he galloped away, leaving her in the meadow with her hair down, her hairpins scattered, and her heart in fragments. Retrieving her bonnet from the maple, she had stuffed her hair under it and tied the ribbons tight. Her heart was not so easily salvaged. The walk back to the house, carrying the cans of blackberries, had seemed endless; the boys were unfeeling monsters, chattering away about how they had had to pull Curly from a fox's hole by her hind legs.

At least that meant she had succeeded in hiding her unhappiness from them.

That day the sun continued to shine. The boys were outside most of the time, making the most of what was left of their freedom. Lissa let them ride with a groom or ramble alone — Peter had plenty of common sense and Colin, especially, had an excellent sense of direction — while she did her best to prepare a plan for such of their lessons as would still be her responsibility. She explored the library, burying her misery in printed words. Underneath, the ache went on.

The weather changed. Chilly rain fell in ceaseless sheets. Now keeping the boys occupied indoors left Lissa little time to brood.

On the second wet, cold day, Lady Orton and Lord Quentin arrived at Ashmead. The boys had had their supper and were sitting by the fire in their nightshirts, listening to Lissa read from *Waverley,* when Lady Orton came into the schoolroom.

"Brrr," she said, shivering and digging her hands further into the fur muff she still carried, "I do not believe I shall ever be warm again. Colin, darling, see what horrible weather your mama has endured to see you!"

"Do come and sit by the fire, Lady Orton," Lissa invited her.

Her unexpected arrival came as a shock, for Lissa had forgotten that Colin's future abode was still not settled. What was she to do if Lady Orton demanded their return to town, thus oversetting her brother's effort to remove himself from temptation? However much he loved Ashmead, Lord Ashe could not be expected to rusticate when the Polite World was gathered in London and Parliament was in session.

"Yes, Mama, come and get warm and listen to *Waverley.* It's a rattling good yarn."

"Not now, my love. I just came up to say hello before I change for dinner. You may tell me all about it tomorrow. You look very well."

"I am well. Supergigantenormously well." Colin and Michael had both adopted Peter's invention, and applied it indiscriminately. "We can stay at Ashmead, can't we?"

"As long as Miss Findlay does not mind staying out here in the middle of nowhere to look after you. And she does not leave to nurse a sick mother," Lady Orton added darkly.

Lissa knew her predecessor, Miss Prescott, had committed that grievous sin. "I have no mother, Lady Orton," she hastened to assure her employer.

"You may stay, then, Colin."

So, after all Lissa's worry, that was that.

"And Lord Quentin and I shall be able to marry at last!"

The prospect no longer disturbed Colin. "You'll come to see us, Mama, when the weather is nice?"

"Yes, indeed. In fact, I have had the most splendid notion. It is too bad of your uncle to go off to town when I particularly wished to discuss it with him and your grandmama at the same time."

"He had to go to find us a tutor," Peter apologized.

"We have to start doing lessons all the time," Michael explained, " 'cause of autumn. You can discuss it with us instead if you like."

"What sort of splendid notion, Mama?" Colin asked cautiously.

"I shall come to Ashmead for Christmas, and invite lots of friends to bring their children! With their nurses and governesses, of course, to take care of them, but Mama is bound to say it will be too much trouble. I counted on Rob to persuade her she need not lift a finger herself. She has Cousin Jane and an excellent housekeeper to organize everything, and I daresay you will not object to helping, will you, Miss Findlay?"

"Not at all, ma'am, if Lady Ashe agrees to the party."

"If! That is the only difficulty. I must change and go down to talk to her."

Lady Orton kissed Colin and departed. The boys were far too excited to settle down to *Waverley* again. Lissa tried to calm them by pointing out that Lady Ashe was highly unlikely to be willing to fill the house with unknown children. Even with nursemaids and governesses galore, the disruption of her peace would be *supergigantenormous*.

Lissa's calming efforts were in vain. At last she put Michael to bed, leaving Peter and Colin trying to work out how many children, nurses, and governesses could be crammed into the nursery wing.

As she tucked Michael in and snuffed his candle, he asked in a voice full of foreboding, "Will they bring their own toys, Lissa? We haven't got enough for lots and lots of children."

"If they come, which I consider most improbable, I shall make sure they are advised to bring their own toys."

"Good," said Michael.

Lissa had noted how, more and more, all the boys spoke of "we," and "us," and "our." Colin had not talked of lending his possessions to the others in an age. It was not so much that he had learned to be more sharing, as that he no longer thought of them as belonging particularly to him. He regarded himself as one of three. "You'll come to see *us*," he had said to his mother.

He even suggested occasionally that Peter and Michael should take turns at going down to tea with his grandmama. Not that he minded the event, but sometimes he had to abandon something interesting they were involved in.

However, Lady Ashe made it very plain when she wished to see all three boys, as she did now and then. Otherwise little in their daily lives served to distinguish the master's nephew from the governess's brothers.

Against all the odds, Lissa had found a happy home for Peter and Michael. The cost to her heart, none but she would ever know.

Colin was eager to go down to the drawing room. He had not seen Mama for ages, except for a few minutes last night. Besides, he wanted to know more about the children who were coming for Christmas, so he could tell Peter and Michael all about them.

"Don't forget, your mama wants to know about *Waverley*," Michael reminded him, coming into his room as he combed his hair.

"She doesn't really. Mama doesn't like books."

"Doesn't she?" Michael was aghast. "What does she read, then?"

"Silly magazines with pictures of ladies' clothes. She used to make me look at them, too, before."

"Gosh, what a waste of time!"

"Wasn't it? I hated it." Colin held out his hands. The rain had stopped at last, and though a cold wind was blowing they had been out for a ride earlier that afternoon. "D'you think my nails are clean enough?"

Michael examined his own. "Cleaner than mine, but I 'spect Lissa will make you scrub them."

They both sighed. Colin poured some water from the ewer into the basin and scrubbed his nails, then presented himself to Lissa for inspection. Passing muster, he hurried to the drawing room.

The weather was still horrible, so he was not surprised to find no callers. Grandmama, Mama, Cousin Barbican, and Lord Quentin sat close to the fire, Mama shielding her face with a hand screen. Though she smiled at him, she looked rather cross. Lord Quentin looked pleased, and Grandmama looked just the same as usual.

Making his bow, Colin wondered what they

had been talking about before he came in.

"Come and sit here, darling," Mama said, patting the footstool beside her.

A footman had followed him in with tea, lemonade, and biscuits and cakes. Colin saw there was cherry-cake, which Michael had finally decided was his favorite. He hoped some had been sent up to the nursery. It wasn't fair that he got all the best treats just because Peter and Michael didn't have a grandmother.

As Grandmama poured tea and Lord Quentin handed the cups and biscuits, Colin whispered, "Mama, why are you cross?"

"Grandmama is not well enough to have a lot of children to stay."

How clever of Lissa to guess! He should have listened to her, then he wouldn't be disappointed. "But you will come for Christmas all the same?" he begged.

"Yes, darling. I shall just have to think up something else amusing to do." She put on her thinking face, one step nearer a frown than her cross face.

"Well, young man," said Lord Quentin cheerfully, "what have you been doing all summer?" He didn't like children, so he was glad about the Christmas party.

Colin knew he didn't like books, either, and he nearly decided to bore him with the story of *Waverley*. But that would be rude, and being rude on purpose wasn't nearly such fun any more now there were so many things to do that were lots of fun. Colin politely told Lord Quentin about the ponies, and Curly, and picking blackberries, and watching Uncle Rob's bridge being built.

Lord Quentin wasn't really very interested. He soon started talking to Grandmama about a summer ball he and Mama had gone to. Colin thought Grandmama looked bored. He certainly was, and awfully hot, too, sitting so close to the fire. He finished his lemonade, but he was still too hot.

"Mama, may I go and look at Grandmama's china? I'm dying of heat."

"Your face is very red. Are you sure you have not got a fever?" She felt his forehead.

"No, I'm perfectly well, just hot."

"Very well, run along, my love, but do not take the china out of the cabinet to play with."

"I wouldn't!"

He crossed the room to the glass-fronted cabinet where Grandmama kept her figurines. Most were dull shepherds and shepherdesses, but there were some dogs, a merry-go-round, a Punch and Judy, and even St. George killing the dragon, Colin's favorite. He put his hands behind his back so as not to be tempted to turn the tiny key and open the doors. One day, when Michael was chattering with Grandmama, Colin and Peter had made up a grand story about the dragon attacking the merry-go-round. It was a pity they weren't allowed to take them out and play with them.

"Play!" he heard Mama exclaim. "That is it.

The very thing!"

"My dear Lady Orton," said Lord Quentin, "what do you mean?"

"Amateur theatricals, at Christmas."

Wondering what amateur theatricals were, Colin missed what Grandmama said next, but he realized she sounded disapproving.

"No, no, assure you, ma'am," said Lord Quentin, "quite the thing. In fact, I'd go so far as to say, all the rage. Dashed if we don't find 'em putting on plays everywhere we go these days. In fact I know at least half a dozen people — best of *ton,* I assure you — who have constructed private theatres in their houses, or at least put up stages."

"Such as?" Grandmama asked in her disbelieving voice.

"Oh, Mount Edgcumbe, for one. The earl's never happy unless he's strutting about playing a bumbling Cornish mayor or some such, making people laugh."

"Truly, Mama, it is perfectly unexceptionable. Some people even hire a professional actor or actress to improve the performance. Oh, I have just thought — Miss Findlay will be able to help us, having been on the stage."

"Miss Findlay?" Grandmama was shocked. Colin's heart sank at her tone. "An actress!"

"Opera dancer," said Lord Quentin. "Don't take much acting ability, I'm afraid, Lady Orton."

"Disgraceful!" snorted Cousin Barbican. "I knew from the first the girl was up to no good."

"An opera dancer?" Grandmama said faintly. "Ashe's light-o'-love, I collect."

"Don't think so, ma'am. He swore she wasn't his ladybird."

"I did wonder at first," said Mama, "but as Rob pointed out he would never introduce his *chère amie* to his sister, still less to his mother."

"Bad *ton*," Lord Quentin agreed. "Not that sort, Ashe."

"I hope you are right, but if not his then someone else's." Grandmama sounded horrified. "I cannot — *will* not — have an opera dancer in the house. She must go. I shall send her, all three of them, away first thing tomorrow morning."

"Quite right," Cousin Barbican confirmed.

"How could you let her take charge of your son, Daphne! She will corrupt his morals and . . ."

"I say, ma'am," interrupted Lord Quentin, catching sight of Colin as he turned, recovering from the paralysis that had struck him at Grandmama's dreadful words, "child present, don't you know. Daresay he won't understand, but . . ." He shrugged.

Mama jumped up and hurried over to Colin, looking flustered. "It is time you went back to the nursery, my love."

"But, Mama . . ."

She swept him towards the door. "Run along now, Colin darling. And remember, pray, it is very wrong to repeat what you overhear."

218

His world shattered, Colin plodded up to the schoolroom. He told the others about the children not coming for Christmas, and they thought that was why he was so quiet and mopish. They tried to console him. As though he cared a fig! Christmas would be just as much fun without a lot of people he didn't know. More fun, probably, with just Peter and Michael. And Miss Findlay, of course. But without them . . .

He *couldn't* go back to the lonely life in the London house. It would be better to live in that nasty house in the dirty street in Lambeth, with Lissa and Peter and Michael. He wouldn't mind being poor, he wouldn't even mind being ill, if he was with them.

Uncle Robert would come and visit them there, even if Lissa wasn't his light-o'-love, which was a pity. It sounded such a nice thing to be. Colin imagined a candle set in a window to show the way to the person you loved. Being a ladybird would be fun, too, having red wings with black spots. He wasn't sure what a Jeremy was, but of course Lissa wasn't one because it was a man's name and she was a lady, so Uncle Robert couldn't possibly introduce her as Jeremy to Mama.

Mama wouldn't like to visit him in Lambeth, he thought, but perhaps he could go sometimes and visit her. She would probably marry Lord Quentin if Colin went to live with Lissa. That wouldn't be so bad, just for visits. Lord Quentin wasn't a monster like Michael's papa.

Colin couldn't remember his own papa very well. He had been sad when Papa died, but perhaps it was lucky, because when he was twenty-one Papa's estate would be his. The Findlays could go to live with him there and not be poor anymore.

Maybe Uncle Robert would go on giving him — pocket money — which was really his own money, after all — when he went to live in Lambeth. Then they wouldn't be quite so poor, and Lissa wouldn't have to work so hard.

The trouble was, Mama and Grandmama would never let him leave with Lissa and Peter and Michael tomorrow morning.

So he must be gone by then. He must take himself to Lambeth. If he was waiting at the house when Lissa arrived, she would take him in, and hide him if they came to get him. She was good at hiding people. Michael's papa had never found him and Peter. If Lissa was a man, she'd be a gallant knight like Sir Lancelot, galloping around rescuing people. Sir Jeremy, Colin thought, and smiled.

"I am glad you have cheered up a bit, Colin," Lissa said. "We shall have a merry Christmas anyway, just wait and see."

"I know. I'll be happy as long as I'm with you and Peter and Michael."

She smiled at him. "Good. Now eat your supper, pet."

Afterwards, thinking about the long journey to Lambeth, Colin wished he had saved some of his supper. He had some sugarplums in his chamber, he'd take those. And he had a few shillings he had saved to buy a pretty handkerchief for Lissa, because she'd lost her best one. She wouldn't mind if he bought bread instead. Peter said bread was the best value.

Should he take his pony? Galahad was in the paddock, not the stables, but he would have to get the tackle without waking the grooms. He'd have to saddle the pony himself, too. Luckily Uncle Robert had made them learn how.

"Bedtime, boys. Go and get ready and I shall come and say good-night."

Where had the evening gone? It would soon be time to run away. Had he thought of everything?

Colin smuggled a pencil and a sheet of paper into his bedchamber. He'd leave a note, so that no one would worry about him.

When Lissa came to say good-night, he gave her a big hug. "I love you, Miss Lissa."

"I love you, too, pet." She kissed him. "Now put your book away and lie down."

"I'm not very sleepy. Please may I read for a few more minutes?"

"Just a few, and make sure your candle is quite out. Good night, love."

Writing with the paper propped on his book was not easy. He tried to make his writing neat, but Lissa would say it was poor penmanship. He'd be extra careful of the spelling to make up. Lambeth was a problem, he had never seen it written so he had to guess.

At last it was done. He folded it and wrote "To Everyone" on the outside. Putting it on his nightstand where it could not be missed, he blew out his candle.

Moonlight shone through a crack between the curtains. Good, he would be able to see his way. Now he just had to wait for the household to go to sleep.

Sixteen

"Lissa, Colin's run away!" Peter burst into her chamber, waving a sheet of paper, as she was pinning up her hair.

Her heart stood still. "What? He cannot have run away. Pray don't hoax me like that, Peter. It is neither funny nor kind."

"I'm not hoaxing. He's gone. I went to see if he was up yet and he's not there and I found this by his bed. It says 'To Everyone,' so I read it. Here."

Lissa took the note with trembling fingers. " 'Please don't worry,' " she read. " 'I can't stay when Miss Lissa is sent away and Peter and Michael, so I'm going to Lambith. Don't worry about me. Your loving Colin.' "

"What does he mean, when we're sent away?" Michael asked fearfully, standing in the doorway behind Peter.

"I have no notion, pet, but we cannot be concerned about that when Colin is somewhere out in the cold. And wet," Lissa added, glancing at the window. The wind had brought up a new set of clouds and a thin, dismal drizzle beat against the glass. "With his weak chest . . . What can have upset him so? Oh, how I wish Lord Ashe were here!"

"We'll have to find him," Peter said in a businesslike tone. "Hurry up and get dressed, Michael. Ask Nanny to help you put on riding breeches. I'll change and we'll take the ponies."

Michael disappeared and Peter started to follow.

"I wonder if Colin took Galahad?" Lissa struggled to collect her wits, scattered by the shock. "He might have ridden miles by now. Peter, wait. This is too much for us to deal with. Run down to the stables and see if Galahad is gone. Ask Mr. Trumbull to come at once to see me in the front hall." The head groom was the best man to organize a search. "Hurry."

Peter ran off.

Grooms and stable boys: Lissa was not sure how many there were but mounted they could cover the ground quickly. The footmen must go out too, she decided. On foot they would look in places riders might not think of.

Colin might go across country rather than staying on the roads. He might go the wrong way, so searchers must head in both directions, not just towards London.

Why Lambeth? Shaking her head in puzzlement, Lissa abandoned her hairpins and hastily tied back her hair with a bit of ribbon. On her hurried way to the stairs, she stuck her head into Michael's chamber.

"Michael, you need not put on riding breeches. The grooms will search for Colin."

"But I want to help, Lissa!"

She racked her brains. "Ask Nanny to help you put on your best clothes, as if you were to go to the drawing room for tea. Lady Ashe is going to be very distressed. She is fond of you, so you may help to comfort her." She sped on, not waiting for Michael's response.

The butler, Parrish, was horrified to hear of Colin's flight, as was Mr. Trumbull when he came in a moment later with Peter, who reported Galahad missing. Lissa was explaining what she thought should be done, and asking the men's advice, when Michael dashed down the stairs, half dressed.

"Lissa, Lissa, Nanny says someone must go for the apothary, in case Colin's ill when he comes home."

"I'll send one o' my lads to Bascombe after the 'pothecary, miss," rumbled Mr. Trumbull.

"Better tell him to go on to Stow-on-the-Wold," Parrish suggested, "to fetch her ladyship's doctor. Now don't you be fretting, miss. We know what to do. We'll find Master Colin and have him back in your care in no time."

"That we will, miss," Trumbull affirmed, "never fear."

"Thank you, both of you." The most important weight off her mind, Lissa contemplated the next step with dread. As the men hastened off, she sank weakly onto the nearest chair. "And now I must break the news to Lady Orton and Lady Ashe."

"I'll tell Lady Ashe," Michael volunteered.

"Shall I tell Colin's mama?" Peter asked, blenching.

"You are both the dearest boys!" Lissa put an arm around each and hugged them hard, remembering how Colin had told her last night that he loved her. "But I must do it myself. I just wish I knew why he went! He said nothing to either of you?"

"Not to me," said Peter thoughtfully. "Remember how quiet he was last night, after tea? I wager he heard something in the drawing room which overset him."

"Lissa, they won't send us away?"

Should she reassure him, or prepare him for the worst? She could not think about it with Colin on her mind. "I expect Peter is right, that Colin overheard something yesterday, but he may very well have misunderstood. I have not been told we are to leave, and I see no reason for so sudden a decision."

"No, 'cause Colin likes us, doesn't he?" Michael said, cheering up, to Lissa's relief.

"It's as if we were three brothers instead of two," said Peter. "Can't I go and help to look for him, Lissa?"

At that moment, a groom burst into the hall from the back passage. "Miss, Galahad's come home wi'out the young master, and Mr. Trumbull said to tell you the dog, that Curly, 's missing!"

"At least Colin's not alone," Peter said. "Curly will keep him company. Can't I go, Lissa? She'll come when I call and show us where he is."

Lissa gave in. With strict instructions to stay right with the groom, Peter ran off. By then, the housekeeper and their ladyships' dressers were all waiting to speak to Lissa.

She addressed the housekeeper first. "If you please, Mrs. Cardew, a good fire in Lord Orton's chamber, plenty of water kept hot, and prepare a warming pan and hot bricks."

"Very good, Miss Findlay."

Though she used Lissa's name, rather than the more respectful "miss," thank heaven she, like the men, accepted a governess's authority where the well-being of her charge was concerned.

"And if you have any remedies specific to chest complaints, pray look them out," Lissa added before turning to the abigails. "Have your ladies heard about Lord Orton?" she asked them.

"Not Lady Ashe," said the plump, grey-haired, motherly looking woman who served the baroness. "Her ladyship doesn't leave her room till noon, and doesn't see a soul till then but Miss Barbican and me. And what this'll do to her, there's no knowing, Miss Findlay, what with her weak heart and all."

"Do you think we might be able to keep it from her until noon? Surely Lord Orton must be found by then!"

"If Miss Barbican don't tell her. I'll do my best to keep her out, saying the news might kill her ladyship, troubled as she already was last night, poor dear."

"Oh dear! Yes, please do your best. What about Lady Orton, Miss Marlin?"

"Her ladyship's awake but still abed and don't know yet."

"She cannot be kept in ignorance when her son is missing."

"I won't take it on myself to break the news, Miss Findlay," Marlin said grimly.

"No, I must break it to her myself, and at once."

"Can I come?" Michael asked in a small voice, looking lost and near tears.

"No, pet, I want you to do something much more useful. Poor Nanny Bessemer will be fretting. Will you go and tell her about everything that is being done to find Colin?"

"I'll tell her Colin has Curly to look after him."

"Yes, do."

As Michael scurried barefoot up the stairs, Lissa followed more slowly. How she wished she could think of a reasonable excuse to postpone informing Lady Orton of her beloved son's disappearance. It seemed all too likely Lissa would be blamed for the escapade, though what she might have done to foil it she could not imagine.

If she was not already about to be dismissed, then Colin's mistaken belief might well precipitate exactly what he feared.

Marlin led the way to Lady Orton's dressing room. Leaving Lissa there, she went on into the bedchamber "to prepare the way," to Lissa's heartfelt gratitude.

The dresser said something about bad news, then she reappeared and admitted Lissa to a charming pink and white chamber. Lady Orton was sitting up, alarm on her lovely face beneath a pink-ribboned cap. A letter she had been reading dropped, forgotten, on the ruffled counterpane. Seeing it, Lissa realized she still had Colin's note clutched in her hand.

"Miss Findlay, what is wrong? Has my boy fallen ill again?"

"No, Lady Orton. He has run away. I promise you, everything possible is already being done to find him." Lissa gave her the note.

"Run away?" She read the note and promptly burst into tears. "Oh, this is all my fault," she wept.

Perplexed, Lissa sat down on the edge of the bed and put a comforting arm about her employer's quivering shoulders. "Your fault, ma'am? How is that?"

"I told Mama you used to be an actress. I knew very well she would be furious. I simply was not thinking. Colin was there and he heard Mama say you must leave in the morning. Oh, can you ever forgive me? My poor little boy!"

So Colin was right. Heavyhearted, Lissa tried to concentrate on Colin's plight, not her own. "We must pray he suffers no lasting harm. I daresay he found shelter when it began to rain, but in case of need a groom has ridden for the apothecary and the doctor. All the rest of the grooms and footmen are out looking for Colin."

"You have done everything, Miss Findlay. You take such good care of him, and I have ruined your life." Lady Orton sobbed harder than ever.

Marlin moved in. "Now calm yourself, my lady," she said firmly. "I've sent for a tisane. Giving yourself the headache won't help Master Colin. Like your ladyship says, Miss Findlay's done all the needful and she'll tell us the minute he's found." The dresser nodded to Lissa, who thankfully accepted her dismissal.

She went out through the dressing room. Opening the door to the hallway, she found Lord Quentin, in a crimson velvet dressing gown embroidered with Chinese pagodas, with his hand raised to knock.

"How is she?" he asked anxiously.

"Will you go and comfort her, sir? Her maid is with her. She blames herself."

"Herself?"

"Colin ran away because he heard I . . . I was to be dismissed, Lady Ashe having discovered my past."

Lord Quentin flushed. "My fault, too," he said, abashed. "Lady Ashe might have swallowed an actress in the house, but I let slip you was an opera dancer. Did assure her there was no . . . er . . . carrying on between you and Ashe. Don't know if she credited it, I'm afraid."

So Lady Ashe believed her son was Lissa's lover? Lissa's head whirled. She closed her eyes and put a hand to the doorjamb to steady herself.

"She was in high fidgets," Lord Quentin went on, "said she couldn't bring herself to talk any more about it last night, meant to leave it till today. I say, are you going to swoon?" he asked in alarm.

She took a deep breath. "No. I cannot, must not, think of anything but Colin for the moment."

"Then bedamned to propriety, I'll go and see if I can cheer Lady Orton up a trifle." He bolted past Lissa and she heard his knock on the connecting door.

He was a bit of a fool and something of a libertine, but he truly loved Lady Orton. As she went to check on the housekeeper's preparations, Lissa wished with all her heart that she could turn to Lord Ashe for comfort and support, though love was out of the question.

Lissa was in the day nursery with Nanny and Michael when Peter burst in.

"We found him! I called and called, and Curly came, just as I said. She led us back to him, where he took shelter under a hedge. Mr. Trumbull's carrying him up."

Springing to her feet, Lissa hurried to him and drew him out into the passage. "How is he, Peter?"

Peter sobered at once. "He looks dreadful, white as a sheet and not moving, except he keeps shivering and shivering."

"Wheezing?"

"Yes, pretty badly. Not as bad as when we left London, I'd say."

"Is he conscious?"

"His eyes were open, but he didn't seem to hear what we said to him. He'll be all right, won't he, Lissa?"

Lissa bit her lip. "I hope so, Peter." She turned at the sound of a heavy tread on the stairs. "Here he is. Will you go to Michael? Tell him all about the search and finding Colin. Don't say anything about how ill he seems."

Peter nodded solemnly and went back into the day nursery.

Trumbull followed her into Colin's chamber and deposited his burden, wrapped in a couple of men's coats, on the chaise longue she had had moved in. He glanced around at the blazing fire in the grate with the copper hip-bath standing ready before it.

"You'll need a hand moving the poor lad, miss."

"I shall help Miss Findlay," said the housekeeper, coming in, followed by a footman with the first two buckets of hot water for the bath.

On her knees by the chaise, Lissa tore her gaze from Colin's bluish lips. "If you please, Mrs. Cardew," she said thankfully. "Bless you, Trumbull, for finding him so quickly."

"If there's owt else I can do, miss . . ."

"Yes." She laid her hand against Colin's icy cheek. His eyes seemed to look right through her. "I think . . . I think Lord Ashe must be informed. I shall write a note as soon as I have a moment."

"There'll be a man waiting to carry it, miss," the head groom promised and removed himself as a second hot-water bearer arrived.

With Mrs. Cardew's assistance, Colin was quickly stripped. His skin was so chilled, Lissa decided a really hot bath would be too much of a shock to his system. They wrapped him in blankets until the water was brought to a moderate temperature.

As they lowered his limp body into the warm water, Lady Orton hastened in, Lord Quentin on her heels. She took one look at her son and burst into tears.

"Oh, my poor little boy!" she wailed.

"Told you it wouldn't do," said Lord Quentin. "Not in a fit state to be any use to the child. Leave him to Miss Findlay. Miss Findlay will take the best possible care of him."

"Indeed I shall, Lady Orton," Lissa assured her, with a grateful nod to Lord Quentin. The last thing she needed was a weeping mother getting in the way.

He gently but firmly removed her ladyship.

"Maybe he'll do for Miss Daphne after all," Mrs. Cardew observed. "There, lamb, we'll have you cozy in your bed in no time. Look, Miss Findlay, I do believe his lips are losing that nasty blue cast already."

"And he is not shivering quite so convulsively. Can you hold him for a minute while I pour his drink?"

Colin turned his head towards her. His frightened eyes held a plea and his lips shaped the words, "Don't go!"

"I'll fetch it, miss."

The housekeeper brought barley-water with lemon and honey from the spirit lamp where it was keeping warm. Then she lifted the lid from the bowl before the fire and pungent fumes of camphor drifted through the room. She returned to hold Colin while Lissa urged him to drink. He managed to swallow a few sips.

The bathwater cooled. They moved him into the well-warmed bed, propped up against pillows. He was still wheezing, but his color was beginning to return, and though he could not speak his stupor had clearly passed.

Lissa wondered whether she need send for Lord Ashe after all. Part of her wanted to use the excuse to see him again. Part of her recognized the unwisdom of seeing him — and dreaded, besides, that he might view her summons as encouragement.

A treacherous voice in her head whispered that Lady Orton could send for him.

No, to suggest such a thing to the already distraught mother would be bound to confirm her fears for her beloved child. As long as Colin continued to improve, Lord Ashe must remain in ignorance.

"Mrs. Cardew, I believe you might take a comfortable report of Lord Orton to his mama."

"I will, miss, and then get on with my own affairs, if you can manage without me, for the household's all at sixes and sevens. Send for me at once if you need me."

The housekeeper had scarcely left when Colin was seized with a violent fit of shivering. Alarmed anew, Lissa realized he was still chilled inside though warmed on the surface. Not knowing what else to do, she turned up the spirit-lamp beneath his barley-water. She was helping him to drink when the apothecary from Bascombe arrived.

He examined Colin and told Lissa cheerfully, in the boy's hearing, that she was doing everything right. Her relief did not last long. Taking her aside, the apothecary said he was as good as certain an inflammation of the lungs was inevitable. He gave her some medicines, advised her on what to expect and what to do, and warned her not to let the doctor from Stow-on-the-Wold bleed Colin.

"The lad's going to need every drop of blood he has," he said gravely. "I've other patients to see, but send for me at once if you have any doubts about how to go on."

Bidding her good-day, he departed. Lissa sat down at Colin's bedside to write to Lord Ashe. Whatever the cost to herself, she could not conceal from him that his nephew was in sore straits.

She was struggling over the wording when Lady Ashe's dresser came in. Glancing at Colin, who had closed his eyes, she whispered, "How is the lad, Miss Findlay?"

Lissa told her what the apothecary had said.

235

"Does Lady Ashe know yet?" she asked.

"No, I've managed to keep it from her, but she wants to see you in her sitting room," the woman said apologetically.

"Even though she does not know Colin ran away? You will have to break it to her yourself, for I cannot leave him now. Pray tell Lady Ashe she may dismiss me when her grandson is out of danger!"

Seventeen

Ashe scowled at the stage. Not one of the pretty, lively dancers attracted him in the least. He had no desire whatsoever to win the leading lady, the gorgeous, flamboyant Damask Rose, from her current protector. Even the dashing blond widow he had invited to join him in his box, along with a respectable couple to preserve her reputation, did not interest him, though she was as lovely as Daphne. She was also as vapid as Daphne without half his sister's charm and with none of his sister's artless innocence.

After the performance, he treated his guests to supper at Fenton's Hotel. Then he took the widow home — on the way to delivering the couple to their residence. In spite of her hints, he did not propose any future meetings.

"Home," he ordered Burr.

The widow and the theatre had been a last resort. For the past several days, Ashe had spent each afternoon immersed in working with Voss on his next speech for the Lords, each evening and half the night at his club. The company of his friends and political associates; the gaming tables; enough brandy to require Mills's special remedy next morning (a rare occurrence since his salad days): nothing sufficed to drive from his mind a slight, brown-haired girl whose lips were blackberry-sweet and who faced the world's trials with love and gallantry.

Love for her brothers, for his nephew even, not for him. He did not expect it. But he felt she liked him, enjoyed his company, and had she not, for just a moment, responded with passion to his kiss?

There were worse foundations for an alliance, if he could but persuade Lissa of it. If he could only win back her trust.

The town carriage drew up in Dover Street. Ashe sprang down, his mind made up.

"We leave for Ashmead in the morning, Burr."

"Yes, m'lord," the groom said woodenly.

Ashe had told everyone — servants, secretary, family, friends — that he was fixed in town for the present, for the Little Season and the new session of Parliament. His sudden departure was bound to cause some comment, but he did not care. The prospect of seeing Lissa again made his blood sing.

The next day started cold and dry, though a chilly wind was bringing in clouds from the west with a promise of more rain. The roads, even the turnpikes, were in a sorry state after several days of near constant rain. There was no question of doing the journey in a single day, as Ashe had when he fled Ashmead, trying to hide from his feelings. Now he had made up his mind and was determined to let no obstacle stand in the way of getting what he wanted, the delay was irksome but unimportant. Lissa would be there when he arrived. That was all that mattered.

He reached Ashmead late in the afternoon of the second day. A thin, chill drizzle was falling, autumn anticipating winter, in stark contrast to the summery warmth of the day he had kissed Lissa.

The memory of that kiss heated him through and through. What a fool he was to have tamely let her go, apologized, run away!

The front door swung open before he reached it.

"My lord!" The footman looked astonished.

"What's the matter, James?"

"The groom only left midday yesterday to fetch your lordship," the young man blurted out, recovering himself enough to take Ashe's hat, gloves, and greatcoat. "I wouldn't've thought he could hardly have got to London yet. We was expecting the doctor, not your lordship so soon."

"The doctor? Her ladyship is taken ill?"

"Master Colin, my lord. Lord Orton, I should say. Out all night he was, poor little lad."

"Out all night!" Ashe turned as his butler came hurrying up. "What's going on, Parrish?"

Nodding to the footman to resume his post at the window overlooking the carriage drive, Parrish said in a discreetly lowered yet agitated voice, "Master Colin ran away, my lord. Why, I couldn't take it upon myself to say. He's taken an inflammation of the lungs. The apothecary's come again but Miss Findlay wants the doctor's advice, too."

"He's bad? I'll go up at once."

Ashe took the stairs at a run. Not sure which was Colin's chamber, for the boys had a room each here, he looked into the schoolroom.

Michael sat at the table, fast asleep, rosy tear-stained cheek pillowed on his arm and his dark hair even more rumpled than usual. Peter, standing at the window, turned as the door opened. Hastily brushing his eyes with the back of his hand, he ran to Ashe.

"Sir, I *am* glad you've come! I try to keep Michael entertained, but he keeps on crying. I told him and told him it's not our fault. We haven't done anything bad enough to be sent away."

"Sent away?" Ashe was once again shocked. "You had best come and sit down, Peter, and tell me all about it."

Michael raised his head and rubbed his eyes. Ashe went over to him, picked him up, and, crossing to the fireplace, settled in a chair with the child in his lap. The feeling in his breast when Michael clung to him was beyond words.

"Quickly, now, Peter. I must go to your sister."

Peter slumped into the opposite chair. "Colin ran away, sir. He left a note, but it didn't say much, just that he was going to Lambeth. I expect he thought we would go back there, don't you think? You see, he heard his grandmama say we had to leave."

"Why?" Ashe asked bluntly. "Why should my

mother want you to leave?"

"I don't know." Peter looked bewildered. "We broke some glass in the kitchen gardens with a ball — it went over the wall. But Colin hit it, and anyway, the gardener said he wouldn't tell Lady Ashe, just Lissa. And Curly chased a pheasant, but even Lissa doesn't know about that. She doesn't care about pheasants. We were going to tell you when you came back, weren't we, Michael?"

"Yes, and I kept the feathers for you, sir. Curly caught its tail in her mouth."

"But my mother doesn't care any more about pheasants than Lissa does. Are you sure she said you must go?"

"Oh yes. Colin's mama told Lissa. Lissa said Lady Orton was dreadfully upset about that, as well as Colin being missing. That was before we found him. Curly may have saved his life, sir, so you won't punish her for the pheasant, will you?"

"Good Lord no! I am quite sure the pup has forgotten the pheasant incident, so punishment would be useless."

"I did scold her."

"Good. She found Colin, did she?"

"No, she went with him, and when he sheltered from the rain under a hedge she curled up with him and kept him warm."

"So isn't Curly a good name for her?" Michael demanded.

"Perfect," Ashe agreed solemnly.

Peter resumed his explanation. "I helped to

search for Colin and when she heard me calling she came out and showed us where he was. He was dreadfully cold and wet by then even though she stayed with him."

"And now he's dreadfully ill." Michael's face crumpled and tears started to flow again. "He might die!"

Ashe hugged him. "We'll do our best to prevent that. I must go. Just be very sure, both of you, that you will not be leaving Ashmead as long as I can persuade your sister to stay."

They showed him which was Colin's chamber. Close to the door, he heard a murmur of voices within. He tapped lightly and opened the door. Camphor vapors wafted to meet him.

For several moments he saw nothing but Lissa's tired face, lit up from within as she looked around and saw him. Then his gaze went beyond her, to Colin's leaden flush, dull eyes, and heaving chest. With swift steps he crossed to Lissa and took her hands in his.

"I'm here to help. Tell me what to do." He searched her face, trying to see whether her pleasure in his arrival was for her own or only for the boy's sake.

A spasm of coughing shook Colin and she turned back to her small patient.

The following week was a nightmare of coughing spells, fever and chills, pains in chest and abdomen which made Colin cry out though he could ill spare the breath. Ashe and Lissa administered oxymel of squills, hot linseed and onion compresses, elixir of cinchona bark, camphor from the steaming bowl on the hearth and a lard and camphor rub, and endless quantities of barley water. Doctor and apothecary agreed that the more liquids they could pour into the child's small body the better.

Maids and footmen came and went, changing soaked sheets, building the fire, fetching and carrying.

Ashe saw little of Lissa. She stayed with Colin from noon to midnight, and he took over from midnight to noon. After Daphne's visit to the sickroom, shortly after Ashe's arrival, when she burst into helpless floods of tears, he neither expected nor wished for her assistance with the nursing. At least her failure was due to too much sensibility, not too little.

In answer to the appeal in Lissa's eyes, that first afternoon, Ashe escorted his sister from the room.

"You must not come up," he said gently, leading her down the stairs. "Your distress disturbs Colin and you will make yourself ill. The last thing Miss Findlay needs is a second patient, my dear."

"She is an angel, Rob," Daphne wept, "and I have done her such a disservice, but I did not mean to, indeed I did not!"

Ashe directed her tottering steps to the library. He sat her down, removed the soaked, twisted scrap of handkerchief from her fingers, and substituted his own. Sitting beside her, he asked

243

sternly, "What did you do? How did you harm Miss Findlay?"

"It was accidental, truly. I did not think. I was so pleased with my notion, and so pleased she would be able to help, the words just popped out."

He ran an exasperated hand through his hair. "What words, Daphne? Cut line, do!"

"I thought we might have a Christmas house party with lots of children invited, to amuse Colin. And Miss Findlay's brothers, of course. But Mama put her foot down and said it would be too much for her. I know she is not well, but she need not have had much to do. I could have organized everything, with Cousin Jane and Miss Findlay and Mrs. Cardew to help."

"It's not a bad notion," Ashe mused, momentarily sidetracked, "if you would really abandon town early to do your part. However, I cannot see how that harmed Miss Findlay, unless you somehow led Mama to believe it was her proposal. Mama would think that shockingly encroaching."

"Oh no! Miss Findlay told me she had no objection as long as Mama approved. And the boys were *aux anges*."

"I daresay Mama did not like your having discussed it with them before mentioning it to her, but I hardly suppose she would blame Miss Findlay."

Daphne had stopped crying, and now her face of misery changed to one of guilt. "No, but perhaps I set up her back when I argued. You know how she always used to tell me a lady never argues. So she was already displeased and ready to *cut up rough* when I spoke of Miss Findlay being an actress."

Appalled, Ashe sank his head in his hands. "Daphne, you didn't!" he groaned.

"And then Lord Quentin made it worse by saying she was not an actress but an opera dancer. I do think you might have told me so, Rob," she said in an injured tone, but when he glared, she went on hastily, "but Lord Quentin did not think before he spoke any more than I did, I promise you. He is almost as mopish as I am, for we both thought we had found someone at last to whom I might entrust Colin, so that we could marry."

"You did?" Ashe said thoughtfully. "Well, don't despair yet."

"But you do not understand, Rob. Mama absolutely refuses to have an actress in the house! Not even for a week or two to help stage an amateur production."

"To *what?*"

"Did I not explain? I thought, since we could not have children to stay at Ashmead, we might enliven Christmas with putting on a play. Everybody does it."

"Ah, so that's how the subject of Miss Findlay's having been on the stage came up. I wondered."

"Yes, and Cousin Jane said it was disgraceful,

and Mama immediately jumped to the conclusion that she was your *chère amie.*"

"As you did," he reminded her.

"I did not know her then," Daphne excused herself. "Anyone can tell she is a lady. And Colin has been so happy with her, and now he is dying, and Mama says she must go! Oh, I am the most wretched creature in the world!" She dissolved in tears again.

Swallowing his irritation, Ashe put his arms around her. "Miss Findlay will save Colin if anyone can, my dear," he said, patting her back. "As for Mama, you may leave her to me."

Despite these bold words, not without qualms did Ashe, having turned his sister over to the joint ministrations of her abigail and Teague, approach his mother's sitting room. Unlike a number of people he knew, who ruled their families with threats of imminent collapse, Lady Ashe suffered from a genuine disability.

Frosty air, sudden exertion, climbing stairs, all brought blue lips, breathlessness and a tumultuous pulse as evidence of the acute pains in her chest. So did emotional distress. Ashe knew he must tread carefully if he was not to have his mother's death forever upon his conscience.

Yet his instinct was to fling open the door and rush in to berate her for causing so much unhappiness with her stiff-rumped, finicking notions of propriety.

Restraining himself, he tapped softly and, bidden to enter, did so at a moderate pace. From vases of white, yellow, pink, and rust red blooms rose the tangy scent of chrysanthemums, reminding him of the harsher odor of camphor. Amid the flowers she loved, real and embroidered, his mother reclined on her sofa. She looked unwell, and older than a mere week ago.

She set down her needlework and held out her hand to him. "Robert, thank heaven you have come. How *could* you introduce a loose woman into your own home? You must get rid of her at once. The dreadful creature is pretending Colin is desperately ill and has actually persuaded Daphne the child is in danger of his life!"

"He is, Mama." Ashe took her hand and stooped to kiss her cheek. "I have seen him, and spoken to the doctor. Surely you cannot disbelieve your own physician?"

"Then she has made him ill. Her unkindness drove him to run away."

Gritting his teeth, Ashe pulled up a chair. His mother was usually perfectly reasonable, but once she took a notion into her head, her tenacity was extreme. It dawned on him that she was trying to evade the responsibility for Colin's flight.

"Now think, Mama," he said with what patience he could muster. "Has Colin seemed in the least mopish these past few months? I believe you must acknowledge he has never been happier, nor in better health. I am quite convinced, as is Daphne, that Miss Findlay is responsible."

"But an actress, Robert! Worse, an opera dancer!"

"Only for a few months."

"What difference does that make? She cannot possibly be a good influence upon the boy."

"Come now, admit you saw nothing amiss before you discovered she had been on the stage."

"Too young and too pretty," Lady Ashe reminded him.

"Dreadful faults, to be sure, but for which she can scarcely be blamed. You saw nothing amiss in her manner."

"N-no."

Encouraged, Ashe said, "Circumstances forced her to seek employment to keep herself and her brothers, and she took the best she could find. Surely she is to be admired, not condemned?"

"She should have found a respectable position."

"That's easy to say, Mama. You, I thank the Lord, have never been in such straits and cannot imagine what it's like. It went sorely against the grain with her. She is a lady by birth, instincts, and upbringing, I am certain."

"She cannot have remained virtuous," his mother said uncertainly.

"She has." Ashe put all the sincere conviction of which he was capable into his voice. "When I met her, she and the boys were slowly starving to death, yet she refused even to consider accepting my protection."

"Oh, Robert, you did not . . . !"

"I did."

"They were starving?"

"Michael was so hungry he had pains in his stomach, yet when he found a penny in the street and bought a bun, he shared it with his brother and sister."

"That delightful little boy?" Tears rose in her eyes. Ashe quailed but she blinked them away, reaching for her smelling salts. Alarmed, Ashe rang for her dresser. "I wish you had told me. Now Colin is desperately ill, all because I misunderstood. I shall never forgive myself if he dies."

"We must trust to Providence, Mama, and to Miss Findlay. I had rather trust to her to nurse him through than to anyone else in the world."

Ashe trusted Lissa, but she could not accomplish miracles on her own and he trusted himself more than any other. Armed with her detailed instructions, he spelled her twelve hours on and twelve hours off. He saw her briefly, twice a day.

When he left Colin at noon, before he went riding to rid his lungs of the sickroom atmosphere, he always looked in on Peter and Michael. He knew Lissa spent most of each morning with them. They were always eager for the latest news of Colin.

"Much the same," he told them every day.

"Not even a little bit better?" Michael asked one day, hugging Curly, who had the freedom of the schoolroom now, after saving Colin. "After all this time?"

"At least he isn't worse," his brother consoled

him. "So he isn't going to die, is he, sir?"

Ashe did not wish to depress them, nor to give false hope. "He is fighting bravely, and he was in good health to start with, but he is sadly pulled down. The outcome is still in doubt, I fear, but since he has not yet succumbed, there is a good chance of recovery. You must not expect him to be well all at once, though. He will need a long convalescence."

"What's con . . . that?" Michael wanted to know.

"Getting stronger," Peter explained. "Colin won't be able to run or ride or do lessons for ages. I suppose we shan't have a tutor till he is quite well, sir?" he asked wistfully.

"I'd quite forgotten! I told my secretary to keep looking out for a suitable fellow. If he finds the ideal man, I certainly shan't put him off and risk losing him. You feel in need of a teacher, I collect, Peter?"

"Yes, sir. There's not much else to do but read, and I get awfully stuck with the Greek. I'm really keen to start Latin, too."

Remembering his own reluctant acquaintance with the Classics, Ashe wondered at the boy's enthusiasm. At the same time, his curiosity reawoke as to the oddity of Lissa's knowledge of Greek — and lack of Latin. As soon as Colin was out of danger he meant to pursue the matter.

In the meantime, "As soon as Voss finds someone, you shall have help," he promised, noting that, though in comparison with Colin

250

they were fit as fiddles, their cheeks had grown wan. "Do you not ride in the afternoons, or at least go out to play?"

"If we build forts or climb trees, our clothes get dirty and torn," said Michael, "and Nanny fusses so! And Peter says it wouldn't be right to ride, 'cause the ponies aren't ours and the grooms aren't ours, and Colin's not there to need us to go with him."

"Such scrupulosity does you credit, Peter. However, I wish you to exercise the ponies, or they will grow fat and lazy. Take turns with Colin's Galahad. In fact, I'm going riding now. Will you accompany me?"

The boys were only too delighted.

The woods were all bronze and gold now, splashed with the red of bird-cherry. Leaves drifted singly or in flurries from the trees. Michael simply had to dismount and try to catch some, which meant Peter had to join him to show him how — with no greater success. Ashe nearly gave in to temptation, would have, had he not brought a groom along. He left them scrunching through piles of crisp leaves, throwing armfuls at each other and an ecstatic terrier, and went on to gallop the fidgets out of his mount and his own bones. They met again at the new bridge, pronounced construction to be progressing nicely, and rode home together.

Happy to see the bloom restored to the lads' cheeks, Ashe realized it was not only for Colin's welfare he wanted them at Ashmead, nor even because Lissa would not stay without them. He had grown remarkably fond of her brothers.

A note awaited Ashe at the stables. He unfolded and read it: Miss Findlay begged Lord Ashe to repair to the sickroom at his earliest convenience.

His heart pounding with fear, Ashe raced up the stairs.

Eighteen

Ashe paused outside Colin's chamber and braced himself. A note rather than a message suggested Lissa wanted the servants kept in ignorance, unnecessary if Colin were dead, he tried to persuade himself. Yet she wouldn't want Daphne or Lady Ashe to hear about it except through him.

Had Colin given up the fight and slipped away? Had he simply taken a turn for the worse? Or was he fallen into a delirium, struggling too violently for Lissa to hold him?

No delirious cries came to Ashe's ears — but Colin had no breath to spare for outcries.

He opened the door. The child lay still, propped against his pillows, eyes shut. Lissa sat beside him holding his hand. She glanced up, and came to meet Ashe, a strange look on her face.

"Lord Ashe, feel his forehead."

Three strides took him to the bed. Colin's skin was cool and dry. The chill of death?

No! The boy's stertorous breathing, a constant background for days, now came as a relief. So . . .

He hardly dared say it aloud. "The fever has broken?"

Lissa nodded, speechless, and burst into tears.

With none of the irritation he felt for his lach-rymose sister, Ashe gathered her into his arms. Her forehead buried against his shoulder, she wept while he stroked her hair and murmured soothing nothings.

Her body was soft and pliable in his arms, be-lying the strength of spirit and will he knew to be hers. A surge of desire shook him. He fought it down. This was not the time for kisses, welcome or unwelcome.

She sniffed. "I have no handkerchief."

"Take mine." He remembered the badly monogrammed square of cotton left in his drawer in London. MF — Melissa Findlay. Or FM?

"Lissa," said a tiny, breathless voice, "I'm . . . hungry."

A joyful smile broke through the last tears. Half expecting a rainbow, Ashe smiled back as they turned to the bed.

"Why . . . are you . . . crying?" Colin asked. "Am I . . . going . . . to die?"

"No, love, you are going to get well. Just let me see what the doctor said you are to eat at first. Where did I put that list?"

"Li . . . Miss Findlay, I'll tell Peter and Michael of the change. Shall I inform Daphne and my mother?"

"Pray do! Lady Orton may visit, briefly, if she *promises* not to cry."

"You . . . did," Colin reminded her.

"That was different," Lissa said tartly.

Laughing, Ashe left them.

After cheering the boys with his news, he found his mother, his sister, and Teague in the drawing room. Teague's continued presence surprised Ashe. He would have expected the fellow to be long gone, with sickness in the house and Daphne constantly on the edge of tears. Instead he had stayed on, uncomplaining, to keep her company, occupied if not precisely amused, and out of Ashe's and Lissa's way.

Perhaps he would not be such a bad bargain for Daphne after all.

Ashe paused on the threshold. Daphne and Teague had their heads bent over the Society pages of the *Morning Post.* Lady Ashe was setting tiny stitches in her latest embroidery. She looked almost as worn out as Lissa, Ashe noted with a pang.

"Good news!" he said.

They all looked up. Daphne ran to him.

"Rob, Colin is better?"

"His fever is down, and he's hungry. Miss Findlay says you may go up for a few minutes, if you promise to be calm and not disturb him."

"I promise! Oh, bless her, bless her!" She hurried out.

Teague followed. "Just make sure she don't fall into the vapors," he explained in passing.

Wearily, Ashe dropped into a chair near his mother.

"Colin is truly mending?" she asked.

"Not exactly mending yet. It will be a long road to full recovery, and there are bound to be setbacks. But based on what the doctor told us, Miss Findlay and I believe him out of immediate danger."

"Thank heaven. Will you take tea, or a glass of wine, Robert? You look tired."

"Then imagine how exhausted Miss Findlay is!"

"Yes," she murmured. "Miss Findlay's devotion cannot be denied. Surely she may be spared now. You may trust Colin to others, at least part of the time?"

"That is for her to say. I work under her direction." Ashe grinned at his mother's disconcerted expression. "Yes, Mama, already under the cat's foot, and we are not even betrothed yet."

"Betrothed! Oh, Robert, this is just what I feared."

"I mean to marry her, Mama, be very sure of that. But she knows nothing of my intentions, and before I broach the matter I must find out who she really is."

"Who she is? What do you mean?"

"You are willing to accept that she is a lady?"

"I . . . Yes, I suppose so. But that term covers a great deal. She is probably the daughter of a vicar, or an army officer, or the black sheep of some gentrified family, quite ineligible to wed an Ashe of Ashmead."

Ashe frowned. "A vicar?" he reflected, ignoring the rest. He remembered: Michael named Colin's rocking horse Apollyon, and regarded the learning of "verses" as a punishment; Lissa and Peter had never read any Greek but the New Testament and the early church fathers. But no Latin? "There's a religious connection somewhere," he said. "Her stepfather, I suspect, not her father."

"Her stepfather? You know a great deal about her, I see! The boys are not both full brothers, then?"

"I suspect not. Michael has more of her looks, the dark hair and grey eyes. Perhaps Peter is her stepfather's son by a previous marriage, and Michael by her mother."

"But they all use the same surname. Findlay," Lady Ashe mused, "Scottish, is it not? I know of no noble family by that name. Is it hers, or the boys'?"

"Neither." Ashe smiled at her surprise. "I have long suspected the name is assumed."

"Indeed!" his mother said dryly. "How, then, do you propose to discover who she is, if she refuses to tell you her name?"

"It may be impossible," he admitted soberly. "I do have one or two clues. For instance, I'm fairly certain the boys have always called her Lissa. They have been comfortable with it from the first. I rather doubt, though, that it is shortened from Melissa, as she claims. What else it might derive from should not be too difficult to guess."

"Guess?" Daphne practically danced in, restored to her natural gaiety. "My darling Colin is so much better, Mama. Miss Findlay is sure of his eventual recovery. What are you trying to guess?"

"What is the proper name for which Lissa is the nickname," Lady Ashe told her.

"Melissa," Teague said promptly, following Daphne in. "Heard her tell you so, Ashe. Never would have thought my memory was better than yours!"

Ashe silently cursed. He would have preferred to keep Teague out of the affair. Too late. "That's what she said," he agreed, "but I've a notion it may really be something else."

"Stage name, eh?" He cast a guilty glance at Lady Ashe. "Er-hem, beg pardon, ma'am."

She sighed. "That is quite all right, Lord Quentin. I find I have very nearly resigned myself to a *governess* who was once — briefly — on the stage."

Catching her eye, Ashe realized the stress was aimed at him: she was ready to accept Lissa as a governess, not as a daughter-in-law.

He decided to leave that battle until he had found out who Lissa really was. "Any suggestions?" he said.

"Alicia," said his mother at once.

"Elizabeth," Daphne proposed. "Leticia, Millicent, Elise, Clarissa."

"Wait!" Ashe hurried to the small writing table by the window. "Let me get a sheet of paper to write them down. And go slow. I need Voss and his shorthand!"

"Priscilla, Cecilia," his sister continued. "At

last, a word game I can play! Alison, Sybil."

"Drusilla," Lady Ashe suggested. "Phyllis, Cyrilla, Alcina."

"Crystal," Teague put in tentatively. Ashe scowled at him, recalling an opera dancer by that name who had lived under Lord Quentin's protection for some time.

"I had no idea there were so many," he said ruefully, surveying his list. "Sybil seems unlikely; Cyrilla, Cecilia — the right sounds but backwards."

"Larissa, Casilda." Daphne was in full spate, not to be stopped. "Elysia, . . ."

"I already have Alicia. It's first on the list, Mama's choice."

"Not Alicia, *Elysia*."

"There's no such name."

"There is, too. I know one."

"Children, children, no squabbling if you please. Have you Lysandra on your list, Robert?"

"Let me see, Mama. No, I'll add it."

Ashe recalled the handkerchief. He had been thinking of it as a clue to Lissa's surname, as a guide in seeking her in Debrett's *Baronetage*, or even the *Peerage*. It would be a long task, going through all the *F*'s and *M*'s, looking for someone with a daughter the right age with a viable name — and quite possibly a fruitless task if her antecedents were among the untitled gentry.

But of course the MF, or FM, applied to her Christian name, too. "Millicent is the best so far. Can anyone come up with another *M*, or an *F*? I have it: Felicity!"

"Felicia," said Daphne at the same moment. She glared at him. "There *is* such a name."

"Yes, indeed," said Lady Ashe. "I remember Felicia Warburton, who married the Earl of Woodborough."

"Woodborough? He died several years ago, did he not?" Ashe asked hopefully. "But what is the family name?"

"Milton," said Teague, swelling Ashe's hopes to bursting point. "He died six or seven years ago, with no male heir, to my knowledge."

Lady Ashe pricked the bubble. "Lady Woodborough died years before him, though, Robert. She was not there to remarry."

"Remarry?" Daphne asked, puzzled. "Did you wish her to have taken a second husband, Rob?"

"Lissa . . . er, Miss Findlay has . . . that is, *had* a stepfather. So she cannot be Woodborough's daughter."

"Wait." Teague held up a portentous hand. "Woodborough wasn't much of a man for town life, so I don't know much about him, but I've a feeling *he* remarried. That do you, old fellow? Daresay you've got a *Peerage* somewhere about the place?"

"Yes, in the library. I'll fetch it." A stepmother rather than a stepfather? he wondered. Just another piece of misdirection? But could a woman be as brutal as Lissa claimed her stepfather to have been, driving her to run off with her brothers? Where in the web of lies was

Ashe to discover the truth?

In the boys' fear of savage punishment for misdemeanors, he realized. Someone had made their lives a misery. All Lissa's lies were for their sake as much as her own.

Had their tormenter beaten her, too?

His hands shook with anger. It took a deliberate effort to steady them before he lifted Debrett's *Peerage* down from the shelf.

With little faith in Woodborough as Lissa's progenitor, he also took down the *Baronetage*. The others could help him go through the *F* and *M* listings in both volumes. As he returned to the drawing room, he tucked the *Baronetage* under his arm, opened the *Peerage*, and flipped through until he found Woodborough's name.

Henry Michael Redmond Milton, Third Earl of Woodborough, and a list of lesser titles; *born 1767;* Suffolk and Town houses; *married Felicia Warburton, daughter of . . . . , June 1798* — and Lissa claimed to be nineteen.

His stomach churning with unidentifiable emotions, he stopped on the threshold of the drawing room and read on. Only one child was listed, *a daughter, born April 1799, Felicia Anne. . . .*

Ashe raised his head. They were all staring at him. In a hollow voice he announced, "It would appear that Miss Lissa Findlay is Lady Felicia Milton, only child of the late Earl of Woodborough."

Then he recognized the emotions roiling his

guts: desolation, because she did not need him anymore — had never really needed him; and blind fury, because she had deceived and made a fool of him.

After a few spoonfuls of a custard made with beef tea instead of milk, Colin fell asleep. His face was dreadfully white and thin, but the pallor denoted the absence of fever. Lissa listened to the steady rasp of his breath, so familiar now she usually noticed only if it changed.

She would restore him to health, she vowed. She had done it once, she could do it again. One day he was going to play cricket, and ride his pony, and run with Peter and Michael.

For the moment he had no need of her hovering over him. At last allowing herself to acknowledge her fatigue, she moved to the chaise. She took off the soft slippers she wore in the sickroom and had just raised her legs and leaned back against a plump cushion when the nurserymaid tiptoed in.

"His lordship sent me, miss," she whispered, "to watch over Master Colin so's you can go down to him in the library."

Lissa bit back a sigh. No doubt Lord Ashe was in a hurry to return to town and wished to consult her about Colin's care. She hoped he would stay a few days, in case of a relapse. He was the only person she trusted when Colin was desperately ill.

It was her lack of trust which had driven him to

London in the first place. But only an hour ago, while she cried from sheer relief, he had held her in his arms without attempting the least familiarity. Could she trust him in that, too?

"Miss?"

Sitting up, Lissa heaved her legs off the chaise. She instructed the girl as to what changes in Colin to look for, and made sure the footman Lord Ashe had also sent was stationed outside the door, ready to fetch her if necessary.

"You will find me in the library," she told him. "I shall not be gone long."

If her interview with Lord Ashe was short enough, she might seize the chance to step out for just a moment for a breath of fresh air. She put on outdoor shoes before briefly looking into the schoolroom to assure Peter and Michael that Colin was truly better, as Lord Ashe had told them. The boys would miss him if he removed permanently to town, she thought as she went down the stairs.

When she entered the library, Lord Ashe was moving away from her down the length of the long, book-lined room. He was still in riding dress, brown coat stretched across his broad shoulders, buckskin breeches molding well-muscled thighs. The heels of his top boots thudded impatiently on the polished oak floor as he stepped off the Turkey carpet. His agitated pace gave an impression of leashed anger.

Lissa's heart misgave her. In spite of his promise, had his mother after all laid down the law and insisted Lissa and her brothers must leave now that Colin was on the road to recovery?

Lord Ashe had not heard her soft footfall. Reaching the end of the room, he swung round. The anger in his steps was reflected in his countenance — and when he saw her it did not soften.

Striding towards her, he snapped, "So, Lady Felicia, what have you to say for yourself?"

"How . . . ?" His face swam before her eyes. Blindly she felt for a nearby chair and sank onto it before her legs gave way beneath her. Head bowed, she tried again, "How did you find out?"

"Observation, inference, and deduction. Guesswork, if you prefer. Does it please you to have made a cake of me? How the world will laugh to learn that I was gulled into employing Lady Felicia Milton, only child of the Earl of Woodborough, as a governess!"

"Is that all you care about?" Lissa was angry in her turn. "What the world may think? Rest easy, no one need ever know. *I* certainly shall not tell."

"What the servants know, the world knows," Lord Ashe said wearily, sitting down. "We cannot hope to keep it secret when you remove into a guest chamber, keep company with the family, and are addressed by your proper name."

"No!" she cried in alarm. "I am perfectly content to remain a governess. Nothing need change."

"Everything *has* changed. I cannot, will not, permit this masquerade to continue."

"Let me stay. Colin needs me!"

"Which is why I must beg you, Lady Felicia, to be so kind as to remain at Ashmead to oversee his convalescence," he requested stiffly. "Once Colin is fit again, he must learn to go on with a tutor while you resume your rightful place in Society."

Lissa gazed at him in despair. "You do not understand. I cannot reclaim my place, my fortune, even my name, or he will find us and take the boys away. I know I have lied, cheated, deceived you. You have every right to be angry. But if you will not let us stay and keep our names secret, our only choice is to become fugitives again." Chilled by the dread of once more tramping the streets of London looking for work, she shivered, pulling her shawl closer about her shoulders.

Lord Ashe stood up and took her hands. "Come to the fire," he said gently, pulling her to her feet. "I have no right to be angry. I knew from the first you were not what you seemed. But I never dreamt your real fortune and station in life were so high." He gave her a wry smile. "I beg your pardon for berating you. It's a pity I was startled out of my wits instead of dumbfounded."

Summoning up an answering smile, she took a seat in an easy chair by the fire and held out her cold hands to its welcome warmth.

"There, that's better," he said, sitting opposite. "Forgive me for the tirade?"

"Of course. But truly, I like being Colin's governess."

"And truly, I cannot ignore your rank now I am aware of it, and if I could, my mother and Daphne could not."

"They know, too?" Lissa asked, aghast.

"And Lord Quentin. Miss . . . Lady Felicia, you must know I am fond of Peter and Michael. I would not willingly harm them. Will you not trust me with your story? If I have all the facts, perhaps I may see a way out of your quandary."

Lissa hesitated. He was a man, with all the influence of a titled gentleman. Though Mr. Exton so despised the unearned power and arrogance of rank, might he not be forced to bow to it?

Dared she take the risk?

Abandoning secrecy was difficult after keeping it for so long, but Lord Ashe already knew enough to discover the rest if he put his mind to it. She trusted him to do what he considered best for her and the boys. The question was, would she agree with his notion of what was best?

She looked into his warm brown eyes and read there an earnest desire to help her.

"Very well, sir," she sighed, "I shall tell you."

Nineteen

"I scarcely recall my mother," Lissa began. "She died when I was six. I do remember missing her dreadfully, even though I had a loving nurse and governess and Papa was a wonderful father. When I was not at my lessons, he used to take me with him to visit tenants and neighbors, and just riding about the estate. He was a farmer as well as a nobleman, always working to improve the land. After Mama died, he hardly ever went to London, or anywhere. He just stayed at Woodborough Hall, with me."

Lord Ashe nodded. "I imagine that is why the circumstances of his family are so little known, why it was possible for you to disappear virtually unnoticed. You have no close relatives, I collect."

"Both my parents were only children. I vaguely recall distant cousins being mentioned, but I was not acquainted with any. Papa seemed quite content with the society of our neighbors."

"There is no fourth earl listed. No doubt all the cousins were female, or your mother's."

"Perhaps, though I thought Papa spoke once of an heir, the son of an uncle who emigrated to America, I think. I daresay he would not wish to assume the title, for Papa said the Americans have done away with such things."

Lissa paused as a footman came in unobtrusively to light candles. In the library, dusk had arrived but, glancing at the window, she saw daylight lingering outside. A sudden longing for fresh air overcame her.

A governess summoned to the library stayed in the library until dismissed, but she was Lady Felicia now, whether she would or no. "If you have no objection, Lord Ashe," she said, "I should like to step outside while it is still light."

"By all means. You must be quite as sick of camphor as I am!" he said with a smile. "But don't expect me to wait for your story. With your permission, I shall walk with you. James, send a maid for Lady Felicia's pelisse, if you please."

The footman did not seem in the least surprised, forcing Lissa to realize how futile was her hope of keeping her identity from the servants. Apparently they had known she was unmasked before she did!

"I shall not need my cloak," she said. "I shall only step out for a moment, in case Colin needs me."

"My dear Lady Felicia, have I not made it plain . . . ?"

"You may prevent me from being his governess," Lissa said fiercely, standing up, "but *nothing* shall stop me nursing him until I am quite certain he will not have a relapse!"

Rising, Lord Ashe gazed deep into her eyes as

if searching her soul. She withstood his stare resolutely. He nodded acquiescence. "No cloak, James. If Lady Felicia is sent for in the next few minutes, we shall be on the terrace."

He led her to a room she had not seen before, a long gallery in the older part of the house, facing west. French doors opened onto a stone-flagged and balustraded terrace, with steps down to a formal, old-fashioned parterre. Lissa and Lord Ashe crossed to the top of the steps. Below, laid out in an elaborate pattern around a central fountain, low box hedges edged beds of lavender with fading purple spikes and autumn crocus glowing pink in the evening light. Pink puffs of cloud scudded across the pale blue sky, driven by a warm breeze, a last breath of summer.

In summer this must be a charming place to stroll or sit, open to Lady Felicia as it would never be to a governess. But by next summer, where would she be?

His hand resting in a comfortably familiar way on the head of a curly-maned stone lion, Lord Ashe asked, "When did your father remarry? The *Peerage* made no mention of it."

"I daresay he did not trouble to notify the editors — is that how they know? It was a small country wedding, in 1808, when I was nine."

"And then began your troubles," he observed sympathetically.

"Oh no! I do not believe Papa would have married anyone I did not like. His second wife was a neighbor, Lady Carpenter, widow of Sir Frederick Carpenter. She had always been very kind to me, besides having Peter. He was an adorable baby!"

"So Peter is your stepbrother. Sir Frederick was a baronet? Then the lad is Sir Peter Carpenter!"

"Yes. He has an estate of his own. Papa administered it until he died, but I do not know what happened afterwards. I daresay his lawyer keeps an eye on things, as he does for Woodborough Hall, but lawyers cannot be expected to understand farming, can they?"

"I fear not," Lord Ashe agreed, "and the land has had eight years to deteriorate. When did Lord Woodborough die? No one notified the *Peerage* of that, either, come to think of it. Teague told me."

A lump in her throat silenced Lissa for a moment. As she struggled to swallow it, he took her hand in a warm clasp.

"I don't mean to harass you," he said seriously, "but I cannot help if I don't understand just what happened."

"I know." Agitated as much by his touch as by her memories, Lissa withdrew her hand and started down the steps. "It was in 1810. Papa and my stepmother went on a belated wedding journey — they waited to make sure Peter was settled at Woodborough and I was at ease with the new family situation. They sailed to Jamaica, where Stepmama had inherited an estate she wished to sell. Papa died of a fever, and poor

Stepmama was left quite alone in a strange country."

"An unhappy position!" Lord Ashe's boots crunched on the gravel as he walked at her side towards the fountain.

"Was it not? I try to remember that, and not to blame her."

"Blame her?"

"For marrying Mr. Exton." There, he had the name; she and Peter and Michael were in his hands now. Tense as a setter come to the point, she wondered if he realized. She could not look at him.

Yet despite her misgivings, she felt a great burden roll from her shoulders. With sympathy she regarded the nymph in the center of the fountain, forever bearing a doubtless heavy urn on her shoulder from which water poured endlessly into the marble basin.

"Lady Woodborough met Exton in Jamaica, I presume."

"Yes, he also owns property there. He helped her sell her estate, then offered to escort her home provided she marry him." Bitterly Lissa explained, "His religion would not permit him to travel with a female not his wife, however well chaperoned by her maid. Mr. Exton's religion is not of a forgiving nature."

"I was sure religion came into the picture somewhere," Lord Ashe said thoughtfully.

"Everywhere. When they reached England, Peter and I had to remove to his house, lest living at Woodborough we learn to indulge the deadly sin of Pride. For the same reason our titles were never used. The aristocracy is anathema to Mr. Exton."

"Wait a minute. He is Peter's stepfather, but not yours, merely your stepmother's husband. Surely he had no power to remove you from your home."

"What else was I to do? I had no relatives to turn to. My stepmother was my joint guardian with my father's lawyer. Mr. Oldham sent Mr. Exton an allowance for my keep, but he would have been at Point Non Plus if I had turned up on the doorstep of his chambers!"

Lord Ashe grimaced. "No doubt."

"Nor did I know how to find him. I was only eleven, remember. And things were not so bad while my stepmother lived. To do him justice, I believe Mr. Exton had some fondness for her, in his way. At least she stood between us and his severity as best she could. Michael was born the following year and though Mr. Exton seemed to have no affection for him, his early childhood was quite happy."

"Only that can explain his sunny nature. Lady Woodborough must have been a remarkable woman."

"I loved her," Lissa said simply. "But when Michael was three she died. I tried . . . I *tried* to protect the boys as she had . . ."

"Exton's favorite biblical maxim was 'Spare the rod and spoil the child,' I take it."

" 'He that spareth his rod hateth his son: but

he that loveth him chasteneth him betimes' —
one of his favorites. Another was 'Sorrow is
better than laughter.' "

"Ye gods!"

"He wanted them to be saints, not children. I
could not stop him whipping them, but I tried to
make up to them for losing their mother, to teach
them to love each other, that love is important.
Love, and compassion, and generosity, not just
lack of avarice and pride."

"You succeeded admirably!" Lord Ashe exclaimed. He offered Lissa his arm. Without her
noticing, they had circled the fountain and returned to the steps. Laying her hand lightly on
his sleeve, she glanced up at his face. In contrast
to his words, it was grim. Abruptly he demanded, "Did the brute beat *you?*"

"No." Disconcerted by his obvious profound
relief, Lissa looked away and started up the
steps. "He recognized that he had no real authority over me and never raised a finger to me.
He had no legal duty to give me a home, either.
Mr. Oldham sent money for my keep, but even
so I suppose I ought to be grateful."

"NO!"

"He could have separated me from the boys.
Well, in a sense he did. When my stepmother
died he sent me away to school, a school run by
his church. It is called the Church of the Fiery
Pit, so you can imagine . . . No, I doubt if you
can. They did not beat us, nor starve us, but we
lived in the drabbest surroundings, wore the

drabbest clothes, ate the most tasteless food they could invent. Our minds were to dwell on the certain punishment of our sins by hellfire, not on outward things."

"Is that where you learned to read Greek?" he enquired with interest.

"So that we could study the New Testament in the original, and other ancient church writings. Not Latin, because it is the language of the Roman Church, a hotbed of blasphemy and perversion. Of course, the Anglican Church is not a great deal better," she added dryly.

Lord Ashe grinned. "Don't tell the vicar, pray. Should you like to stroll about the terrace or shall we go in? It's a trifle chilly now the sun is going down."

A wave of tiredness swept over Lissa. Absorbed in the past, she had almost forgotten the exhausting week of nursing preceding the present. Suddenly she felt as if she was wading through treacle.

"Let us go in."

"We'll sit in the gallery if you like. It is pleasant in the evening."

They found a pair of chairs facing the windows. Outside, the sky was turning to rose and apricot and a clear, pale green. Inside, in the twilight, Lissa soon could not make out Lord Ashe's expression. It made it easier to talk about what came next.

"How long were you at the school?"

"Four years, until last year. That is, I returned

to Mr. Exton's house — I cannot bring myself to call it 'home' — in the summer and at Christmas and Easter, though we did not celebrate those pagan festivals. So I saw Peter and Michael regularly, for a few weeks at a time."

"Luckily for them."

"And for me. Their affection meant as much to me as mine to them. Without them, how could I have survived? Why should I have wished to?"

He was silent.

"They are all I have," Lissa went on quietly. "Mr. Exton wanted me to leave them. When I turned eighteen, he found a husband for me, an elder in the church, elder in both office and age. It was an honor to be chosen by such a brilliant preacher of fire and brimstone, he told me. Wed to him, my soul might have some slim chance of avoiding the Pit."

"You refused."

"I refused. Mr. Exton washed his hands of me, said he could not provide a home to an ungrateful, impious apostate. By then I was old enough to understand that Mr. Oldham would be obliged to set up an establishment for me if I arrived on his doorstep. But he has no such obligation to Peter and Michael, and to abandon them was unthinkable! You must see that!"

"I do," Lord Ashe said reluctantly.

"Then you must also see that I cannot abandon Colin. Do not make me leave him!"

"You cannot remain as governess, now I know your true rank. There must be a solution." Restlessly he rose and took a turn about the darkening room, while Lissa scoured her weary brain for arguments. Returning, he stopped in front of her and said tersely, "You had better marry me."

Astounded, for one brief moment Lissa let herself believe it was possible to accept. But she did not deserve to have her prayers answered, after all her lies and deceit. He did not wish to marry her. He just saw it as the easiest way out of the predicament she had landed him in.

"That is not necessary," she said stiffly, her gaze fixed on the floor at his feet. "I am perfectly willing to stay as governess. You need not pay me. When my brothers are old enough to be safe from Mr. Exton, I shall reimburse you for our expenses."

"My dear girl," he burst out, "don't be totty-headed! Money has nothing to do with it. You must see the impossibility of the situation." He started to pace again. "You might stay as my mother's ward, and enter county society, but your stepfather will have to be told. I've no desire to go to gaol for alienating minors from their guardian."

"We shall run away again!" cried Lissa, appalled.

"Taking Colin too, this time?" he threw at her, swiftly crossing the gallery towards her. He seized her hands. "We'll think of a way to do it. Trust me! I shan't let them be taken from you. There is no need to reveal your whereabouts."

She was too tired to go on struggling. "How

will you manage that? They will trace us through you."

He let go her hands and sat down, leaning forward eagerly. "To start with, I shall do everything through lawyers. I shall have my man, Plumditch, approach your father's solicitor without mentioning my name. A letter from you to Oldham — that's the fellow's name? — asking him to explain your position to Plumditch, that will do the trick. Once I understand what's what, I can plan further. Do you know if he is also Peter's solicitor?"

"I think so. I am not sure."

"If not, he'll know who is. Never fear, I shall sort it all out."

He was so positive, Lissa began to believe that somehow he might prevail. With a faint smile, she was about to tell him so, when the footman she had left on duty outside Colin's chamber came in.

"Miss . . . My lady, you're wanted above stairs."

She sprang up in alarm. "Lord Orton is worse?"

" 'Tis not what I were told, my lady. Seems his lordship had a nightmare, dreamt as your ladyship was gone. He's a-crying fit to bust and he won't believe you're still here till he sets eyes on your ladyship for himself."

"You see?" Lissa said to Lord Ashe. "He will cry himself into an attack." She hastened out.

Ashe returned to the drawing room. His

mother had left, but his sister and Teague had their heads together over a collection of fashion plates.

"Rob," cried Daphne, "is it true? She is Lady Felicia Milton?"

"She is," he confirmed.

"How delightful. Heavens above, she must have some new clothes at once! Lord Quentin and I are quite agreed on what will suit her best. I shall take her to my modiste." Sudden tears filled her beautiful eyes. "Oh, but Rob, what about Colin? Even if he were perfectly recovered, how am I ever to find another governess who suits him half so well? We shall never be able to be married!"

"As to that, I cannot help, but at least you need not fret for the present — Lady Felicia will not leave him now. Her situation is complicated and will take some time to straighten out."

"There, what did I tell you, dear lady?" said Teague soothingly. "The chit . . . er, Lady Felicia is devoted to the child. Wouldn't desert him while he's not in plump currant."

"Then I cannot take her up to London," Daphne reflected. "I shall just have to order her gowns myself. It shall be a surprise!" She clapped her hands. "Fortunately Marlin has her measurements, I believe. Lord Quentin, pray remind me to ask her when we go to change for dinner."

Consulting his watch, Teague said, "Time to go up now."

They started towards the door. Halfway, Daphne turned to enquire, "Does Lady Felicia ride, Rob?"

"I'm not sure. She grew up in the country."

"Then I expect she does. She must have a habit. *A la militaire,* do you think, Lord Quentin?"

They went out together.

Not requiring half so long to change, Ashe headed for his mother's sitting room. On the way, he recollected that Lissa had told him she did not ride. Very likely it was another of her taradiddles, another attempt to deflect suspicion. How could he ever have been angry with her for her deceit? She had acted throughout solely in what she saw as her brothers' best interests.

Her stepbrothers', rather. Or was Michael even that? The son of her stepmother and a subsequent husband . . . Exton's son. With a suddenly sinking heart, Ashe wondered how he could possibly justify keeping the child from his father. Had he promised Lissa more than he could perform?

Twenty

"Is it true, Robert?" Lady Ashe lay on her sofa by the fire, looking every day of her age. "The girl is Woodborough's daughter?"

"It's true." Ashe sank into a chair on the other side of the fireplace, his sleepless night at Colin's bedside catching up with him. "Daphne's immediate response was to plan a new wardrobe for her!"

"Naturally."

"I did not care to discourage her — she needs cheering after the stress of Colin's illness — but paying for it may prove a difficulty. If necessary I shall shell out the blunt, but will you pretend it comes from you? I doubt Lady Felicia would accept it from me, even as a loan."

"Do you imagine she has so much proper feeling after what she has done? What on earth can have driven a gently bred young woman to such reprehensible behavior?"

Ashe flared up. "Would you have had her abandon them to that monster?"

His mother looked confused. "Monster?"

"Oh, you mean her theatrical career."

"I do indeed. Daphne may be a featherbrained pea-goose but *nothing* could persuade her to tread the stage."

280

"No?" he said ironically. "Was it not her intention of doing just that which brought down your . . . disfavor upon Lady Felicia?"

"In her own home! Quite different, though I cannot approve even that." Her cheeks tinged with pink, she dropped the subject. "What monster?"

"I was under the impression you wondered what had driven her to abduct her brothers."

"To what!" She reached for her smelling salts. Jumping up, Ashe reached for the bellpull, but she waved him down. "I do *not* want Jane or my maid fussing over me," she said crossly, sniffing at the vinaigrette. "I shall be perfectly all right, I vow, if you will only tell me a straight tale instead of dropping startling tidbits."

"Your pardon, Mama." He gave her a brief summary of Lissa's history. "So, you see, cruelty drove her to kidnapping, and, as I told you before, hunger drove her to the theatre."

"So you said, but perhaps she made up the story of the penny bun to win your sympathy."

"Mother, I was there when Michael, wakened in the middle of the night, apologized for eating more than his share! I saw the scrap of currant bun with my own eyes. None of them had any way of knowing I would be there . . ."

"In the middle of the night!"

"She tried to stop me going with her. I insisted, though by then I had given up . . . my original plans for the night, shall we say. In any case, we were well chaperoned by the boys." He

281

pondered a moment. "You know, at the time I thought it was a sort of waiflike charm which attracted me to her, but now I believe it was always her air of gallantry. Why else should I have so easily conceded defeat? Even then, I wanted to protect her from every distress and misfortune."

"Oh, Robert," cried his mother, "she may be a lady, and in need of succor, but need you marry her?"

"I have already asked her, Mama," Ashe said in a stifled voice. "She will not have me."

Unable to believe anyone could possibly refuse her son, Lady Ashe promptly came about. "My dear boy, this was scarcely the time to make a proposal of marriage, with Colin still ill and her affairs all in confusion."

"Becoming my wife would solve most of her difficulties."

"Is that what you told her? Is that in fact why you wish to wed her? Pure chivalry?"

"Good Lord, no!" Under her probing eye, he flushed. "I love her."

"Did you tell her so?"

"No," he admitted. "I said something about finding a solution, and then popped the question."

"No wonder she refused, then. I daresay Lady Felicia has the pride proper to her station. Taking a husband simply to be rescued would not suit her at all. Nor would you care for a wife who married you for such a reason."

"I'm not so sure of that," Ashe said wryly.

"Fustian! You must extract her and her brothers from their entanglement with that most undesirable preaching person — shockingly vulgar! — and then make another offer, explaining your sentiments properly."

Hiding a smile at his mother's complete *volte-face,* Ashe agreed that dealing with the abominable Exton was the first order of business. He knew Michael was a prime favorite with her, so he kept to himself his doubts about his ability to wrest the child from his father.

He had to manage it somehow. Even if he could bear the thought of returning the little boy to the horrors of such a home, Lissa would never marry him if he failed.

She might well refuse him again anyway, he reminded himself. An attempt at seduction was hardly the ideal way to introduce oneself to a well-brought-up young lady!

Too late to remedy that. The sooner he dealt with Exton, the sooner he could set about courting her in due form.

"If Colin is well enough to do without me, I shall go up to town tomorrow."

"Then I trust you mean to dine with us this evening," his mother said tartly. "You have slept through the dinner hour every day since your return."

"I'll try to stay awake, Mama," he promised, rubbing his eyes, "but first I'll just make sure Lady Felicia does not wish me to stay up with Colin tonight."

Lady Ashe went through to her dressing room to change for dinner. Before repairing to his apartments to follow suit, Ashe went to the nursery wing. In the day nursery, he found Nanny Bessemer sitting by the fire, nodding over some mending. She roused as he entered and blinked at him in bewilderment.

"Good evening, Nanny."

"Evening, Master Robert. Why, you're quite grown up."

"Yes, Nanny. I'm looking for your present charges. Where are Peter and Michael?"

"Master Michael's abed," she said firmly, "and staying there. 'Tis past his bedtime, and the child plumb wore out with all the excitement, what with Master Colin dreaming his friends was all gone away. Nowt'd satisfy the poor lad but to see 'em all together, Miss Findlay, too. You won't let 'em leave, will you, Master Robert? I don't know how Master Colin'd go on without 'em, and that's the truth."

"I'm doing my best to make sure they stay, Nanny, but it turns out Miss Findlay is actually Lady Felicia Milton."

The old woman nodded, accepting the news with the imperturbability of one whom a long life had inured to surprises. "A proper lady, allus kind and polite and bringing her boys up likewise, all three on 'em. Master Peter's reading to Master Colin now."

Ashe went to the sickroom. Colin was asleep, Peter at the bedside reading to himself, the nurserymaid by the fire sewing a rent in a small pair of breeches. The boys always needed new clothes, Ashe noted with a smile.

Peter came over to meet him. "Did you want to see Lissa, sir?" he whispered anxiously. "She was so tired I sent her to bed. I can easily wake her if Colin needs her, but I'd rather not disturb her just to talk to you, if you don't mind."

"You have answered my question. If she's willing to leave him to you and the girl, then I need feel no qualms about retiring to my own bed after dinner. I shall arrange for reliable servants to take turns through the night. It must be nearly your bedtime, is it not, Sir Peter?"

The lad flushed. "Lissa said she told you everything, sir. Even the nurserymaid seems to know. I . . . I'm sorry we had to lie to you. Michael's still little, you see. It wasn't right to let my stepfather treat him like that. Sir, do you . . . do you think we'll all burn in Hell for telling so many lies?"

"Certainly not!" Ashe exclaimed, much louder than he had intended. He glanced at the bed, and Peter swung round to do the same. Colin slept on.

"Sshh!" Peter reproved.

Ashe drew him out to the passage. "Certainly not," he repeated quietly, "if there is any justice in this world or the next."

"Lissa said that sort of lying isn't a mortal sin. She said lots of what my stepfather taught us is nonsense, like all children being already damned

285

when they're born, before they have even had a chance to be wicked. She made it a sort of game, *his* rules and *real* rules, Reasonable Rules, that ladies and gentlemen follow, like being kind and polite to everyone. But some are the same, and sometimes it's hard to tell which is which."

"My dear boy, I fear I am not up to a theological debate at present, if ever! You will do better to continue to consult your sister. I must go and change now. I shall send someone to relieve you with Colin. I'm off to London in the morning to set about extricating you from this muddle."

"Oh, I nearly forgot, Lissa wrote a letter to the lawyer she said to give to you." Peter extracted a folded sheet of paper, a trifle crumpled, from his pocket. Smoothing it, he handed it over, then laid a hand on Ashe's arm and looked up at him pleadingly. "You won't let *him* take Michael back, will you, sir? Even if I have to go?"

And Ashe found himself promising, "I shan't let him have either of you, my word upon it."

A gentleman's word was his bond. He would keep his promise even if he had to kidnap the boys and flee the country!

Not even his imprudent promise could keep Ashe awake. Having sought his bed immediately after dinner and fallen asleep within moments of laying his head on the pillow, he was up early on the morrow. He was glad to escape the house before any but servants were about.

Thus he avoided accompanying Daphne and

Teague, who had announced at dinner their intention of leaving for town in the morning if Colin had suffered no setback. They would likely not set off until noon, and their leisurely notions of travel did not suit Ashe's present impatience.

He also avoided — cravenly, he admitted to himself — what was bound to be a battle royal between his mama and Lissa. Lady Ashe, quite properly, intended to remove Lady Felicia from the nurseries to a more comfortable and elegant chamber.

Ashe was perfectly certain she would refuse to be removed. Whose stubbornness would win the day he was happy to wait until his return to discover.

Another beautiful October day allowed him to reach Dover Street by late the same evening. First thing next morning he sent for his solicitor. Occupied in court that day, Mr. Plumditch returned a message that he would be delighted to call upon his lordship at five o'clock in the afternoon, if convenient.

Frustrated, Ashe agreed.

The lawyer arrived on time and a footman ushered him into the library. A tall, spare man, he had a very high forehead, and his bushy eyebrows looked like furry caterpillars trying to crawl up the empty space, giving him an air of permanent astonishment. He apologized profoundly and profusely for keeping his lordship waiting.

"An unavoidable delay, my lord, though I need hardly say that had your lordship intimated a situation of extreme urgency . . ."

"No," Ashe cut him off, waving him to the chair facing the desk, "not extreme, though I am eager to get the business under way. Do sit down. Madeira?" he offered, feeling a sudden need of a little fortification before he broached that business.

"Thank you, my lord, a small glass would not be unwelcome."

Halsey had efficiently provided a decanter in case it was wanted. As he poured, Ashe asked, "Do you happen to know a lawyer by the name of Oldham?"

"Of Weldrum, Oldham and Weldrum, my lord? I am acquainted with the senior partner, and know of Mr. Oldham by reputation. Your lordship has business with him? Not, I trust, of an adversarial nature?"

"Not exactly. I hope not." Ashe passed him a glass. "What sort of man is he?"

"Competent and conscientious, I believe, my lord. The firm is well thought of, and the practice is an extremely busy one. Almost as busy as my own."

"Busy enough not to enquire into the welfare of a partner's wards?"

"Welfare, my lord?" Plumditch countered warily. "I own I should be extremely surprised to hear that Oldham had neglected any financial affairs entrusted to him."

With an impatient gesture, Ashe brushed this aside. He was glad Lissa's and probably Peter's estates had been well cared for, within the limits of a solicitor's knowledge of such matters, but that was not his present interest. "I'm talking of their health and happiness."

The caterpillars crawled upwards. "Happiness, I regret to say, is not within a lawyer's purview. Moreover, a busy man may be trustee of a large number of estates in the legal possession of minors. He cannot possibly enquire into the personal circumstances of all his wards. Unless unacceptable conditions are brought to his attention . . ."

"Yes, yes, I daresay." Ashe refilled his glass and tossed back the wine. Time to get down to particulars. "I wish to bring 'unacceptable conditions' to Oldham's notice, but my name is not to appear in the affair, at least for the present."

As he explained, with no names and a minimum of detail, Plumditch's eyebrows moved ever higher, in horror.

"My lord," he gasped, "harboring fugitives . . ."

"They are children, not criminals! What I need to know is whether, if I tell you who they are, you would feel obliged, legally or morally, to reveal their whereabouts — that is, my name — to Oldham."

"Certainly not, my lord," Plumditch said stiffly. "You are my client. Anything you tell me in confidence I reveal to nobody."

"Splendid. Then here's what I want you to do."

Three days passed without Plumditch appearing to report his findings to Ashe.

Daphne arrived. Though at once absorbed into the entertainments of the Little Season, she set about ordering a new wardrobe for Lissa.

Voss presented a number of candidates for the post of tutor to Lord Orton, already screened as to their liking for small boys as well as their educational accomplishments. Ashe interviewed them. Several were in orders, and he made a point of examining their beliefs about hellfire, much to their bemusement. Choosing the one who seemed best able to allay Peter's fears, he packed him off to Ashmead.

A letter from Lady Ashe brought comfortable tidings of Colin's recuperation. Lady Felicia was delighted with his progress, but very much on edge over her own and her brothers' plight. Had Robert no news for the poor girl?

Ashe sent a footman running with an impatient message to Plumditch.

The lawyer responded that he had succeeded that very afternoon in approaching Oldham. He would do himself the honor of calling on his lordship next morning, if convenient.

Jack was dispatched again with a demand — softened on second thoughts to an urgent request — that Plumditch present himself immediately. As an additional sop to the solicitor's dignity, Ashe added an invitation to dine in Dover Street. Changing early, he went down to pace the library.

Plumditch was ushered in at last. Ashe strode to greet him.

"What luck? What have you discovered? Sit down, man, take a glass and tell me. Did Oldham cooperate?"

"He did, my lord, upon presentation of the written instructions of his ward. His elder ward, I should say, since he is also Sir Peter's co-guardian." The furry caterpillars lowered in a frown. "It is distinctly odd. Mr. Oldham assured me he was quite unaware of Lady Felicia's having removed herself and Sir Peter from the care of Mr. Ernest Exton. No hue and cry was raised."

"Not even over young Michael's disappearance? Odd indeed! I should say, rather, extraordinary."

"Mr. Oldham knows nothing of Michael, who is none of his concern, but I believe he would not take it amiss were I to confide that he is in agreement with your lordship: extraordinary! He was much distressed by Lady Felicia's flight, and much relieved that she had fallen into what I assured him were good hands."

"I should hope so! What of her future?"

"As you supposed, my lord, her ladyship was well provided for in the late Lord Woodborough's will. In fact, with the exception of various comparatively small sums to servants, his late lordship bequeathed all unentailed property to his daughter, to the tune of some four thousand pounds per annum. Furthermore, the only male heir being deceased — somewhere in the Colonies, I understand — with none but female issue, Lady Felicia is by default the present owner of the entire estate. She is, my lord, an extremely wealthy young lady."

Twenty-one

Rain lashed the carriage windows as Ashe set out once more for Ashmead. The news he bore was good, from Lissa's point of view. If he was blue-devilled, it was solely on his own account.

He had been right to assume she had no further need of him. She was so wealthy, his own not inconsiderable fortune paled before hers. Oldham had agreed to let her set up her own establishment, with a suitable chaperon, until the leases on Woodborough and her town house expired and she could remove to her own property. He was even willing to entrust Peter to her care. If Exton, as co-guardian, objected, the lawyer was ready to go to court to allege negligence since he had not been informed of the boy's leaving home.

Oldham had no say over Michael's future, and therefore no interest in it. Plumditch advised Ashe to send the child home.

Ashe refrained from telling him that course was unthinkable. He saw no reason why Lissa should give Michael up, when Exton had made no apparent effort to retrieve him. Time enough to worry if the fellow started making enquiries.

The more he considered it, the more Ashe

thought the lack of a hue and cry was not merely extraordinary but incredible.

Exton had washed his hands of Lissa. He might delay reporting her departure so as to continue to receive the generous allowance for her keep. Conceivably he was glad to relinquish the responsibility for Peter, his stepson, for whom he also received an allowance.

But surely, however lacking in affection, a man did not simply ignore his small son's disappearance? It was unnatural, devilish queer — in fact, downright smoky!

Rain lashed the windows of Colin's chamber, but in the grate a cheerful fire held the gloomy afternoon at bay. Seated on the hearth rug, Lissa played lotto with the boys.

The new tutor had brought the game, which used Greek letters instead of the usual numbers. In just two days, Michael was well on his way to learning the alphabet, painlessly; Colin had refamiliarized himself with it; and Peter was challenged by having to think of a word beginning with the called letter before he was allowed to cover it on his board.

Lissa approved of the new tutor.

"Lotto!" cried Michael. "Look, I finished this row. It's my turn to call the letters."

"You don't know them well enough," Colin objected.

"Nearly. I know the sounds. I just can't always remember what they're called. When I grow up,

I'm going to be a man who makes up new games for children."

Peter suddenly jumped up, overturning his board. "Here's Lord Ashe," he cried, bowing towards the door. "Hello, sir!"

"Good afternoon, Lady Felicia, gentlemen."

Flustered at being found sitting on the floor, Lissa put a hand on Colin's shoulder as he started to rise. "Your uncle will forgive your not standing," she said, a tremor in her voice. Conflicting emotions paralyzed her, embarrassment at her undignified position, hope and dread of the news he brought, sheer joy at his return. He must not see the joy lest he guess how much she loved him. She kept her face averted as she struggled to master her expression.

Michael had no such qualms. Beaming, he scrambled to his feet, performed a perfunctory bow, and ran to take Lord Ashe's hand. "I'm glad you've come back. Do you want to play Greek lotto with us?"

"Not just now, Michael. I'm still in all my travel dirt. I beg your pardon, Lady Felicia, I should have changed." He sounded puzzled, as if he was not quite sure why he had rushed to the nurseries without cleaning up first.

Or perhaps he was taken aback because Lissa had not greeted him, she thought, abashed. Turning her head to smile at him, she said, "No matter, sir. You were eager to see Colin, I am sure," and she endeavored to rise gracefully.

Swift strides brought him to her side in time to

help her up. Once she was on her feet, he kept her hands in his for a moment, steadying her. She blushed as he grinned down at her.

Colin rescued her. "I'm much better, Uncle Robert. I walked here from my bed without any help."

"Good for you."

"But you have been up long enough," Lissa said firmly. "Peter will support you back to bed."

"I can walk on my own. Just help me stand up, Peter. My legs are a bit wobbly still. Now watch me, Uncle Robert."

With Peter hovering at his side, matching him step for step, Colin crossed the few feet to his bed. Lissa kept her eyes on him, sighing with relief as he flopped down to sit on the edge.

"Miracle-worker," Lord Ashe breathed in her ear, sending a quiver down her spine. "I thought he would be confined to his bed for weeks yet."

"So did the doctor, but he would only get weaker and weaker without exercise. I am very careful not to let him overexert himself," she said defensively.

"I don't doubt it. I recollect what your prescription of exercise did for the boy even in London."

"He still needs me," Lissa insisted. "I cannot desert him. What . . . what happened in London?"

"We cannot talk of that here. I shall go and change, and make my bow to Mama. Will you meet me in the library in an hour?"

The hour seemed endless. Lissa went down a few minutes early. Candles had already been lit, a branch on the massive oaken writing table and sconces above the mantelpiece. Warming her hands at the blazing fire, Lissa contemplated the painting above, a double portrait of the late baron with the dowager on his arm.

One day the present Lord Ashe's portrait might hang there, his wife at his side. Wistfully Lissa wondered whether she had been an utter peagoose to refuse his proposal. He had offered his hand on the spur of the moment, as a matter of chivalry, the easiest solution to her problems. Yet they were friends, and his kisses argued a physical attraction to her. Had she accepted, might he not have come to love her?

Or would he have come to bitterly regret those careless words? No gentleman could truly wish to be tied to so deceitful a female, so wanting in conduct, so lacking in propriety, as to have run away and trodden the boards, however good her motive.

Lissa sighed deeply. She had been right not to take advantage of Lord Ashe's momentary lapse from common sense.

Hearing footsteps behind her, she turned. How handsome he was, his dark hair glossy in the candlelight, brown eyes reflecting the flames, resolute chin, sensuous mouth which had touched hers with fire. She must not think of that now. She must concentrate on what he had learned from the lawyer.

"What did he say? What did Mr. Oldham say?"

"That you inherited your father's entire estate," he said soberly. "The cousin in America died without sons."

"Oh, I do not care for that!" Agitated, she clasped her hands and sank into a chair. "I mean, I am sorry he died, but though I am glad Woodborough belongs to me, what I really want to know is about Peter and Michael. Can Mr. Oldham stop Mr. Exton taking them away from me?"

Lord Ashe sat down across the hearth from her, forehead creased in a frown of perplexity. "According to Oldham, Exton has apparently made no effort whatsoever to find the boys. I find that understandable, if deplorable, in Peter's case, since he is not a blood relative."

Hope blossomed in Lissa's heart. "Peter has a title, too, and I told you he abhors titles."

"True. But to give up his own son without making the least attempt to retrieve him strikes me as unnatural to the point of madness."

"Perhaps he is mad," Lissa cried. "What does it matter as long as both the boys can stay with me? I must go and tell them." She jumped up.

He caught her wrist. "Wait, Lissa . . . Lady Felicia. Sit down and listen, if you please. I have been thinking hard about this, and the only explanation I can conceive is that Michael is not in fact Exton's son."

Bewildered, Lissa returned to her chair. Noting the high color staining Lord Ashe's cheekbones, she said hesitantly, "Surely you cannot mean to suggest my stepmama . . . played him false? She would not do such a shocking thing!"

"Good gad no! That is the last thing I should suppose. I . . . er . . . Do you . . . hm . . . Are you aware that . . . er . . ."

"What is it? I am sure you need not scruple to speak plainly, if you recollect the circumstances of our first meeting!"

A crimson tide flooded his cheeks. "I wish you would forget that," he said crossly. "However . . . When is Michael's birthday?"

"February," Lissa said, puzzled.

"He was seven last birthday? Your father died in 1810, do you know in what month?"

"Yes, September. The eleventh. Why?"

"September?" Lord Ashe counted on his fingers. "October, November, December, January, February — five months."

"Yes, but what . . . Oh!" She flushed in her turn, feeling childishly ignorant. "The girls at the theatre talked about *nine* months and . . . and babies. I never perfectly understood. But do you mean . . . ?"

"It seems to me more than probable that Michael is your father's son!"

Lissa stared at him. "My brother? My *real* brother?" she said incredulously.

"Half-brother. He does, after all, have your coloring, an additional bit of evidence. You realize that would make him the present Earl of Woodborough?"

"Michael Lord Woodborough? Good heavens!" Lissa could not help laughing.

"You had no notion? Why should Exton have kept it secret? And how, for pity's sake?"

"We just called him Michael," Lissa pointed out, "and the servants called him Master Michael. He is only a little boy. There was never any need to use a surname, and despising the nobility as he did, Mr. Exton deliberately suppressed the use of my title and Peter's. Concealing Michael's altogether is but one step further."

"I suppose so, though to conceal it from the lawyer is taking it to extremes! However," Lord Ashe said thoughtfully, "having been born in wedlock, I daresay Michael would be presumed in law to be the legitimate child of Mr. and Mrs. Exton. An excellent reason for widows not to remarry too soon, at least when there is property in the case!"

"But does that mean Mr. Exton is still Michael's legal guardian, even if Michael is Papa's son?" she asked, dismayed.

"I fear so. To prove Michael's claim to the title, we'll have to obtain records of his birth, your father's marriage to Lady Carpenter and his death, and your stepmother's marriage to Exton."

"How?"

"No doubt Exton has them, or at least knows where to find them. We shall have to tackle him after all."

"No! He may seem not to care where Peter

and Michael are, but if he finds out he may change his mind."

"Would you deny Michael his inheritance?" he said gently.

"I shall willingly give him Woodborough, and the money. Everything! The title is not important, especially compared to his happiness. If he wants it, he may pursue it when he is of age and safe from Mr. Exton."

"In fourteen years, evidence may disappear, or be destroyed. Exton may die and be unavailable to answer questions. Without proof of his birth, Michael might refuse your generosity, or if he accepts he must always feel indebted. And have you considered his heritage, as distinct from his inheritance? Do you mean to keep his true parentage secret from him? To let him grow up believing *Exton* is his father?"

Shaken, Lissa buried her face in her hands. "I don't know!" Her voice trembled. "Oh, what am I to do for the best?"

He came to sit on the arm of her chair, a large, warm, comforting presence, one hand on her shoulder. "Michael shall not be returned to Exton. I have promised Peter. Whatever needs to be done to keep you and the boys together, I shall do it, legal or illegal."

"Truly?" She looked up at him.

He gave her a crooked smile. "Truly. Word of a gentleman."

Taking a deep breath, she said, "Will you go to him, then, and get the proof for Michael?"

"I would, gladly, but I believe you ought to go. Partly because you have a far better claim to the information than I do. Partly because it seems to me you will never rest easy until you have confronted him, faced him down, and discovered his intentions from his own mouth."

She clutched his hand. "You will go with me?"

"Of course. Now, whom shall we take to chaperon you? Cousin Jane?"

Lissa noted with relief the twinkle in his eye. Miss Jane Barbican disapproved of Lady Felicia Milton almost as heartily as she had of Miss Melissa Findlay.

Alas, Cousin Jane was the only person Lady Ashe considered suitable to chaperon Lady Felicia, with a maid to attend them, naturally, and a footman for good measure. However, Lissa was far too apprehensive about meeting Exton to care much who were her travelling companions, as long as Ashe was one. Her reliance upon him renewed his hopes.

Several days passed before he judged the weather improved enough for the ladies to embark upon the cross-country journey into Leicestershire. During that time Colin continued on the mend, his strength increasing to the point where Lissa was content to leave him for a few days to the ministrations of others. Ashe was glad to see one burden removed from her slender shoulders.

He would have preferred to ride alongside the

carriage, but that would expose her to Cousin Jane's often acid tongue. His presence silenced Cousin Jane; hers silenced Lissa. It was a quiet journey.

They reached Leicester after a long day, and put up at the Dudley Arms for the night. In the morning, leaving Cousin Jane and the maid at the inn, Ashe and Lissa set out for Coalville. To satisfy his cousin's notions of propriety, Ashe hired a horse and rode, now that he would rather be within.

Beneath a grey sky, the mining villages were drab and soulless. Even the recent rains had not sufficed to cleanse the countryside between of a pall of coal dust. Perhaps the Church of the Fiery Pit was a natural outgrowth of these surroundings, Ashe thought. His own name, which he had always associated with the green ash-tree on his coat of arms, here seemed more a symbol of the destructive power of fire, its dreary leavings. Ashes to ashes . . .

He was growing morbid. How must Lissa feel? He stopped the carriage, tied his horse on behind, and climbed in with her.

Pale-faced, she turned to him with a blind, lost look. He took her hand in his, felt it tremble like a captive bird.

"Frightened?" he asked softly.

"Terrified."

"Don't be. You have defied Exton before. You told me yourself he has no authority over you. Just remember how you taught me not to lick the dust beneath Aunt Busby's feet."

That brought a faint smile. He rattled on about his aunt and the feat of smuggling the boys into and out of her house, until they reached the outskirts of Coalville and the carriage came to a halt.

A spike-topped wrought-iron railing fronted the lane. Behind it a mass of laurels with black-grimed leaves half hid an uncompromisingly rectangular house in the starkest style of the last century. Whatever the original color of the brick walls and tile roof, they were now grey. So was the front door and the paintwork of the sash windows — practical no doubt, Ashe conceded grudgingly.

Their footman had jumped down to open the iron gates. The carriage turned into the drive. Lissa shuddered as the gates clanged shut behind them.

They were shown into a carpetless front parlor furnished with hard wooden chairs. The white walls were hung with texts from the most lurid parts of *Revelation*. The empty grate added to the chilly, cheerless atmosphere.

"They hold prayer meetings in here," Lissa whispered.

With a grimace, Ashe gestured at the fireplace. "A little hellfire would not come amiss."

Perhaps it was just as well she did not hear, her attention on the sound of footsteps in the hall. He turned as the door opened.

Expecting a massive bully of a man, Ashe was

startled to see on the threshold a short, bony figure, clad all in funereal black. Even his plain white shirtfront was scarcely visible between the black cravat and black waistcoat. Exton's hands were long and bony, like an eagle's talons. Sparse, greyish-yellow hair topped a thin-lipped face remarkable chiefly for the coldness of the pale eyes.

This was no ruffian who flogged children in a fit of temper. He would mete out punishment with an icy calmness impossible to oppose or evade.

Ashe decided only the contemplation of hell-fire kept the blood moving through Ernest Exton's veins.

"Well?"

The monosyllable was directed at Lissa, on whom the pale eyes were fixed. Ashe was ready to step in, to introduce himself and explain their errand. Lissa forestalled him, performing the introductions with admirable composure.

"So you have caught yourself a handsome face and a title, a vainglorious profligate," Exton said contemptuously, "and now you expect me to take your brothers off your hands? It is too late for that."

"You do not want them?" Lissa asked with incredulous hope.

"I strove to beat their sins from them as I strove to teach you to despise earthly vanities, to save you all from roasting in hellfire for eternity. For their mother's sake, I have done my duty.

You, unregenerate, have led your brothers into the paths of unrighteousness. Upon your head be it! They are no kin of mine. No more is demanded of me."

Stunned by the astonishingly easy victory, Lissa stared, dumbfounded. Ashe took over.

"You assert Michael is not your son?"

"Certainly not," Exton snapped. "You cannot pass him off on me. His mother was with child when she married me, solely for the sake of her children, born and unborn — I labor under no illusion on that account! But Michael was conceived when she was the lawful wife of Lord Woodborough. I have proof: marriage lines, sworn copies of birth and death entries in parish registers . . ."

"Splendid," Ashe interrupted affably. "That is precisely what we came for."

Once more the gates clanged shut behind the carriage, but this time it was outside. As the wheels began to turn again, Lissa emerged from her daze.

"I have left my gloves behind. I must have dropped them."

"Do you want to go back for them?" Lord Ashe asked, grinning.

"No!"

"You can afford a new pair, you know."

"Oh yes." Lissa felt for her reticule, wherein reposed several months' allowance, handed over by Mr. Exton with a self-righteous denial of ever having intended to keep the money. "How right you were," she said wonderingly, "to insist on confronting him. I am very glad you made me go."

"So am I, because you no longer fear Exton. But I am very glad you don't blame me for your losing Woodborough."

"Of course not. I told you I meant to give it to Michael. It was never truly mine."

"He will get considerable funds also, I believe, but you will still have sufficient income to support yourself in comfortable independence," he assured her, then hesitated. With unwonted uncertainty, he continued, "That is, if you won't marry me."

Was he asking her again, or merely reminding her that she had rejected him? Confused, Lissa was silent, her gaze fixed on her bare fingers, interlaced in her lap.

He reached for her hands, his own ungloved now. A lightning shock raced through her at his touch, followed by an all-pervading warmth. Surely he must guess how much she loved him! Half against her will, she looked up at him, dreading to see pity in his face. After all, however wealthy they might be now, she was still a female alone in the world with her brothers to bring up.

His dark eyes smiled at her. "I warn you, I shall be a far more persistent suitor than I ever was seducer. Be my wife, Lissa?"

Everything within her cried out to consent, to accept his support and friendship if she could not have his love. But she blurted out, "You are not asking me just for the boys' sake?"

"What a suspicious creature! Though I suppose I have given you good reason to doubt my motives, right from the first," he added ruefully. "No, my sweet, I wish to marry you because I adore you and cannot imagine life without you."

Pulling her into his arms, he provided quite convincing evidence of his assertion. His previous kisses had been poor imitations of the real thing, Lissa realized, head spinning, bones melting. And this time, though she had not actually given him an answer, she did not have to try to make him stop!

All too soon Ashe stopped of his own accord, letting her settle, breathless, back in her seat.

"I don't know whether you feel you might ever come to love me," he said seriously. "I want you, even if you only accept for the boys' sake. I am very fond of them, too, and shall gladly be a father — or an elder brother — to them. I daresay Daphne will marry Teague and leave Colin in our care, also."

"I shall not accept for the boys' sake!" she cried. "I saw the results of that when poor Stepmama married Mr. Exton. With her example before me, I would never make such a dreadful mistake."

"I see," he said flatly. "I was too sanguine. I beg your pardon for mauling you."

The despair in his face at once shocked and

elated Lissa, giving all the proof she could desire of his love.

"I *will* marry you," she hastened to assure him, "but not because the boys need you, though they do. I need you, too. I love you quite as much as you can possibly love me!"

And flinging her arms around his neck, she did her best to prove it.

We hope you have enjoyed this Large Print book. Other G.K. Hall & Co. or Chivers Press Large Print books are available at your library or directly from the publishers.

For more information about current and upcoming titles, please call or write, without obligation, to:

G.K. Hall & Co.
P.O. Box 159
Thorndike, Maine 04986 USA
Tel. (800) 257-5157

OR

Chivers Press Limited
Windsor Bridge Road
Bath BA2 3AX
England
Tel. (0225) 335336

All our Large Print titles are designed for easy reading, and all our books are made to last.